GALAXY'S EDGE

EDITED BY MIKE RESNICK

ISSUE 13: MARCH 2015

I0554549

Mike Resnick, Editor
Jean Rabe, Assistant Editor
Shahid Mahmud, Publisher

Published by Arc Manor/Phoenix Pick
P.O. Box 10339
Rockville, MD 20849-0339

Galaxy's Edge is published in January, March, May, July, September, and November.

www.GalaxysEdge.com

Galaxy's Edge is an invitation-only magazine. We do not accept unsolicited manuscripts. Unsolicited manuscripts will be disposed of or mailed back to the sender (unopened) at our discretion.

Available by subscription (www.GalaxysEdge.com) or through your favorite online store (Amazon.com, BN.com, etc.).

ISBN: 978-1-61242-260-2

Advertising in the magazine is available. Quarter page (half column), $95 per issue. Half page (full column, vertical or two half columns, horizontal) $165 per issue. Full page (two full columns) $295 per issue. Back Cover (full color) $495 per issue. All interior advertising is in black and white.

Please write to advert@GalaxysEdge.com.

FOREIGN LANGUAGE RIGHTS: Please refer all inquiries pertaining to foreign language rights to Spectrum Literary Agency, 320 Central Park West, Suite 1-D, New York, NY 10025. Phone: 1-212-362-4323. Fax 1-212-362-4562

Contents

THE EDITOR'S WORD

by Mike Resnick

Welcome to the 13th issue of *Galaxy's Edge*. We're feeling exceptionally pleased this month: we've completed two full years of bi-monthly publication; we've made an agreement whereby we actually have a Chinese edition; we're the only magazine that reviews short fiction (*Tangent*) chose fourteen stories from our 2014 issues when listing their Best of the Year; and we've come out with *The Best of Galaxy's Edge,* a series we have every intention of continuing every other year.

This issue features new stories by Kathleen Conahan, Fabio F. Centamore, Liz Colter, Eric Leif Davin, and a Sargasso Containment story by Brad R. Torgerson. We also have some wonderful reprints by Jody Lynn Nye, Pat Cadigan, Greg Benford, and Kristine Kathryn Rusch, and a continuation of Michael Flynn's *Melodies of the Heart.* In addition, we have our usual book reviews by Paul R. Cook, our regular science column by Greg Benford, and Barry Malzberg's whatever-he-feels-like-talking-about column. And finally, we have Joy Ward's interview with Jerry Pournelle.

I was recently interviewed on a university radio station and was confronted by a professor who insisted that he, and he alone, knew the true definition of science fiction, and if something didn't fit into his definition it clearly wasn't science fiction.

Well, he's happy with his definition (whatever it may be), but he is far from the first. Let me tell you a little something about our critical prognosticators of the past century.

The first guy to define science fiction was Hugo Gernsback, the man who created the first all-science-fiction magazine (*Amazing Stories,* back in April, 1926). He's the guy our most prestigious award is named after—even though he had some difficulty speaking English, clearly couldn't edit it, and usually refused to pay for it except on threat of lawsuit.

Hugo declared that "scientifiction" (his first term for it) existed solely to interest young boys in science. (Young girls, presumably, were too busy playing with their dolls.) The science had to be reasonably accurate, and central to the story.

Now, at about the same time Hugo was creating science fiction, H. P. Lovecraft was perfecting a fantasy fiction that rarely involved science (although he did sell a few pieces to *Astounding* in the 1930s), and clearly wasn't meant for the impressionable young boys Hugo saw as his audience.

Okay, move the clock (the calendar?) ahead eighty-some years. Lovecraft is just about a household name. Eleven of his books are still in print. You'd need extra fingers and toes to count the movies adapted from or suggested by his work. Science fiction is happy to claim him as one of our own, at least a close cousin if not a wandering son.

And Papa Gernsback of the rigid definition? Not a single word he wrote in his entire life—and that includes novels, editorials, non-fiction, the whole shebang—is still in print.

The first major critic to come along was Damon Knight. Damon knew that science fiction was the pure quill. It annoyed him when science fiction writers didn't know the craft of writing, and it annoyed him even more when they got their science wrong.

But what really drove him right up a tree was when they didn't even *try* to make the science accurate. When, for example, they put the key in the ignition and the spaceship started up just like a car. When, for example, they put an oxygen atmosphere on Mars.

When, for example, they were Ray Bradbury.

Damon acknowledged that what Bradbury did was Art; he knew his craft too much to argue with that. But Art or not, it sure didn't fit his notion of science fiction, and his criticisms and essays left no doubt that Ray Bradbury was a gifted imposter who should either mend his ways or stop posing as a science fiction writer.

The result? Almost every word Ray Bradbury wrote during the past seventy years is still in print, and just before his death the Pulitzer committee honored him for a lifetime devoted to science fiction. Of all the dozens of pure science fiction books Damon Knight wrote or edited, only two are in print today.

The next major critic was James Blish, perhaps not quite the writer Knight was (though a good one, no question about it), and a hell of a lot nastier, but he knew his stuff, and that meant he knew science fiction was **I**mportant (note the capital I), that no practitioner dared take it lightly, that it was just this side of sinful to be flip and flippant, which meant that the greatest offender was probably Robert Sheckley. How dare he make fun of the honored tropes and traditions of science fiction?

Okay, move the clock ahead a quick sixty years and (you saw this coming, right?) there are eleven Sheckley books in print. Of all the books, fiction and non-fiction, that James Blish wrote only two remain in print. Even his *Star Trek* books have gone the way of the dodo.

But more to the point, no one argues any longer that humor cannot be valid science fiction (and indeed, such humorous stories as Eric Frank Russell's "Allamagoosa" and Connie Willis' "Even the Queen" have won the Hugo). Today no one says that the science is more important than the emotional impact of a story, by Bradbury, by Roger Zelazny, by anyone. And no one denies that horror and supernatural fiction (perhaps excepting those vampire novels that are thinly-disguised category romances and outsell science fiction ten-to-one) a place in our family tree.

Now you would think that after the originator of our field and our first two major critics all fell on their faces trying to keep science fiction within their rigid definitions, future generations of self-appointed Keepers of the Flame (or the Definition) would have slunk off into the shadows. But they didn't.

At the midpoint of the twentieth century, everyone knew that sex had no place in science fiction. Our field was like a George Bernard Shaw play, which is to say that an alien reading (or watching) it could learn everything there was to know about human beings except that we come equipped with genitals and an urge to use them. Then along came Philip José Farmer with "The Lovers" and its sequels, and when God didn't strike him dead, all the writers who had been avoiding Topic Number One for years, even such traditionalists as Heinlein and Asimov, began making up for lost time. And by the mid-1960s it was never again suggested that sex had no place in science fiction.

J. G. Ballard got a lot of grief because clearly you couldn't fool with the actual form of the science fiction novel. But after he did it, so did dozens of others, experimenting every which way as the New Wave was born, fought for its right to exist, and was finally incorporated into the body of the literature.

So okay, they lost a lot of battles, but there was one thing the traditionalists knew would never change, and that was that science fiction took place in outer space. Then Robert Silverberg began exploring "inner space" with books like *Dying Inside.* Barry Malzberg explored it with *Herovit's World.* The Defenders of the Faith howled like stuck pigs, and a few years later everyone agreed that Outer or Inner Space were equally valid venues as long as the story worked.

Alternate history was okay for historians like McKinley Kantor and politicians like Winston Churchill, and the *very* occasional science fiction short story, but everyone knew it wasn't really science fiction—until Harry Turtledove began proving it was on a regular basis, and suddenly dozens of writers followed suit. Now there's no more controversy. Of course alternate history is science fiction.

And what's driving the purists crazy these days? Just look around you.

Connie Willis can win a Hugo with a story about a girl of the future who *wants* to have a menstrual period when women no longer have them.

David Gerrold can win a Hugo with a story about an adopted child who claims to be a Martian, and the story never tells you if he is or not.

I can win Hugos with stories about books remembered from childhood, about Africans who wish to go back to the Good Old Days, about an alien tour guide in a thinly-disguised Egypt.

The narrow-minded purists to the contrary, there is *nothing* the field of science fiction can't accommodate, no subject—even the crucifixion, as Michael Moorcock's Nebula winner, "Behold the Man", proves—that can't be science-fictionalized with taste, skill, and quality.

I *expect* movie fans, making lists of their favorite science fiction films, to omit *Dr. Strangelove* and *Charly*, because they've been conditioned by Gene Roddenberry and George Lucas to look for the Roddenberry/Lucas tropes of movie science fiction—spaceships, zap guns, cute robots, light sabers, and so on.

But written science fiction has *never* allowed itself to be limited by any straitjacket. Which is probably what I love most about it.

About the only valid definition that I'm willing to accept is this: all of modern, mainstream, and realistic fiction is simply a branch, a category, or a subset of science fiction.

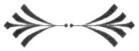

Liz Colter is a 2014 winner of the Writers of the Future Contest, with recent sales to Heroic Fantasy Quarterly *and* Penumbra, *among others. She has two completed fantasy novels and is working on her third.*

THE TIES THAT BIND, THE CHAINS THAT BREAK

by Liz Colter

My first view of Alawea is bittersweet, as always. The beauty is breathtaking, from thin, blue rivulets that stream down the mountain, to the city itself, which leans back against the mountain's rocky base as ruler might lean into the high back of a throne. Spires rise as thin and fragile as a glass blower's straw above the sweep and curve of villas that cascade down the terraced levels. Alawea, the city of my birth and wellspring of my nightmares.

I don't return willingly but, like my parents, I am bi-gender and also a messenger. I go where I am sent. Though for many seasons I have lived in Zasna, serving the tetrarch of that city, if she bids me deliver a message to Alawea, then come I must.

The lowest level of the city is hidden behind the perimeter wall, and so it's the elegant middle and opulent upper terraces that expand and define as I approach. Closer still and the wall looms largest. It blocks all else until I reach the city gate, where metal bars sketch thick black lines through my view of the jumbled shacks and mud-caked cobbles beyond.

Alawea may be my birth-city, but it's the blighted Sabanach quarter, sprawling and stinking, that's my true childhood home. I hate it more than the poor quarters of other cities for that fact alone.

The gate guard takes in the delicate, fair skin of my face with its wisps of dark beard and sideburns, finger-joint long but sparse, like the crest-feathers of a green finn. Her eyes sweep lower to the flatness of my chest and the narrowness of my waist, and lower still, to the Y of my legs where they meet the saddle, no doubt wondering, like all do, what lies beneath the brown cloth of my breeches.

I need no identification other than that which I present to the world each day. She nods to a boy inside who swings the barred gate wide for me to enter. I gather my breath and nudge my mount forward beneath the heavy arch of stone and into the city. Muck spatters from my horse's hooves as I thread the narrow streets. Dung fires—and worse, the refuse burned within those fires—assail my nostrils after many days spent traveling under the canopy of open sky.

I suppose I should be grateful to the 14th Autarch, more than a century dead, who decreed that all messengers would be bi-genders, giving many, if not most of us, a profession. Perhaps I *would* be grateful if he'd also allowed us to climb out of the slums. Or if his incentive had been loftier than devising a means for bi-genders to access his palace to satisfy his well-known perversions.

Past the outer ring of beggar's camps and temporary shelters lies the interior of Sabanach, where many of the short, boxy shacks flaunt strips of bright cloth hanging across low roofs or along either side of the doorways. The extravagant use of cloth is not as wasteful as it seems; it transforms the bleakness into a riot of rich reds and bright yellows, deep blues and emerald greens. It proclaims the uniqueness of the inhabitants and shouts to all who pass by, "I have not been conquered."

That my parents still make their home here gives me the opportunity to remove the dirt of my travels in private before presenting myself to the tetrarch. A rare respite from performing the duty under the eyes of palace servants.

I stop before a squat hovel with faded strips of cloth lovingly stitched into a rainbow of familiar colors. The open door indicates that at least one of my parents is in residence. Horses are rare in Sabanach, but to steal a horse with the trappings of a messenger would be to steal from the messenger's master, which none would dare. I tie him without hesitation to the iron stake hammered to the left of the door.

My eyes fight for focus as I step over the threshold into the dim interior. Against the far wall of the single room a figure crouches on the dirt floor upon hands and knees, folding blankets at the foot of the sleeping pallet.

"Dallu?" It's been three seasons since I was here last and I say the name more to identify myself, knowing I'm silhouetted by the light at my back.

"Jerusha." Dallu drops the blankets and comes to embrace me. My co-parent's small breasts press against me, our cheeks rub roughly. I am bestowed a light kiss on the forehead. "You're here on business." Dallu holds me at arm's length to examine the brown breeches and shirt of a messenger that I wear.

I nod. "I thought to wash before going to the palace. I hope to visit afterward, but one never knows."

"Of course."

I strip off my dusty shirt and find a pitcher of water on the table and a cloth and bowl where I know they'll be stored.

"Where's Beldala?" The past two times I passed through Alawea my birth-parent was away, making it nearly seven seasons since we last saw each other.

"Gone."

Dallu's tone implies deeper meaning than one syllable should possess. Turning with the dripping cloth in my hand, I wait for more.

"Beldala left to deliver a message to Glendower. That was half a season ago."

"Half a season?" The water from the cloth plops drip by drip on the toe of my boot as the news sinks in. "To Glendower and back should take no more than a fortnight; a fortnight and a half at most."

Dallu's voice drops to a hush so low, even standing two arm spans away I strain to hear the words. "I think Beldala left to look for the insurgent army."

"You believe the rumors?"

"Beldala did."

I hope more than I can say that Dallu's suspicion is true, but an attack on the road is far more likely. When the autarch decreed that bi-genders would be messengers the excuse used was that, being neither men nor women, we were safer from the violence men encounter on the road and the other sorts of brutality more often visited upon women. In truth, we're more vulnerable to both. Mono-genders, both men and women, prove their superiority to all but a fortunate few of us in a variety of ways. It happened to me often enough in these very alleys.

A hard knot in my belly forms around the fear for my birth-parent's safety. "What makes you think Beldala wasn't waylaid?"

"I tracked down the one who should have gone to Glendower," Dallu says. "The messenger was not ill as Beldala told me. The errand was traded and the trade requested as a favor."

I digest this in silence. The wet cloth, gone from cool to cold in my hand, pebbles my skin in goose-flesh as I touch it to the back of my neck and face, to the warm skin under my arms. Lastly, I lower my breeches and rinse the rest of the stink of twelve suns' travel from my body.

Dressed again, I nod for Dallu to follow me to the back of the room. Leaving the chair for my co-parent, I take the three-legged footstool Beldala fashioned when I was a child.

"I've heard that insurgents gather to the east of the Barrier Wall," I say, my voice low. "I've also heard they welcome bi-genders to fill their numbers."

"Fantasy," Dallu snorts. "Why would they accept us when no others do? I tried to convince Beldala that what people wish enough for they will invent."

"Or create," I say.

The rumors excite me and I wish I possessed the fortitude of my birth-parent, risking all to seek the truth. I think not only of the lot of bi-genders, but the starvation in our quarters while those above us feast. The torture of innocents on the merest suspicion. The quashing of the old religion for the new. It makes me feel as the great prairie cats held captive in the palaces must feel, pining for the plains where mates and prides roar their defiance and freedom. I want the rebels to be real, the freedom to be real, so that I might someday roar my own defiance.

"My tetrarch has seemed nervous of late," I say. "Perhaps when the tetrarch opens the message I carry I'll learn more. Maybe it holds proof we need."

"Do not say 'we!'"

Dallu's words are too loud and I look to the door, though I see no one lingering there.

"My mate left to chase dreams," my co-parent continues, standing so suddenly that the chair rocks twice before settling on four legs again. "I'll not lose a child to them as well."

The conversation is over and I have made a poor homecoming, but ideas, no more than seeds before, have taken deep root. What if I could someday leave the service and the hatred? Make a new life among equals?

"I don't wish you gone," Dallu says into the awkward silence, the words ironic in light of my thoughts,

"but you should go. You'll be punished if it's found that you delayed delivering your message."

We both know this for truth. Dallu follows me from the dimness of the shack into the sharp, dusty sunlight.

"I hope to see you again before I leave," I say, pulling the reins loose and continuing to the rear of my mount to re-buckle the croup.

Despite a man, woman, and child walking toward us and three men close behind them, Dallu reaches out suddenly, taking me in a quick embrace. There's no law against public affection between bi-genders; like campfires in the high grasses of the prairie one simply knows better. Perhaps Dallu thinks I mean to go looking for the insurgents that very moment. As if I'd know where to start, or have the nerve to try.

The family comes level with us just as the heaviest of the three men behind them shouts a challenge. The father turns and the woman grips the shoulders of what I now see is a bi-gender child. My hands clench into fists reflexively; the taunt and the setting evoking old habits.

"They're new here." I hear sorrow in Dallu's voice and an anticipation of the inevitable.

Though not all bi-gender couples can reproduce, mono-genders have been giving birth to bi-genders more frequently in recent generations. When a high-born child shows the signs—at birth, or later, when puberty reveals the androgyny that external characteristics had not—the family is cast down to live among the lowest classes. The hatred visited upon those both high-born and bi-gender is fearsome.

The child presses close to the mother's body and the father steps in front of them. Memories of my own childhood howl as I watch. It was many years before I grew strong enough to dissuade individuals, old enough to discourage those younger than me, and before every detail of my body was common knowledge among the brutes of Sabanach.

The heavy fellow snatches at the child but the father loops his forearm under the man's and draws a large circle, leaving him surprised and open. The father kicks, first to the belly and then to the face. He is trained in military arts, then. A shame, for he is outnumbered and will suffer for it. We have, most of us, learned when there is a chance of fighting our way free and when there is not.

The mother, and even the child, struggle, scratch, do what they can to fend off the arms of the other two that snake past the father. The fight boils nearer and my horse shies, forcing Dallu and myself away from his rear and into the street. I tell Dallu to get inside. I will follow once I retie my horse.

Suddenly, I hear the unmistakable ricochet of thick bone breaking. The heavy man cradles one forearm in the other, bellowing his anger and pain. The older of the three, a feral-looking man, draws a knife that is half a sword and lunges for the father. Dallu steps closer, an impotent desire to help writ clear in eyes that are wide with concern.

"Get inside!" I hiss again. I grasp for Dallu's sleeve but miss.

The child wriggles from the mother's grip and lifts a broken cobble from the alley just as the father ducks under the attacker's arm. Before the child can throw, the father steps back to counterattack, stumbling over the child's shoes.

I refuse to believe this will go so far as killing. Thugs torment and abuse us—the lowest of the low—with impunity, but murder of any citizen is no mean thing. It would bring down the wrath of the soldiers. Many in Sabanach, participants or not, would suffer.

Dallu must see a different outcome. My co-parent grabs the collar of the off-balance father and pulls the man onto his ass. The knife's trajectory is unchanged and Dallu stands now where the father stood a moment before.

The blow is indeed lethal. An upward strike, sinking the long knife nearly to the hilt.

The feral man freezes like one of the stone statues in the palace gardens. It is Dallu who removes the blade by sliding lifelessly to the ground.

The alley suddenly erupts in pushing, jostling panic. My eyes are fixed on the still face of Dallu, and the last flicker of recognition in those brown eyes, as I kneel beside my co-parent. I don't see the cowards run.

Someone grips my shoulder hard.

"Get out of here," the father is saying to me, "before more people see you."

I hear the words but they wash over me like tepid water, eliciting no reaction.

"I'll help you carry him," he says.

I distantly register the arbitrary pronoun he uses for my co-parent. The man squats and slides his arms under Dallu's back, lacing them around the still and bloody chest. My mind and body are frozen in the moment of the knife strike, unwilling to move forward into the present.

"Soldiers will come soon," he repeats slowly.

When I move my joints are wooden, as if a puppeteer controls what I cannot. I lift Dallu's legs. The father gives me a look like I have done something praise-worthy. He shuffles back and indicates the open door with his head. "This one?"

I nod.

We set Dallu on the sleeping pallet in the far corner. I try to still the torrent of emotions threatening to burst from my chest by arranging Dallu's slack limbs. I brush the high, aristocratic cheekbones with my fingers. I wonder if the fact that Dallu once lived in the upper terraces somehow prompted this fatal rashness.

"What's your name?"

I'm shaken from my thoughts by the man's unexpected question. His wife and child stand behind him, mute with fear and shock.

"Jerusha," I reply, and close Dallu's eyes as gently as possible.

"Was he your father?"

Co-parent and father are a world apart, but I have no strength to teach this man his new language. He will learn it soon enough, if he lives so long. "Yes," I say, standing.

"I swear to you, on my name, Finagor of house Aruldon, I will do anything in my power to repay his sacrifice."

I want to snort at the man's belief that he possesses any power at all now that he is here among us.

Dallu's still body draws my eyes back to the corner. I am overwhelmed anew that I will never again feel my co-parent's embrace. The insurgents, if they exist, are right in seeking to tear the hierarchy apart. And if they don't exist, they should.

The hatred I carry for our lot in life pushes out at my ribs, making my hands shake and my head pound. My lifelong fear angers me even more. Like a tether under too much strain, something breaks. I move so suddenly that Finagor steps back, and I storm outside like Abab confronting the Lashans.

The streets and alleys are as vacant as I have ever seen them. People have gone to hole like the small prairie animals before a great thunderstorm. I strip my saddlebags from the horse with a jerk.

Back inside, I pull open one flap and yank the purple velvet package from within. Opening that, I remove the cream-colored paper, folded twice and perfect in its squareness. In my anger the entire seal tears from the paper below the flap as I open the message I have borne these past many suns. The reading skills needed to carry out my duties are sufficient to understand the words written within.

The rumors are true. My knees go weak at the verification.

There must have been an earlier communication from Alawea to my tetrarch in Zasna saying that Alawea's spies discovered the insurgent army. The message I hold is my tetrarch's answer. She advocates that both cities should unite their forces and strike at dawn on the day after the coming full moon. The location to join forces and the location of the rebels are both mentioned.

Finagor's skin has blanched to the color of yellowed bone. "What have you done?" he asks.

The answer is so large I can no more distill it into words than I could distill the salt from the wide sea. I have taken action on my own behalf. I have confirmed my greatest hope. And I have ensured my own slow death by opening the tetrarch's private message.

The paper drifts from my fingers to the dusty floor and still I make no answer. Finagor stares at the message lying in the dirt as he might at a deadly porah snake. At last he bends to lift it from the ground. His breath hisses between his teeth as he reads.

"They do exist."

In an unsteady voice his wife asks, "Who?"

He hands her the note. The child watches her read it.

"I planned to take my family east," Finagor says, a slow wonder in his voice, "as soon as I could secure food, weapons, and mounts. We would have gone on no more than the hope, but you have given us the certainty. And more than that, the location."

And as suddenly as that, the rumors make sense.

Those cast out from the upper terraces would spurn living as I have lived, given any chance of an alternative. If the families defecting are comprised of men and women with Finagor's education and military training, the new army would welcome them with open arms. Bigotry toward bi-genders would of necessity be suppressed or eradicated as the numbers grew.

My excitement falls to ash, however, as the implications of the message crash home. "Why celebrate knowing their location when they're about to be destroyed?"

"I'd rather die a soldier than be ambushed by thugs in an alley." Finagor looks to his wife and she nods in agreement. "Besides, if this army is as large as rumor has it, they may have a chance. I doubt the Holy Autarch or the western cities have word of them yet."

What he says makes sense. Four of the five cities are widely spread out, standing at the corners of the land to protect the capital with the Holy Autarch in the center. Our eastern provinces would be held responsible for an army forming at our border and would likely keep quiet, hoping to deal with it before the autarch learned of its existence.

And what will you choose, Jerusha?" his wife asks me, finally speaking. "The watch will learn of the murder here and investigate before long. You had best go soon, whether it's to the Barrier Wall or to the palace."

A short huff, nearly a laugh, escapes my chest. "I can do neither. My horse has been seen. If soldiers come and learn I haven't gone to the palace, I'll be hunted down. My mount is tired from the journey. I'd be captured long before I made the wall." I nod to the opened and dusty note in her hand. "My other choice is to deliver that to the tetrarch."

"You're not trusted with your tetrarch's seal, I suppose?" Finagor asks.

I indicate I am not.

"Bring me a light then," he says.

His tone, still that of one from the highest terrace, brooks no argument. I retrieve flint and striker and a small twig from the cookfire pit and hand them to him, wondering what he intends.

He blows what dust he can from the letter and strikes a spark to the twig. With the small flame he heats the seal and carefully begins peeling away bits of torn paper from the edges. I realize that he means to re-seal the message and hope kindles in me, catching like the dry twig.

"Wait!" his wife says, and Finagor extinguishes the tiny flame at once.

"Why deliver this message when Jerusha could deliver another in its place?" she asks.

He looks at her, then at me.

"Would you be willing to deliver a false message, Jerusha?" he asks.

It's hard to imagine the suffering I would endure for such treachery, were it discovered. I look again to Dallu's cold body. The conditioned obedience that broke inside me moments before remains broken.

"I would." My resolve hardens as I say the words.

"You carry stationery?" Finagor asks.

"Yes." A messenger keeps pen and ink as well as blank notes for aristocracy and a supply of stationery made especially for the tetrarch: the thick outer paper, a layer of the tetrarch's color inside, and a fine layer for the message glued to that.

Finagor nods.

"What if the message were to urge forestalling any action?" I suggest. "I'll likely be sent away with an answer, which would give me time to ride instead to the insurgents and warn them."

"The message could say that your tetrarch in Zasna had also discovered this army's location as well as their leader," Finagor muses, "and has infiltrated them besides. Instead of advising a coordinated attack, we could make the message say that your tetrarch has an assassin in place and wants no action taken yet."

His wife smiles and so do I.

I remove a fresh piece of stationery backed with the tetrarch of Zasna's deep maroon and hand it to him, then retrieve pen and ink.

Pulling the chair to the small table and sitting, Finagor rubs his sleeve across the table's surface. He studies the original message, wipes his hands on his pants, and secures the blank message with thumb and middle finger.

"My tutor taught me my letters by having me trace the writing of scholars and then imitate it freehand. I believe I have not lost the talent."

The old gods I still pray to must have given me this man when they took Dallu from me, for even had I envisioned this course, I could never have managed what he creates.

"Sand," he says, when his artifice is complete.

I reach into the saddlebags and hand him a small pouch tied with a thin ribbon. He opens it and sprinkles a light dusting to dry the ink, then taps the paper edgewise on the table. Blowing off the excess, he holds it for the rest of us to examine. I myself would not know it for a forgery had I not witnessed the act.

He hands the message to me to fold with the ritualistic precision I have practiced since childhood. Relighting the twig, he sets to work on the original message again, this time to remove the seal entirely. Carefully prying it up with a fingernail, he shifts it to the new stationery with the delicacy of balancing a finn's egg on the tip of his finger.

"If I press it hard I'll distort the seal. Have a care, messenger, it won't hold well."

Taking it from him I place the ersatz message gently inside the velvet pouch.

"Give me a blank note," he says when I am done. "I need to write a message to a friend of mine in the palace proper."

My look must convey my thought, that he has no friends there. Not anymore.

"His son and mine are of an age," Finagor explains. "They played together. Martine began binding his son's chest two moons ago."

It doubles my risk to deliver a second note, but our fates are twined now like the roots of a mayak tree; what endangers me endangers him as well. I do as he asks.

He scratches a note in his own hand, the letters narrower and finer than the last. I catch enough to see that he is requesting horses and supplies. He folds the note in half, writes "Martine of House Saber" on the front, and uses a tiny remnant of wax on the twig to glue the two sides together.

Finagor hands it to me. "If this reaches him, perhaps both he and I will see you east of the wall. And now you must go. You have delayed too long already."

He is right, though the events since my arrival have taken less than a tick of the sun, Dallu's death adds yet another layer of danger. I pack the additional message and sling my saddlebags over one shoulder.

"If you're still here when I return to take Dallu's body to the cremation pit," I say, "then you will know all went well."

"You shouldn't come back," his wife says over Finagor's shoulder.

"She's right," he says. "You risk enough already. Let me see to that burden for you."

I feel guilt but no sorrow that it will be Finagor throwing the body into the sulfurous refuse pit instead of me, but I must at least make my goodbye. I cross to the pallet and kneel to kiss Dallu's cool forehead one last time.

Finagor follows me to the door when I am done.

"Fortune to you," I say to him, as I leave my childhood home for the last time.

He surprises me by reaching out. We grip forearms in the way of equals.

I walk out into a street that is as still and quiet as the prairie at midnight. Gathering the reins of my horse, I mount and ride for the uppermost terrace.

The stillness has rippled out perhaps four streets in all directions. Beyond that perimeter of fear, Sabanach hums with its normal activity as if nothing of consequence has occurred today. Children play in the muck; a few pile round rocks until they fall, others run and scream as one pushes an inflated pig's bladder with a stick. Laundry flutters in the light breeze, absorbing the stench of the quarter into the drying cloth.

I ascend the hill and pass unchallenged through the middle terrace gate. The guards laugh and joke among themselves, sparing me only a glance. Bigenders, being impossible to counterfeit, are not worth their concern; a fact, I'm sure has kept us as messengers generations after the death of the 14th Autarch.

The sky of the middle terrace is the pale, pearly pink of the interior of an oyster shell, though it can only be seen from the vantage of this terrace. By order of the tetrarch, a fine dust is sprayed upward daily from multiple points. It ascends no more than three times the height of the tallest building, and yet it appears to color the sky by catching the light in some way I don't understand.

The road winds upward through the shops and villas. The brown clothes of a messenger protect me here, unlike Sabanach, where impotent anger at the world outweighs sense or caution. At last, I arrive before the third and final gate. Waved through again, I pass under the stone arch and emerge to a dome of pale lavender sky, the color most favored by this tetrarch.

The color is everywhere, in the piled hair of the gentry, in the stain of windows in the elaborate villas, and worked into the clothing of both men and women.

The palace of the tetrarch crowns the city with only the backdrop of the mountain beyond. The whole is gilded in a glittering gold material, the manufacture of which is long forgotten. Seven spires rise in the pattern of the seven stars of Agrenost and kiss the pale purple sky with needle-thin tips as delicate as crystal and as strong as iron.

My resolve doesn't waver but anxiety toys with my breath nonetheless, catching at it as I enter the courtyard. I dismount and hand the reins of my horse to a boy who spares me no look. The horse belongs to the tetrarch, but I am less than nothing.

The palace halls are well known to me and I wend the maze of twists and turns to the heart of the labyrinthine building. The tetrarch is not in the throne room, but a soldier at the door knows his whereabouts and directs me to the Room of Dreams. One of the soldiers there confirms that the tetrarch is within and opens the door.

The walls and ceiling of the room are egg-shaped and the color is that of rich cream. Golden gilt bands the center of the room. The ceiling is painted the pale blue of a third season sky on the plains, with clouds rendered so realistically they seem to drift if one watches them too long. I enter, and my performance begins.

The tetrarch sits on the floor, as children of his age are wont to do, but I see why the soldier saw no need to escort me inside. Next to the tetrarch a giant prairie cat lies at his ease, propped on strong elbows. Eyes that were half closed in repose open, piercing me with orange and gold.

I have heard it rumored that the cats are prescient, if so, then perhaps I am doomed no matter how well I play my part. I do my best to mask my face with calmness, though the cat and the handler standing nearby—training stick in hand—make it more difficult still.

An attendant brushes the tetrarch's brown hair. It has never felt the touch of shears in the eleven years of his life, and spills across the floor behind him. I sink to one knee by the door and bow my head as I have so many times before. Were this the Holy Autarch, I would prostrate myself. I reach into the pouch and withdraw the folded paper as carefully as possible. "A message, Exalted One," I say, proffering my lie.

Too late I see that the much abused wax of Zasna's tetrarch is loosened and raised all across the lowest side. It remains sealed by the barest margin. Visions of the chambers of torment below the palace dance before my eyes, all the more vivid for never having seen them.

He nods and I approach, my arm still extended. I tense my muscles to keep from shaking as I hold the message and force myself not to stare at the defect in the seal. Both cats and children are sensitive to signs of uneasiness that adults might miss.

I hold my breath as the boy-ruler takes the message from my hand.

He will not fail to notice the defect when his attention reaches the seal and my dreams of freedom evaporate like morning mist. I spend a last wish hoping that Finagor will escape suspicion for his part in this duplicity.

In the heartbeat between the tetrarch slipping a finger beneath the fold and the imminent examination of the seal to break it open, the cat stretches forward to sniff the bottom of the paper. My heart lurches as I think he points out the falseness to his master.

Sweat trickles beneath my arms as the great ruff about the cat's neck caresses the message, obscuring nearly half the folded paper. He nuzzles at it almost as if reading it with his nearsighted eyes. One hind leg extends as he leans forward, the joint reversed from other four-legged creatures. It's said the cats can stand on their hind legs in the way of people, though I've never witnessed this.

The tetrarch glares at the cat and strikes the animal's head with one thin elbow as he breaks the seal. The trainer is there in an instant. He jabs the cat hard in the hindquarters with the metal point of the stick. The cat jerks but suppresses a growl.

The message is open and no one has seen the defect. Relief leaves me lightheaded. The tetrarch reads the message quickly and nods to a servant at the far end of the room. In the way that the most familiar and well-trained servants have, the man discerns his master's intent and brings one of the small burning braziers, holding it carefully by its long, narrow stem. To my profound relief, the tetrarch tosses the message in and watches the flames devour it.

"I wish to reply," he says to me, and holds out one long-fingered and uncalloused hand.

The servant runs to a gilded box on a desk and returns with stationary and pen. The tetrarch disdains the offered board from my satchel and writes instead against the floor. I remain on bended knee until he has finished, then fold the message and wait while he seals it, marking the wax with the imprint of his ring.

Bowing my head once again I stand and back to the door, the new message in hand.

The Holy Autarch has noticed me on occasion, and the bright blue gems of his eyes disturb me. The tetrarch of my adopted city often acknowledges me. But this tetrarch has never once looked into my eyes. His cat does, though. He lifts that massive head, the chain about his neck clinking softly, and stares into my soul in a way that says he knows my secrets. I stumble but catch my balance, and am relieved to hear the snick of the door as the guard pulls it closed behind me.

Two hallways from the Room of Dreams my heart still labors. I wish nothing more than to run from the palace and ride from the city out into the empty lands and then to the east. But one last promise I must fulfill before I leave.

A tetrarch's messenger may attract unwanted attention delivering a note to Finagor's friend and so I spiral toward the outer halls, keeping watch for a local messenger. At last I pass one I know. My heart has slowed to normal and my voice, when I speak, is steady and matter-of-fact.

"I was given a message for Martine of House Saber by someone too rushed to find a palace messenger."

We are the only two in the hall and I receive a small roll of the eyes that some find us so interchangeable. The messenger takes the note and reverses direction, unaware of the seditious contents folded within that paper.

And just like that, it's done. My last duties as a messenger completed. Zasna's tetrarch will wait at least a fortnight for a reply; Alawea's tetrarch even longer. I can be with the insurgents long before that.

The final set of doors loom ahead, leading outside and to freedom. My eyes are so fixed on that egress that I don't hear or see the great cat step from the shadows of the cross hall until he is an arm span or two from me. His chain is still looped around his thick neck, but there is no handler at the other end.

I have never seen one of the great cats in any of the palaces absent a handler. His approach is unnerving, the more so for the odd motion of his forward-jointed hind legs. I wonder if I have come so close to freedom only to die within sight of it.

His yellow and gold eyes fix me, as if he reads me like my masters have read the written words I have carried. His mouth is open slightly as he pants, and fangs longer than my fingers gleam wetly.

I suppose it doesn't matter if I die now. I would have liked to have tasted freedom even for a short while, but the only messages that have ever meant anything to me have been delivered today. Even if the beast perceives what has occurred, unless he possesses some way to communicate it, then it cannot be undone. I resolve to die content.

He comes close enough that his great ruff tickles my hand. Lifting himself with a casual show of back and abdominal strength, he stands almost as straight as I and taller by a head. I try to step back but one heavy paw slaps my shoulder and pulls me forward until my face is close to his. His breath is not rank, as I would have imagined, but sweet and earthy. His whiskers twitch as his mouth stretches and relaxes, and he makes soft grunts deep in his chest. Yellow-gold eyes fix my own, piercing me, willing me to understand.

I think I do.

"I won't forget you," I say, "or your brothers."

Perhaps I'm wrong and he only wanted to wish me well in the freedom I can escape to that he cannot. Or perhaps he knows what Finagor and I have done today, or even what is yet to happen, and wished to advise me. But I choose to take this as a sign that our plans will succeed.

His paw pushes down hard on my shoulder for balance as he steps back and drops again to all fours. On impulse, I reach forward and touch the great head, though I have never seen a tetrarch or a handler so familiar. My hand strokes back, over the thick fur and to the chain at his neck. It is tight to the point that I cannot slip even a finger beneath it.

"I will unchain you myself if I can," I tell him.

He looks up at me and gives another soft grunt. Then he turns and disappears in the shadows of the cross hall. When I hear the drag of the chain no more I walk out the doors of the palace, lower than the lowest servant, for the last time. From the vantage of the palace I can see beyond the eastern wall, and the sight swells my heart.

Pat Cadigan is a two-time winner of Britain's Arthur C. Clarke Award, as well as a Hugo winner. This is her first appearance in Galaxy's Edge.

JOHNNY COME HOME

by Pat Cadigan

There was nothing for me to do in Moscow but drink.

Well, that and look for Johnny, and I no longer really had to do that. The Sense told me he was in the city, eventually our paths would cross and I would reel him in. But until that happened, I had to do something and drinking was it. Bars as Westerners know them were still relatively new in Moscow. Most of them little more than empty storefronts with the bare essentials; if you wanted atmosphere, you brought it with you. Or, if you were an especially wealthy tourist, you could go to one of the headjob parlors, where they gave you a happy-hood and a couple of gloves so you could enjoy your Stoli in whatever virtual environment they were running that night—provided, of course, you'd made your reservation the required six-to-eight months in advance.

I figured it was artificial reality either way and, not being an especially wealthy tourist, I opted for the austerity plan. Besides, in Moscow, it was the booze that carried importance, not the place where you drank it, and Stoli seemed to have a deeper understanding of the drinking organism. It certainly understood me—besides being mellow and friendly, it had the salutary effect of enhancing the Sense. The bad news was that sobering up dulled me, but that was easy enough to take care of.

So there I was, boozing and cruising in Moscow. They all envied me back home—my turn to fetch Johnny, and I got to go to Russia to do it. First time I'd ever been off the North American continent, too. But here's a little Home Truth for you (and why not Home Truth, seeing as how we've had the Awful Truth, Nothing But the Truth, and Cheap Truth, God help us each and every one): one place is pretty much like another, and once I understood what I could do in Moscow, I might have been

anywhere, the language difference notwithstanding. Even now—or maybe especially now, in the last weeks before the millennium turned. Well, not a full turn—next year would be the real first year of the new millennium, but everyone in the world seemed to be stuck on the idea that 2000 was the Big year. Certain ideas died hard, and others wouldn't die at all. Like Johnny's ideas.

He could live a thousand years himself and never give up on those sweet, mad ideas. Master of my fate, captain of my soul, world full of miracles, tomorrow's another day (or another millennium), anything can happen and it probably will.

Yah. Dream about it, Johnny. He'd be doing that right now, somewhere in Moscow, living in his own brand of artificial reality, dreaming hard enough to kill someone while I held my place at a bar that had once been some kind of counter—kitchen? grocery?—it was hard to tell in this light—in another dingy ex-storefront.

As usual, there were lots of foreigners. Some were tourists and business travelers, but a good many of them were what the government was calling 'temporary long-term.' No doubt plenty of those were skating along on forged papers, hoping to find some way to establish residency later. Russia had been through a lot of changes in the 90s right along with the rest of the world, but people themselves never really change, no matter where they are. Nor do situations. That's some more Home Truth, and you could figure that one out even without the Sense.

So I maintained, anyway. The Sense is not one hundred percent infallible but the group back home believed it was a constant, all-over advantage. I was of two minds, you should pardon the expression, about that, myself, and it sometimes caused more friction among us than Johnny's periodic coop flying. 'Loyal opposition' is not an easy concept to put over to organisms like us, but we all understood disloyal opposition. We had Johnny. Or we would when I brought him home again, tired, disillusioned, and hung-over from his freedom bender, to play docile prodigal and rejoin. Until all those sweet, mad ideas built up enough to set him off again.

I was on my third Stoli, watching the bartender sort out orders and make change, when the front door opened wide with a blast of frigid winter air.

Over the multi-lingual gabble, someone started calling for papers in six different languages, and the person on my left dropped like a stone.

I looked down. A pretty, heart-shaped face framed by dark blonde hair looked back up at me, eyes wide.

"Pamageeteh menye," she whispered. Help me.

I was on the verge of telling her I wasn't Russian. Then I moved so that I was standing directly in front of her, my ankle length coat spread to hide her. She had been at the end of the bar next to the wall, so perhaps no one had seen her duck. Even if someone had, this was not the type of crowd that would alert the immigration officers now moving through the place and shining flashlights on documents held up for inspection.

Chatter became hushed and most movement ceased, except for the sweep of the flashlight beams standing out hard in the smoky air, like light-swords in some old science fiction movie. The bartender moved slowly down the counter, picking up empty glasses, running a rag over the chipped Formica, until he came to where I was standing. Folding his arms, he leaned against the wall and looked around in an aimless, bored way before letting his gaze rest pointedly to my left.

I showed him my passport and shrugged. He made a fist, wincing. His thoughts were like a bellow in my skull, a mostly incoherent expression of anger, at me with my coat so obviously spread, at the woman hiding behind it, at the immigration officers, at the world in general for interfering with him. He was very young, one of the post-glasnost generation, with no memory of a different time, when this empty storefront would have been equally empty even with a store in it, when he might have begged the blonde's blue jeans from her to sell on the black market and ended up crouching in the dark with her, hiding from KGB, not immigration.

Or perhaps he was a member of a hate-group. I could get no clear indication from him. Even with plenty of warm, Sense enhancing Stoli in me, his tension was an occluder.

The bartender's gaze shifted and I turned to look at the immigration officer now standing on my right. Without moving my elbows from the bar, I showed her my open passport. In the peripheral glow from the flashlight, her face was calm, unworried; she might have been an acquaintance looking at pictures of my family.

She moved the flashlight beam to my face. I stared past it to the two pinpoints of reflected light, all I could see of her eyes now. Everything stopped.

After awhile, she said, "Thank you, Maria Tell," her accent making the words musical. She held her head high as she turned around. I could feel the bartender staring hard at me as the woman made her way to the door, where the other officers were waiting. They filed out in another blast of Moscow winter wind that cleared a little of the smoke and briefly overrode the ancient space-heaters. I could still Sense her aching feet, her fatigue, her discomfort in the cold, her wish that they could just give this foreigner watering-hole a fast once-over and leave empty-handed, through for the night; and if by chance there were refuseniks with forged papers among the crowd, then please don't let her have to find them, let it be one of the others who would have to stay up the rest of the night inputting and contacting embassy officials and whatnot. All she wanted was to go home and see what had been downloaded from the International Net.

That made me the genie who had granted her wish. No wonder she'd thanked me so politely.

The blonde emerged from under my coat, swiping at her mussed hair and looking dazed, as if she had just awakened with no idea how she'd come to be here. "God, I had no hope that would work, I was just desperate and crazy—" She saw the bartender and her expression became wary. But instead of throwing her out, he leaned on the bar and looked directly into my face.

"Do you have a brother?" he asked in heavily accented English.

And then, of course, I knew exactly what Johnny had been doing all this time in Moscow.

"I'm in it for the same reason as anybody else," said the blonde, puffing along beside me in the cold. "Artistic freedom."

I made a polite noise, or tried to. My lungs felt frozen. The blonde's name was Evie Gray, and she was now my friend for life.

"The Russians understand," she went on. "They know what repression really is. They make movies here where people drink and use drugs, they can make fun of religion. They've got *Huckleberry Finn* in the libraries—it's pretty weird in Russian, but they've got it in the original English, too. And God, rock music! All kinds of stuff you can't hear in the States any more, old rap, new rap, heavy-fuck-ing-metal that tells you to kill yourself, for chrissakes. And in the happy-hood parlors, it's anything goes, hard-core, soft-core, violence, whatever you want, and no goddam Council for the Prevention of Mind-Control to come in and pull the plug on you—hell, you can even get abortions on demand here, did you know that? On demand. All you have to do is walk into a clinic and you don't even have to give them a reason—"

"Still can't burn the Russian flag on the steps of the Kremlin," I said. "But I guess nobody's perfect, eh?"

She didn't hear me. She ran on and on about the Constitution being fucked like the air and water and land had been fucked and how it was just going to get worse and worse. Whether she was saying all this for my benefit or her own wasn't clear even to her. Not that it mattered any more. Her visa had run out three weeks before and she was now officially refusenik, subject to arrest and deportation.

I wondered if she was aware of the original meaning of refusenik, but I wasn't curious enough to use the Sense to find out. There were scads of these new refuseniks running around Moscow and elsewhere in the Soviet Union. I couldn't decide whether they were yet another premillennial nut-group, the start of a real movement, or just more people living in their own brand of artificial reality. But then, I predated the Berlin Wall and, at my age, sometimes everybody looked like just another nut. Even when the Sense told me they were all quite sane, if not especially wise.

What Evie Gray was more than anything else was especially wealthy. I didn't point out to her that this was the only way she could have managed this dramatic flight to freedom. It's yet another Home Truth that only the richest and the poorest ever attain freedom, the richest because they can afford it, the poorest because nobody's ever looking for them.

"You don't share a brother-sister resemblance," said the woman with the long, straight hair. "More like mother and son. If you'll pardon my saying so."

I smiled at her; she didn't smile back. Russians were sparing with their smiles. Whoever had taught her English had been from Boston. "He's adopted."

"Excuse me?" She looked puzzled.

"Nothing. Yuri at the Kropotkin hard currency bar gave me this address."

Her gaze slid to Evie Gray. "Did something happen at the Kropotkin?"

"No. Almost, but it was averted," I said.

"Good answer," Evie murmured.

"I understand." said the woman, stepping to the dark velvet curtain behind her. She sounded friendlier but she still didn't smile. "You realize this is a very exclusive mesto; foreign visitors who come here must reserve many months in advance and the wait list is already a year long."

The bundle in Evie's outthrust hand was obscenely thick. "I can pay."

The woman made it disappear almost before my new American friend realized she had taken it. "Next time, you should be more discreet. Put it in a little sack and pass it. If others saw, you could be marked as worth robbing."

"I wouldn't let that happen," I said, "but we promise we'll be more careful in the future."

"Harashow. This way." She pulled the curtain aside and stepped into the headjob parlor.

I liked the simple descriptiveness of their name for it: mesto—literally, place. Some place else might have been more like it. The Russians had embraced virtual reality with a religious fervor. Having been through only a few days of a Russian winter and hearing it called unseasonably warm, I could understand. But virtual reality was just as major in the States and any other country developed enough to maintain the technology. I could understand that, too. It was merely the next logical step after television and video games, really.

The mesto wasn't much like an American arcade. Instead of little single or double booths, there were rows of what looked like old barber chairs, about fifty altogether, all of them occupied by people wearing headpieces and action-gloves. Lots of weird hand-motions going on, some I could guess at and some I wouldn't have wanted to. There were no individual units—all the cables from the equipment disappeared into the floor. Centralized transmission;

no variety, but it would make the mesto's operating costs a lot cheaper, increasing the profit margin to something that even an old 80s greed-is-good throwback would call more than respectable.

"How long have you been operating?" I asked the woman as I followed her to the end of the last row of chairs.

"Almost a year," she said.

At the end of the row was a vacant chair, the only one in the room, with a head-piece sitting on it like an abandoned crown. "Your companion bought you an hour's worth," the woman said, gesturing at it. "Take your pleasure."

I blew out an irritated breath. "That's not what I'm here for."

"If you want to see your brother, you'll take the hour." She picked up the head-piece and held it out to me.

It didn't make any sense, and I was having a hard time with the Sense as well. The long, cold walk from the Kropotkin had sobered me up and I was dull. But the little flicker that I managed to get from her indicated that somehow, she was telling the truth. Maybe Johnny wanted me all tangled up with wires and distracted with fancy pictures before he'd talk to me, figuring that would keep me from sussing him out. As if this artificial reality could come between us any better than the one he'd made for himself. Dream on, and on, and on, Johnny.

The woman helped me with the gloves and then started to put the headpiece on me. "I'd like some Stoli, please," I said.

"This is not a voluta bar," she said. "We don't serve anything. If you wanted drinks, you should have brought your own."

"Get her some vodka." Evie slipped a hand into her pocket. "You can get me some, too."

The woman hesitated.

"And bring a straw. You know, one of those hollow tube things you can suck liquids through?" I added, in response to her blank look. "Unless you're hiding some dispensers for the head-pieces?"

"Yeah, it's the same fuck-the-tourists crap all over," said Evie.

"Shut up," I told her.

"Sometimes there's a bottle back in the office. A straw—" the woman shrugged. "I'll see what I can find." She took something from Evie—discreetly enough, I supposed—and slipped out a nearby door. Evie moved to help me with the head-piece.

"Hold it," I said.

She drew back a little, looking stung.

"I can't go on helping you indefinitely, you know."

"Can't?" She gave me a fast, pained grin. "You mean won't, right?"

"Look, I can fix it so tired cops don't see what they don't want to see. But I don't forge residency papers. And I'm not staying in Russia any longer than I have to."

"But you could make someone forge papers for me, couldn't you?" I wanted to shake her. "Is this place really so much better than the U.S.? You think Russia is heaven just because they've got *Huckleberry Finn* on the shelves and rap music on the radio and abortion on demand? Does the name 'Stalin' many anything to you? How about 'Pamyat'? They were just another anti-Semitic hate group in the early 90s, but now even their staunchest sympathizers are afraid of them. And they're not the only haters running around loose, all of them with their own agendas, but two things they all agree on: they hate Jews and they hate refuseniks. You think all of the missing ones are just blending in with their forged papers? Plenty of them are lying on slabs in a Moscow morgue, gutted like cattle, courtesy of Pamyat."

"Pamyat is a bad word around here. Don't use it." The woman reappeared and thrust a bottle that was a little over half-full at me. "Scares away our business. Sorry, no straw. And I have no idea what you'll do with it when you're inside."

I took a couple of healthy swigs and stuck the bottle between my thighs. She shrugged and looked at Evie. "I'll wait right here," Evie said.

"Hurry up and take your hour. There's a long line behind you." She pushed the head-piece all the way down so that my face was covered and the eye-screen lit up immediately.

I joined a standard dolphin's-eye sequence. As soon as artificial reality had become feasible for the mass-market, everyone had gone for the dolphin and whale stuff. Out of guilt, maybe: sorry we killed so many of you, so we'll be you, or pretend we are. I would have been bored except the quality was way beyond anything I'd ever seen before. The Russians must have been cranking away on hardware r&d, boosting definition and whatever else. But the head-piece hadn't looked like it was anything so extraordinary.

The perspective cruised past a formation of opalescent, eye shaped bodies that turned right and then left as one, lifting themselves out of my path like a curtain. Near a boulder, a fleshy squid ignored me, its tentacles rippling. Seaweed drifted, sank away into the shadows. Nothing new here, nothing in the least, but the quality—my inner ear kept flashing swimming messages to my stomach, where the disloyal Stoli had turned on me with a threat. Disloyal opposition. I hung onto the arms of the chair and tried to keep part of my awareness tuned to where I knew my body was, waiting for Johnny's presence to press in on the Sense.

I might have been cruising the ocean for ten minutes, or almost the whole hour; my sense of time had slipped away like one more darting ocean creature. But the novelty was wearing off and I felt bored, impatient, and slightly dizzy.

The perspective made a sudden wide arc to the left and passed through a multi-colored rock formation. Something with nasty-looking jaws peered out of a dark hole but never moved as I passed.

Just beyond the rocks was a giant clam, the ridges of the shell perfectly formed. It began to open as I approached—more standard stuff—displaying the giant pearl in the giant clam was usually the climax and indicated a change to the next sequence. So much for my hour and finding Johnny, I thought, watching the clamshell rise. When I got out of the chair, I was going to chug the rest of the Stoli and use the Sense to make the mesto hostess do cartwheels until she dropped.

<<Sadistic idea. Not like you, Maria.>>

The clamshell was gaping wide and it wasn't a pearl displayed there but a man, curled up in the fetal position. He unfolded slowly and gracefully, the way everything moves underwater, and turned to look at me.

Same old sweet, mad Johnny. His shoulder-length brown hair was floating around his head, his hazel eyes were like stars in his lovely, open face.

<<The Sense couldn't get a good fix on you until you jerked the cop in the voluta bar. I used the Sense

on the cops just that same way myself, till I found something better.>> He smiled at me. <<Come for to carry me home, sweet Maria? Sorry, not this time. This time, I beat you. I beat you all.>>

<<You always say that, Johnny. What is it now, a woman, or another man again? Even without the Sense you could make them fall in love with you. Lots of people can do that. But you can't make them love you. That's something very different from falling in love, Johnny, and after the last three times, I'd have thought you'd have known that. You'll end up killing this one with your needs, too. Just like the others. The group forgives your sin because we understand. But nobody else will. At the very least, they'll put you in jail and there you'll be, far from us and us far from you, all of us feeling the Lack. That's bad, Johnny. Remember how bad it is to feel the Lack? After your lover isn't falling in love with you anymore and you're without us?>>

I was working the Sense on him, of course, and he was pushing back just as hard, maintaining the balance of pressure as only those endowed with the Sense could. It was a balance he couldn't have with someone outside the group, the give and take of the Sense that we all needed, whether Johnny wanted to admit his own need or not.

<<It's different this time, Maria. I let my lover go right after I found this.>>

<<Found what—artificial reality? You can get that anywhere. Come home and we'll buy you your own booth.>>

<<But they don't have centralized transmission back in the States. A multitude all looking at once, invisible to each other but all visible to me. And I can have them all, not just one at a time but together.>> He spread his arms. <<I found this lonely technician, got her to scan my likeness into the simulation. The scanning equipment here is so much better than ours, they've been working so much harder on it. And between me and my likeness—>>

He didn't have to explain. Even without the Sense, I could have felt how it was, I think. Johnny's likeness might as well have been him. It had its own power within the artificial universe, blocking our little exchange from the rest of the clientele. A hundred people looking and none of them saw. I would have said a connection between a living being with the Sense and a likeness was impossible, except obviously none of us had tried it until now.

<<Of course, I have to stay in…keep the head-piece on, and the gloves. They're making a whole suit for me, it's almost finished. What I've done for business here—it was great before but now it's taken a real jump. We're going to expand. More of them for me, more and more, wanting to be in some beautiful, otherworldly place, one that I create. They give me their wanting and needing and I feel no Lack, none at all. I don't have to stay locked into the group any more, Maria. I'm free now. Free.>>

<<Why, Johnny? Why do you have to have them? Why don't you just come home and get the same thing from the ones who really know you and understand you?>>

He looked away from me, dreamily reaching up to run a finger along the belly of a passing shark.

<<Because it is always the same. I want different. I want to wake up in the morning knowing that I might see anybody, be with anybody, go anywhere. This way, I can. I don't want to be chained to the group, the way so many of them are chained to lives they never wanted. This way, anything really is possible. It really is a world full of miracles.>>

<<Dream about it, Johnny.>> I worked the Sense harder on him. <<It's still only a dream, and when you wake up, you'll still be what you've always been.>>

The push came so forcefully that I would have sworn he'd found someone else with the Sense and the two of them were ganging up on me. The likeness, I realized; Johnny had invested a great deal in it as the would-be escape hatch from the prison of his life, and wherever Johnny went, the Sense went with him. I had Stoli, but Johnny had this, and it was bigger.

Still, I strained for him, trying to make him—him and his likeness?—acknowledge the connection between us and fortify its existence.

I almost had him. Perhaps I had had him—his miracle world was more wonderful, but I was more familiar.

And then rough hands tore the head-piece away and I heard the mesto hostess say, "Time's up."

The cold was what really brought me to, though I was already staggering along Gorky Street. Famous Gorky Street, I remembered; every few years, the Russians would change the name to something else but for some reason, they'd always end up changing it back again. Evie Gray had her shoulder wedged under my armpit and my arm slung across her shoulders. She was chattering away but my head was too bad to make sense (or Sense) of what she was saying and the traitor Stoli in my gut was like a washing machine on the heavy soil setting.

Somehow, little old Evie knew—I say it's a Home Truth that in times of stress, everybody's got a tiny spot of the Sense—and got me to an alley where I could throw up in peace. Good-bye Stoli, and good-night, Gracie. Or Evie. I was dulled out.

After awhile, Evie got me moving again. She was still chattering—Christ, this woman never ran out of breath, I guess—and I caught the word problem.

"The real problem, Evie, old girl," I said, talking loudly over her, "the real problem here—and I think the Russians really do understand this—" I swing my free arm out to gesture at an empty storefront and almost sent us both down on the cold pavement "—the real problem is, people think life is a ladder, and it's really a wheel. That's a real Home Truth and we ignore it. It's there for us to see, everything is there for us to see, we've got Home Truth coming out of our ears, we know everything there is to know to get us through the day in one piece, and we ignore it like it doesn't exist. Hell, the earth is round, it turns, you'd think anyone could take a hint that blatant, but even someone with the Sense, who's supposed to know a little more than the average pilgrim, can still look Home Truth right in the kisser and say, 'No, thanks, artificial reality for me, please.' I don't know what to do about that, Evie. Even with the Sense, I just don't know what to do about it."

I heard her clear her throat. "Why don't you just shut up?"

She took a real chance dumping me at Intourist. She could have just left me on the street for the authorities to pick up—probably nothing would have happened, I wasn't refusenik, after all—and the fact that she got me indoors before she disappeared indicated a sweet generosity of spirit within that foolish chatterbox exterior. I liked her retroactively, for all the good that would do her.

I got a plane out the next morning—all I had to do was find an Aeroflot ticket agent with a xeno-phobic bent and give a little push. The genie of the bottle grants your wish and leaves your country.

The layover in London was supposed to be just a few hours, but Gatwick shut down indefinitely with a bomb scare—bomb scares were coming more frequently as December 31 approached—so I took the train into London, figuring I might as well be comfortable. Besides, I'd never seen London.

Forgot my own Home Truth: one place is pretty much like another. There was nothing for me to do in London either but drink. But London really understands the drinking organism the way Moscow was trying to. The pubs were warm and mellow. Guinness was even better on the Sense than Stoli had been, and I almost didn't care when Gatwick stayed shut another day and another, and Heathrow with it.

I didn't call home. They'd all know by now, anyway. I would only be telling them the details, and those could wait.

Those could wait and I could drink, and like anyone in artificial reality, I lost track of the time, which was how I came to be in London on Christmas Eve, looking down a week to the (artificial) dawn of the (artificial) new millennium. Feeling the Lack and filling it with Guinness. Travel was impossible now. There were riots every day, and not just in London. The Messiah was coming, they said; the Messiah was coming.

Then the transmission from Russia began. But I didn't bother trying to tell anyone that it wasn't really the Messiah. Just Johnny.

Happy-hood parlors all over London filled up, left the pubs empty (more for me, I thought, wavering at times between bitters and Guinness). Centralized transmission. No variety, but the quality… oh, the quality. Lost nothing bouncing off a satellite, not with Johnny on the job. Johnny on the spot, all the spots. The (artificial) dawn of the (artificial) new millennium. What everyone wanted all along, I guess.

And as to what Johnny wanted…not to be chained, to be free. He got both, thanks to the Sense, in any reality he chooses.

The Sense is a funny thing, and it can even be a good thing. I worked it pretty hard on him, but as I told Evie Gray, nobody's perfect. We'll get what we wanted, too, me and the rest of the group back in the States, when the transmissions to America begin, when poor, sweet, mad Johnny finally comes home.

Copyright © 1991 by Pat Cadigan

Zombies and Werewolves in space
What could possibly go wrong?

Though a relative newcomer, Brad R. Torgersen has had quite an impact on the field, with a Campbell nomination, a Nebula nomination, and three Hugo nominations, all in the past three years. His first novel is now out from Baen Books, and he has two collections available from Wordfire Press.

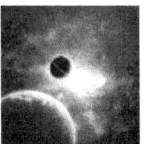

a
Sargasso Containment
story
www.SargassoLegacy.com

GYRE

by Brad R. Torgersen

The red-lettered sign over the tube to my berth clearly said NO PASSENGERS.

Yet there she was on the ramp: petit, stern-faced, and clasping a suitcase in both hands. Sweat beaded her forehead and her chest rose and fell quickly.

"If you can't read, it's not my problem," I said to her as I nudged past, pushing a cart loaded with lockers.

"This is dock six-oh-six," she said, "which means you're the courier pilot?"

I stopped halfway down the tube and turned back to face her.

"Yes, I am. The commercial spacelines are over on the third node. This is freight and cargo territory. You're in the wrong part of the station."

"Actually, Mr. Teller, I found you right where they told me to find you."

I raised an eyebrow.

"Whoever *they* are, they neglected to mention that couriers don't carry people."

"I'm not here for myself, Mr. Teller. I am here for this."

The young woman opened the suitcase to reveal a foam-packed interior. A shining, metallic cylinder was tucked into the foam, like an egg in a nest. There were no stickers or barcodes on the cylinder, and the young woman looked at me expectantly, as if the cylinder's mere presence explained everything.

I sighed.

"Fine, I still have room for small stuff. Whatever it is. But you'll have to go back and get it cleared through customs first. Then take it to the yard purser and have the transit fees deposited and transferred to my corporate account. I am assuming whoever sent you with this, also sent you with money?"

"They did."

She locked the suitcase back up and stepped down the ramp toward me, waiting until we were practically chest-to-nose before reaching into her shirt pocket and removing a transaction card. She raised the card up to my eye level.

"There is enough here to ensure that neither customs nor the purser need be involved. I was told that you are a man of discretion, Mr. Teller."

Who in the hell had this girl been talking to?

She apparently knew far more about me than I was comfortable with her knowing. I was about to beg off when I looked up at several people in bulky armor who were approaching the tube's mouth.

They all carried guns. And they didn't look like the normal uniformed patrol.

The young woman, noticing my eyes, jammed the transaction card into one of the open pockets on my flight vest, then spun and faced up the ramp. With one hand she held the suitcase protectively behind her. With the other she reached back to deftly guide my fingers around the suitcase's handle.

"What the hell—?" I began, but she cut me off.

"There are instructions on the card, Mr. Teller. You must ensure that this package arrives safely at the Sargasso Grid. Whatever else happens."

One of the armored men saw the young woman. He hand-signaled to the others with him. They brought their weapons up in unison, and I distinctly heard the sound of safeties clicking off. She screamed and ran at them, getting a quarter of the way up the ramp before multiple shell blasts took her down. Blood went everywhere.

I stood gape-mouthed and deafened, the suitcase still in my hand.

The barrels of their weapons retrained on me as the men advanced down the ramp. When they reached the young woman's corpse, one of them bent to check the body. He rolled her over on her back, causing one of her arms to flop loosely. A

STARTING AT $999!
(All-Inclusive)

INCLUDES:

✳

Your luxury cruise from Miami to the Bahamas
(including all meals on board)

✳

Critique of your manuscript by
Toni Weisskopf (head of Baen Books)

✳

Critique of your manuscript by Nancy Kress
(New York Times bestselling Hugo/Nebula winning author)

✳

Secrets to writing for the 1632 Universe by Eric Flint (creator of the 'Universe'
and New York Times bestselling author of "1632")

✳

One-on-One meal with a faculty member of your choice
(first-come-first-serve basis)

✳

Guaranteed purchase of at least one story from the pool of students attending
by *Galaxy's Edge* magazine

✳

and Much More!

✳

PLEASE NOTE:
Prices are expected to increase on March 31, 2015.

Sail to Success

RETURNING FOR A THIRD YEAR BY POPULAR DEMAND
A UNIQUE WORKSHOP FOR SPECULATIVE FICTION ON BOARD A CRUISE SHIP

THE SAIL TO SUCCESS WRITERS' WORKSHOP
DECEMBER 7-11, 2015

www.SailSuccess.com

FACULTY INCLUDES

MIKE RESNICK

NANCY KRESS

ERIC FLINT

TONI WEISSKOPF

ELEANOR WOOD

MIKE RESNICK is the winner of more awards for short fiction than anyone else in science fiction, living or dead, including five Hugos from a record 36 nominations. He currently edits *Galaxy's Edge* magazine.

NANCY KRESS is an award-winning, bestselling author and a regular columnists for *Writer's Digest*. She is also a regular teacher at Clarion, Taos and The Writer's Center in Maryland. She was the 2008/9 Picador Guest Professor for Literature at the University of Leipzig's Institute for American Studies.

ERIC FLINT is a *New York Times* bestselling author and the creator of the 1632 universe, one of the most inclusive universes in science fiction with more than 100 different authors participating in the project.

TONI WEISSKOPF is the head of Baen Books, a major publishers of science fiction in the United States. She will personally give feedback on student manuscripts.

ELEANOR WOOD heads one of the most prestigious science fiction literary agencies in New York. Her client list reads like a who's who in SF and Fantasy, including the estate of Robert Heinlein.

black sphere tumbled from her lifeless fingers, and all of the armored men looked down at it in alarmed surprise.

Whatever else happens . . .

I spun and threw the suitcase onto the lockers and began pushing the cart with all my strength. Two meters farther there was a line of yellow and black caution tape that stretched all the way around the tube: the demarcation for the emergency cut-off seal. I slapped at the red panic disc on the tube's wall.

Decompression doors snapped shut behind me.

I didn't wait to see if they'd be grenade-proof.

✧

The yard was in pandemonium. Ships were decoupling right and left. I dodged on thrusters while various voices from traffic control screamed in my headphones.

"—unconfirmed reports of additional decompression at—"

"—they're rioting on the mezzanine, the constabulary are—"

"—unable to regain control. Telemetry is hazed—"

I tuned out the chatter and focused on driving. It took about ninety seconds of sweat-inducing manual navigation to clear completely off the node, then I punched the primary drive and felt the fusion reactor's vibrations through the base of my spine.

Ahead lay the blackness of interplanetary space, and beyond it . . .

There's a dragon down below . . .

Every experienced pilot knew that interstellar space was closed to us. As if the whole of the universe had been kept safe from human meddling, behind an invisible, locked door. Men had tried to penetrate the Sargasso Grid, and died for their ambition. Part of me wondered if we'd ever solve the mystery, and actually venture beyond the solar system; to explore other stars. But that was a challenge for others—better paid, with superior research budgets—to tackle. My personal goals were much more humble. Transport item A to point B, receive money C. Rinse and repeat.

No glory. But then, not much danger either.

Until now.

The transaction card was a stiff rectangle in my vest. I fished it out and stuck it into the reader slot on my dashboard. A new voice flooded into my ears, overriding all others. I sucked in breath, recognizing the man instantly.

"I regret the necessity of this maneuver, Sal. It's been a few years since you visited Earth. I know you never cared about our local politics down here, but things have gotten bad. Really, really bad. This Rust drug is like a plague. The whole planet is going crazy with it. Literally. If you're hearing this message then it means I am dead, and I've left it to my daughter to get both this message and its attached cargo into your hands. You're the only courier I trust, Sal. Everyone else is on the take from someone. Or caught up in Rust-created illusions. But I know you, just like I knew your dad. You'll do the right thing. I've included enough funds to make it worth your while, too. Five megacredits. There is another ten meg waiting for you when you reach home port, after the long trip out to the edge of the Grid. But go to Saturn first. I'm including coordinates, and a cypher key, on this card, for clearance. I'm sorry I can't tell you more, but the less you know, the better. For all our sakes. You are a professional. I am sure you understand."

The voice recording faded out, and I double checked the balance on the card to verify if what Jeran Velasquez had said was true.

It was. *Five million.* Almost enough to put an entirely new secondary drive into my ship. Dump the clunky, outdated converters. Open up additional room for more cargo. Faster times in and out of orbit. My mental calculator began whirring on the figures. Whatever else Jeran had gotten me into, he'd definitely made sure I wasn't going to do anything out of charity. This was a transaction, first and foremost. It was just a damned shame his daughter had had to die in the process.

His daughter. *Damn.* I'd never even found out her name.

I closed my eyes and saw her lifeless young body being rolled over, like a side of beef. It gave me the shivers, and I couldn't make them stop. I eventually told the autopilot to continue pouring on the thrust, then got out of my pilot's crèche and used the handrails and foot pads to go to the forward cargo compartment.

The lockers and the suitcase had spilled wildly during pull-out from the orbital station, and it took me a few minutes to get them re-arranged and strapped down. The suitcase I took with me back to my personal cabin, where I popped it open and gazed again at the metallic cylinder.

It didn't look like a standard data drive. There were no jacks, lines, nor obvious seams in the metal to indicate that the cylinder could be opened or accessed. For all I knew it was a solid piece of brushed steal. Only Jeran's message convinced me that there was more to the cylinder than met the eye.

I closed the cylinder back in its case, and told myself I'd not let it out of my sight.

Jeran had been right about one thing, I didn't care about the political situation on Earth. I made my money hauling butt between Jupiter, Saturn, the asteroid belt, and occasional trips to Mars. My reputation with Space Patrol was clean. I was good at my job, played by the rules that mattered, and there were no questions asked. Not even when the local situation got messy.

As I'd just seen it get messy in a very deadly way, back at the node. I certainly wouldn't be returning to the spaceyards of Europa any time soon. Not until I knew more about what had happened. Or why an old friend from Earth had sent his daughter all the way to the Jovian moons to die.

Rust. Jeran wasn't kidding. The stuff was causing mayhem. And Earth had plenty of company in the chaos department. The courier free-exchange news network had been lighting up for weeks. One safe harbor after another had been red-lined, due to outbreaks of what could only be described as fatal addiction and delusions, due to drug consumption and spore contamination. Whole colonies had been quarantined. There was talk that the death toll in the asteroid belt alone was well over a thousand, and climbing like a rocket.

What had Jeran's daughter given me, precisely?

If the metal canister in the case held an equivalent volume of the potent black Rust, then it was worth more than my entire ship, several times over.

But that didn't make any sense, with Jeran involved. The man was not a narcotics dealer. He was an honest businessman turned politician. Clean, sober, and proud of it too. One of the few pols I actually trusted to try to make things better, not worse. The chances of him being involved in anything truly illegal were so remote as to not even be worth considering.

I shook my head. Questions just made things messy, and were bad for business. Dad taught me that. And I'd seen little in the ten years I'd been doing the job to convince me that my dad was wrong. Keep your eyes open and your lip zipped. Stick to the contract. Be a pro. Point A to point B, for money C. Live a long, prosperous life. And nobody bothers you. As long as you don't bother them first.

Except, the old wisdom held little comfort for me now.

I laid on my bunk and wrapped a blanket around my body, still unable to stop the shivering.

✧

They caught me just fifteen minutes shy of the official governmental boundary. Two ships. They were using EM and radar suppression because I didn't see them until I saw the flashes from their thruster systems. I potted my own secondary drive to one-ten and felt my teeth rattle, as I warned them off via radio.

For my trouble I was told they'd have one of their kinetic weapons put a hole through my fuel torus— if I didn't heave to and await official latch-on.

Such a threat was a blatant violation of the interplanetary courier charter, which granted all licensed members of the Courier Guild the equivalent of diplomatic immunity. By threatening to attack my ship, these people had placed their entire government in danger of being blacklisted by the Guild—which would practically cut them off from civilization.

The contents of that suitcase must have been important.

Rust. Was that really all it came down to?

Cussing up a storm, I potted down the secondary drive to zero, spun the ship, then potted the secondary back up for braking. Then I went to wait calmly at the main hatch as the two Space Patrol ships matched with mine, and extended grapplers. I felt my craft jarred slightly as the grapplers took hold, then the *thunk-clunk* of the ship-to-ship tube as it sealed on the outside of the hull.

I opened my hatch expecting more guys with guns. This time, the official kind.

What I got was a well-toned older woman in a tight spacer's suit, flanked by four bulky men wearing ceramic armor. Their insignia marked them as Space

Patrol. Their eyes were hidden behind dropped sets of flash visors.

The woman's face—

I averted my eyes as we shook hands. Despite the reconstruction surgery, her face was difficult to look at. Whatever had happened to her, it had been bad.

"Mr. Teller," she said.

"That's correct," I said hesitantly.

"I'm O'Riley. Space Patrol tried to contact you numerous times via radio, but you weren't answering our hails. Under the provisions of the interplanetary theft ordnance—which your Guild recognizes—I was obligated to prevent you from departing Jupiter space with dangerous contraband onboard."

She stepped into my ship without being invited. I stepped back, not sure I could have prevented her in any case. Her movements were those of someone accustomed to the deck of a ship. Her eyes appraised the interior of my vessel as she moved.

"I'm not sure what you're talking about," I said, trying to keep up with her.

"Mr. Teller, neither of us is dumb enough to believe that. The young lady who gave you a suitcase before suicide bombing your berth didn't hand you a bouquet of flowers, did she?" "Like hell," I said. "She was murdered. Those weren't cops who gunned her down."

"Did you know her?"

"Not at all. In fact I told her she was in the wrong part of the station to be seeking passage. Then she was shot to death. I didn't wait around to see much of what happened next. Didn't feel like being a collateral casualty."

I looked to each of the four men who accompanied O'Riley. They seemed alert, but not necessarily menacing. They were taking their cues from the woman.

I finally got ahead of her and put an arm across the corridor, blocking her passage. I don't know who she thought she was, but I wasn't going to just let her ransack me without sufficient cause and documentation.

"By commandeering a courier en route," I said firmly to her, "you are walking on very thin ice. The internal security problems of Jupiter's moons are *your* concern, not mine. All data and cargo on this vessel is secured under the Guild's own Common Confi-

dentiality Clause. You can't seize any of it without first petitioning the local Guild office for a writ."

"I know," she said, not smiling. One of her men stepped forward and handed me a piece of hardcopy.

Son of a . . . it even had the Guildmaster's signature on it.

I thought of Jeran's daughter being shot to death, and clenched my teeth to keep from filling the air with obscenities.

"Come with me," I said, and led them aft.

☼

O'Riley held the metallic cylinder in both hands.

"Satisfied?" I said.

"Yes," she replied.

"Then the conditions of the writ have been met. I'll have to ask you to leave my ship and allow me to resume my voyage, immediately."

"Of course, Mr. Teller. Thank you for your professionalism."

I wanted to tell her she could shove it up her ass, but held my tongue.

The six of us walked back to the hatch in silence. O'Riley gave the cylinder to one of her men, then they walked back across the threshold.

She turned to face me before she went.

"Ordinarily, we would seize whatever monetary funds were used in the course of an illegal shipment. In this case, however, I recommended that we write them off. I don't think you knew what was being entrusted to you. Believe or not, I know a boarding like this is galling, Teller. I've been there a time or two myself. But Space Patrol has to be sure. Rust is no laughing matter. It's getting far too many people killed. Or worse. This is a pandemic the whole solar system is afraid of now."

She turned on a heel without allowing me to retort, and I watched her walk swiftly across the ship-to-ship tube without saying another word.

I closed the hatch and heard the tube decouple and withdraw, followed by the release of the grapplers. I climbed back into the pilot's crèche and navigated away on thrusters, distancing myself from the two Space Patrol ships until it was safe enough to engage the secondary and resume my trip to Saturn.

It wasn't until ten minutes later that my radios suddenly came alive with another hail.

"Yes?" I said, flipping on the video as well as the audio.

"You deceitful bastard," O'Riley spat at me, her face pink with anger.

"Beg pardon?"

"Shut down your drive and prepare to be re-boarded."

"What for?"

"You defied our search."

"Bull. I obeyed the stipulations of the writ. You got what you wanted."

She brandished the metal cylinder in my field of vision.

"It's a worthless piece of mill stock!"

I stared at the screen image of the cylinder for a moment, then realized that the empty suitcase itself still lay on the floor of my cabin.

The suitcase . . .

Without taking my eyes of the screen, I gently manipulated my controls and began potting up the primary drive. It would burn a lot of reaction mass, but at this point I needed raw thrust. The secondary had a fuel-efficient specific impulse ratio that served me well in most instances. But now? Now I just needed to keep space between myself and the Space Patrol. Whatever this was about, it wasn't my business and it wouldn't matter once I was out of O'Riley's jurisdiction. Clearly Jeran hadn't given me Rust, if that was what she was after. And I wasn't going to cool my heels in a brig cell on Callisto while they pulled my ship apart, looking for something I didn't have.

O'Riley's ship and my ship had been going in opposite directions for more than ten minutes. In the time it would take them to decelerate, do an about-face, and engage their drives—even as powerful as those drives were—I'd be out of reach.

Or so I hoped.

"Shut down immediately or there will be dire consequences, courier."

I frowned at her.

"I fulfilled the writ. You can't search me again without obtaining a second one. Look it up in your treaty with the Guild."

I clicked off the feed without giving her a chance to retort, and kept the primary drive running strong. The two Space Patrol ships did slow, stop, turn, and

slam their own pots to the max, but it was too late. They couldn't get me before I hit the boundary.

Whatever Jeran had intended, his sleight-of-hand had provided me with enough time to make my break.

✿

Saturn space. I swung my ship around until I could aim the drives for deceleration. The down-thrust toward Enceladus would take almost a day, at this range, and I wasn't in any hurry.

What I did do was unstrap and go back for the suitcase itself, which still sat—open and forlorn—on the floor of my cabin.

I shook it out, examined the interior pockets, and found nothing.

Returning to the pilot's crèche, I re-activated the transaction card—still plugged into the dash—and waited while the card executed a routine that triple-checked data with the navigational system.

I put my headset back on in time to hear Jeran's voice.

"Looks like you made it halfway, Sal. Excellent. You may have also figured out my little trick. Sorry about not letting you into the loop sooner. I knew there was a high probability you'd be boarded before you could leave Jupiter space, and I didn't want there to be any chance that you'd give away the goose. I had to make sure you were as convinced as they were. Of what, I still can't say. All you need to know is that you need to dock at Enceladus and ask for the Intra-System Ambassador's office. Take this card and the suitcase. The office should already have your name, and will know what to do.

Once my ship's computer was talking to Saturn's in-system network, I moved the five million off the card and into my corporate account, threw the card into the empty suitcase, and closed the case tight.

The ride down into the gravity well of Saturn was uneventful, allowing me to grab some sleep, a shower, and a fresh flightsuit. After that I made some advanced calls to the yard at the Enceladus, checking on prices for replacement of the secondary drive. I haggled with a few companies before we agreed on an amount, then I set myself up at a business hotel on-station for the two weeks it would take to have the work done.

Sliding into the traffic control net, then my berth at the orbital yard station, also went without incident.

I didn't have a clue what was up until I opened the hatch and three Guild officers grabbed me and threw me up against the bulkhead, cuffing me unceremoniously.

"They'll strip you for this, Teller."

"What the f—" I said out the side of my mouth, my head pressed painfully to the wall.

"Collusion with a drug-runner is one thing, but these are Rust freaks you're carrying water for. What were you thinking? This puts the reputation of the entire Guild on the line. At a time when we can least afford it. Rust craziness is slowly dismantling the chain of commerce throughout the entire solar system. We need the Guild to stay clean. You're lucky we don't dump you out the airlock."

So much for the warm welcome. My pleading to see the Ambassador's people went unheeded, and I was shuffled off to a locked room at the Guild's office where I was allowed to talk to no one, nor see anybody, for at least two days. During which I could only guess at my fate. Nobody would talk to me. Not even the woman who brought me my meals. She wouldn't even look me in the eye.

On the third day the locked door opened, and the Guildmaster entered, along with a familiar individual.

"Oh crap," I breathed.

"Surprised to see me, Mr. Teller?" O'Riley said, her face just as difficult to look at, as the last time. Her eyes practically dripped with anger.

"A little," I admitted.

"Don't be. Did you think we'd just let you go?"

"Let me guess. You radioed ahead of me, claimed I was still carrying contraband, and had the Guild hold me until you could catch up."

"Very good. You're not as dumb as this situation makes you out to be."

I turned to face the Guildmaster.

"Sir, I'm a little curious. Since when has the Guild answered to any planetary government—even Space Patrol—without there being an internal investigation first?"

"Shut up, Teller. I knew your father. He was one of our best. He'd have never allowed himself to get involved in something like this. They were *using* you."

"They *who?* Sir, I don't know *what's* happening. Did O'Riley tell you how this started? A woman was

murdered right outside the hatch to my ship. I'd be dead now too if I'd not gotten across the emergency line in the docking tube before things blew."

"A Sargasso cultist acting in concert with other Sargasso cultists," O'Riley said stiffly. "We didn't become aware of Mr. Teller's collusion until it was revealed he'd acted in false faith during our search under writ."

"Sir," I said, ignoring O'Riley, "I think this all might become a bit clearer if you just contact the Ambassador's office and give them my name. I've seen what happens to Rust addicts. The women who was killed? Stone-cold sober. And the people who did it? Hardly Space Patrol. Something very wrong is going on. And I think this O'Riley woman might be very wrong too."

"We have the suitcase, and the card, and we did contact the Ambassador's office. They've never heard of you, Teller. Like I said, you've been *used*. You'll be fortunate if all we do is confiscate your ship and revoke your license."

"You have the suitcase?" O'Riley said to the Guildmaster. Her voice sounded surprised.

"We seized it upon Teller's arrival."

"May I see it, please?"

"What for?"

O'Riley looked at me for a moment.

"I'd rather not say in front of the collaborator."

Frowning, the Guildmaster walked out of the room with O'Riley, who had begun to whisper something to him in his ear. Two plainclothed Guild officers remained behind, watching me dispassionately.

"This is all crap," I said to them, not necessarily expecting a response.

"We know," the two women replied in unison.

"What?"

One of them held an index finger to her lips while the Guildmaster re-entered with O'Riley in tow—the suitcase in her hand.

O'Riley flipped it open on the room's single, plain desk. The transaction card clattered out.

"Where is it?" O'Riley asked, hurriedly sticking fingers and hands into the interior pockets on the suitcase's lining.

"It?" I said. "There's nothing in that suitcase but air."

O'Riley made a snarling noise as she upended the suitcase and shook it violently, finally swinging the case by the handle and slamming it against the desk, snapping the hinges and cracking the exterior.

A single, tiny plastic disc spun out of the crack and rolled across the floor.

All eyes in the room went to the tiny disc. O'Riley's face lit up, and she turned to chase after the disc, when the Guildmaster waved a finger at one of the two guards, who stepped to the door and instantly closed it.

"Are we secure?" O'Riley asked.

"For now," the Guildmaster said. "Still think Teller is dirty?"

"I never really did," she said.

"Somebody better explain what the hell this all means, or I am going to start throwing fists!" I exclaimed, launching out of my chair and eyeballing the four of them.

"Calm down," the Guildmaster said.

"Sir, you have no idea what I've been through. A woman murdered on my doorstep, being boarded and searched, then accused of criminal collusion, and finally getting stuck in this cell for the past three days. Call me crazy, but I think I remember having some *rights* that everyone has happily trampled over in the past five days."

"Sorry," O'Riley said. "It's just that . . . how much do you know about Rust?"

"Fancy new organic drug. Showed up on the black market not too long ago. Commands a steep price. The high is better than anything, or so I am told. Except when it gets you dead. Which is often. But that's part of the thrill, they say. High addiction rate. Apparently the spores have been infecting food shipments, and contaminated hydroponics are causing all kinds of outbreaks."

"You pay attention to the Guild news, that's for sure," the Guildmaster said.

"Here's what you don't know," O'Riley said. "On Earth, it's even worse than the official news will dare say. They're talking about possibly putting whole cities under martial law. In the asteroid belt, or out here in the Jovian moons, each and every settlement is practically self-quarantined. One location goes bad, you simply redirect traffic. Seal it off. They don't have that option on Earth. The Rust is now getting out into the general farming and food supply. Before long, hundreds of millions of people might be affected."

"So what does this have to do with the woman who got shot after she handed me that suitcase?"

"There are very well-financed and highly-positioned people who are making a lot of money on the Rust black market," O'Riley said. "This little disc? Do you know what's actually on it?"

"No," I admitted.

"The planned genomes for several counter-viruses," the Guildmaster said. "Basically, the blueprints for a genetically-engineered time bomb that can dismantle Rust down to the last spore. Assuming we can get to a pure source."

"Pure source of what? The Rust?"

"Yes," O'Riley said. "Once exposed to the organic source, the counter-virus will be able to key properly on all Rust that's been spawned from the source. Red, or black. It may even help cure those who've already become addicted, or infected."

"But why all the games?" I asked. "Where's the source?"

"The Sargasso Grid," O'Riley said. "I watched my brother die from Rust. I've seen it do worse to others. I'm not Space Patrol, but I struck a deal with them to help them fight Rust trafficking. But even I didn't know the half of it, until a man brought a mother and her sick son to me. All three of them looking for Nikki Dark."

My brain lit up.

Nikki Dark. Owner of the *Dreadnaught*. Rather infamous in Guild circles, for her exploits. A scoundrel of many bar stories. Which made her either hated or admired, depending on your particular angle.

"Wait," I said, eyeballing O'Riley's scar-laced face. "Don't tell me *you* are Nikki Dark."

"I am," O'Riley said.

"Nikki Dark and the Space Patrol, working together to fight Rust-running," I said. "I guess stranger things have happened."

"Like the mob buying off people all over the solar system, to hamper efforts to find a way to defeat Rust at the point of origin?" the Guildmaster said. "Even we haven't been safe, Teller. Which is why we had to keep up the pretense of you being a suspect, right up until we were sure you had in your possession what had been promised to us by Mr. Velasquez."

"Who has a dead daughter now!" I burst out, seeing her limp body flash before my eyes.

"Nobody trusts anybody anymore," O'Riley said. "Velasquez was working on a cure at the same time people orbiting Mars were working on a cure. The Mars effort didn't finish their work in time. The Rust-runners had someone on the inside trying to disrupt things. Velasquez had what he thought was a workable counter-viral template, but no way to reach the source. And no way to simply transmit his findings without the transmissions being tapped or blocked."

"The Rust-runners would rather watch interplanetary civilization collapse, than aid in the effort to halt the epidemic?" I asked, incredulously.

"Vultures," the Guildmaster said. "Which is why we finally came down on the side of assisting. Velasquez knew us, or rather, he knew your father. We knew you could get this far, if you set you up with the proper cover story. Now you'll go the rest of the distance for us."

"For what?" I said, pacing back and forth in the cell. "The Sargasso Grid is a no-man's land. You go in, you never come out. Or if you do, you come out crazier than crazy. Like the Sargasso cultists."

"The Sargasso grid, and the Rust, and the cultists, and the mob," O'Riley said, "they're all part of the same thing. Can't you see? The Rust came from the Sargasso. That's our origin. The cultists actively encourage Rust use. The mafia sees Rust as a can't-lose commodity. Worth gigacredits. Velasquez gave us the key to potentially dismantling the entire problem. But we have to brave the Sargasso to do it."

"What, do we go floating out there in the dark and hope something magically happens?"

"No," O'Riley said. "We have a way to exactly track down our target."

Just then the door to the cell opened, and a small gurney was wheeled in. There was a little boy tucked into numerous sheets and blankets. He looked incredibly thin and pale. So much so, I wasn't even sure he was still alive. The slightest rising and falling of the boy's chest told me he was still with us. The woman at the gurney's side was hollow-eyed and lean-looking too. Obviously the mother, from the way she couldn't take her eyes off her son's sallow face.

The two Guild officers with us quickly closed the cell again.

"This man brought the counter-virus?" the mother said.

"Lily Silva," the Guildmaster said, "meet Sal Teller. He'll be taking you and Mateo to the Sargasso Grid, along with Ms. O'Riley."

"Aboard the *Dreadnaught?*" I asked, looking to O'Riley.

"No," she said. "My ship is too well-known. We've already sent it on its way elsewhere, as a decoy. You know that new secondary drive you bought? Well, you'll be surprised just how much your money got you, when we get back to your berth. Your ship was never outfitted to get much past Uranus. Now we could go deep into the Sargasso, and not even come close to a bingo fuel point."

"And what's the ace in the hole?" I said, staring at the sick boy in the gurney. "Do we have a homing signal or something?"

"You might say that," the mother—Lily—said. She leaned over the gurney and spoke quietly to her son.

"Can you still talk to her, Mateo? Can you still talk to Rat?"

"I can *feel* Rat," the boy said, almost too quietly for me to hear him. "But her name's not really Rat. I told you that. She's named Jingfei. And she's with the man who would have been my papa. Carvahlo. And they're with the Other."

I felt the hair go up on the back of my neck.

"Carvahlo," I said. "You don't mean *Victor* Carvahlo?"

"Yes," Lily admitted. "He was—he should have become—my husband. Before the accident in the Sargasso. The one that twisted his mind. How or why he became the point of origin for the Rust is a question I can't answer. I'm almost afraid it's something *I* helped engineer. A piece of research I did, and which Victor twisted for some crazy purpose. Out there in the Sargasso. Now it's like the Rust brings part of the Sargasso back to the solar system. To normal space. Where it's destroying lives and minds. Including my son's."

"Who is Jingfei?" I asked.

"We don't really know," O'Riley said. "We think it was somebody from one of the penal colonies on Ceres."

"Ceres is off-limits," I said. "One hundred percent quarantine."

"This Jingfei girl got off before the blockade," the Guildmaster said. "She was deep under the effects of

Rust contamination when she fled. Somehow, Mateo here is in contact with her. Emotionally. Mentally. He can sense where she is, and where we need to go to find her. Mateo's got Rust contamination too, obviously."

I jerked away from the gurney.

"He's not contagious," Lily said loudly, here tired eyes glaring at me. "If he was, we'd all be contaminated by now. But the Rust is in him, and it's in him good. I thought I had a cure when we fled Mars. Marcus—someone who served time with Jingfei on Ceres—came to me, hoping I had the answers. He took us to Nikki Dark—Ms. O'Riley—and we discovered we only had part of the puzzle solved. What we needed was a way to fight back. With a virus that would actively infect and destroy Rust at the molecular level. The Space Patrol helped relay this to Earth, and Mr. Velasquez said he'd send us the best solution that he could come up with. Rust-runners and corrupt officials permitting."

"If they were willing to kill his daughter like they did," I said, "all of us are in great danger."

"Which is why we had to cook up the game, and make you believe it," the Guildmaster said. "So that if you somehow got caught en route to Saturn, you wouldn't know any better. And you certainly couldn't lead them to Lily or her son. But now that we have the disc, there's no more sense delaying the inevitable. Go. Take your ship, and O'Riley, and Lily, and her son, and find Carvahlo. Through the connection Mateo has with this Jingfei girl. Lily will know what to do with the genetic blueprints on the disc. We already put the synthesizer aboard your ship that she will need to make the prototypes. You just have to get her within spitting distance of the Rust's actual source, she will make the proper exposures, then you have to get the active counter-viral samples back to us. So that we can release them into the wild. And hopefully this nightmare will start to end. For everybody."

I stared at the boy in the bed.

Too sick to live, and perhaps even too sick to die?

A miserable existence.

"Okay then," I said. "If it means getting my ship back, and eventually making good on the ten megacredits I was promised, let's go."

✿

I'd never been this far out. The sun was like an extra-bright star, just barely discernible among all the other stars. Each of which shone like a pinprick of light on an otherwise perfectly black velvet canvas. It had taken several weeks to go the distance. Even with the souped-up drive my ship had been outfitted with. O'Riley and the Guildmaster hadn't lied. They'd replaced my actual purchase with a super-expensive prototype drive the Space Patrol was testing on interdiction cutters. I was the only civilian allowed to have one, or so they'd told me when we broke orbit. And it would get us to the destination and back without having to make any more pit stops—and risk potentially getting sandbagged by Rust-runner goons, trying to keep us from destroying their market.

"Jingfei is close," Mateo's weak voice whispered.

My ordinarily cramped quarters had been cleared out, and now they served as Mateo's hospital room. I slept in the pilot's chair most of the time, while O'Riley took the long-neglected navigator's chair. Lily, of course, kept close to her boy. And Marcus? He'd stayed with the Guildmaster. Giving us only a verbal message to deliver to Jingfei, assuming we actually found her. And Carvahlo.

"He did what needed to be done," Lily told me upon our departure.

Which was fine for me. I didn't think the ship could hold another grown male. Not after taking on two passengers the ship hadn't been designed to accommodate in the first place.

I'd been following Mateo's directions for the most part. Riding an invisible barrier just inside the known limit of the Sargasso Grid, until Mateo was sure that Jingfei—whom he had also called Rat on occasion—was directly ahead.

I didn't dare pot up the drive. Every nerve in my body screamed against plowing my ship into the Sargasso. It was madness. There was no guarantee that we wouldn't all go just as mad as Lily's one-time husband had gone. I'd heard the scuttlebutt around the Guild. Even seen some of the leaked digital imagery recovered with Victor Carvahlo. From the boarding of the *Illico One*.

How had the rhyme begun?

Aye, aye, m'lady?

There's a dragon down below,

Aye, aye, m'lady,
Yet exploring we shall go.

I wasn't the adventuresome type. What the hell was I doing all the way out here, at the precipice of eternity? Every pilot had a pet theory about the Sargasso. Some said it was a barrier created by God, to keep mankind from straying too far beyond our intended domain. Others said it was a dimensional anomaly, held at a certain distance by the curvature of space-time created by the sun. Still others though it was a wholly artificial thing: a sort of psychic barrier laid down by an alien species trying to either keep us in, or prevent others from coming along and letting us out.

I myself? I didn't really care what it was.

I just knew that going into it was suicide.

"Carvahlo is out there," Nikki Dark—O'Riley—said to me, as she stared over my shoulder from the navigator's station. She'd been a sharp second mate, and there'd been no bickering about who gave the orders during the trip from Saturn. Far from being a scoundrel, I thought O'Riley was probably the most professional co-pilot a man could ask for. It was a shame we were going to have to split up and go our separate ways when we got back home.

Assuming we didn't get devoured by the Sargasso first.

"I wish the kid could dog-whistle this Rat girl, and have her drag Carvahlo out to meet us. I mean, what do we expect to find when we get there, anyway? Carvahlo and his minions, welcoming us with open arms? It will be obvious why we've come, once they see Lily. And her virus synthesizer. I can't imagine Sargasso cultists who treat Rust like a holy sacrament will be too pleased to see ship filled with infidels, come to destroy the very thing that gives their lives meaning."

"We're counting on the fact that Victor Carvahlo literally thinks of Lily as an angel," O'Riley reminded me. "You saw the same footage I did, after we left Saturn. The stuff they don't let the news show? He claimed—upon being rescued—that Lily came to him in the form of a literal angel, and protected him from a demon while he was trapped aboard the *Illico One*. That's our hole card. He hasn't seen Lily in years. Crazy or no, some part of him must still love Lily. Enough to let her sway him. If even only for

long enough to let the synthesizer do its job. It only takes one of us to escape and get the counter-virus back to the Guild. After that, every Guild ship will be carrying counter-virus. It'll be spread to every settlement, no matter how remote. And Earth too."

"And what if the counter-virus doesn't work?"

O'Riley frowned, and didn't answer my question.

Which was merely a reminder to me that we'd all been dancing around the uncomfortable fact that this whole plan—already banking on improbabilities—had no guarantee of achieving the desired goal of eradicating Rust. For all we knew, the virus could mutate and turn into something even worse than Rust. Perhaps, much worse?

Although there didn't sound like a death much worse than the one O'Riley had described, when confiding in me about the final hours of her brother.

I thought I understood her motive, at least. She had a son to protect. The Space Patrol offered legal immunity in exchange for her services—to help stop Rust.

Lily too had her son to protect.

Me?

I had nothing.

But over the time it had taken us to reach this point, I kept watching my new navigator out of the corner of my eye, and realizing that A to B to C didn't necessarily describe everything that was worth doing in the universe.

"Ah, screw it," I said, finally putting my hand to the drive's potentiometer. "Waiting around wondering what might happen is almost worse than what's actually going to happen."

My ship pushed into the Sargasso.

And we never looked back.

The space station wasn't really a space station at all. Rather, it was a collection of wrecked ships all piled together on a tiny carbon-molecule dwarf moon. The abandoned technology had been jury-rigged and re-worked until it formed a minimally-functional habitat on the surface. When we flew over the part of the dwarf moon with the most activity showing on the surface, there was no apparent place for use to dock or land.

So far, the dreaded Sargasso hadn't taken its toll on our senses. No angels, nor devils, had risen in our minds to make us want to claw our eyes out.

The single hailing call we'd received, had been answered by Lily. Who'd cleaned herself up and even put on a little makeup, before putting herself in front of a comm unit and responding with the words, "Victor, it's me, Lily. Victor, I have to see you. I want to come home, please."

Since then, we'd seen not a single sign that they might be belligerent. The dwarf moon was inhabited, but by how many, we couldn't say.

Eventually, we picked a clear spot near what seemed to be an open-mouthed hangar, and set down. The dwarf moon's native gravity was miniscule. Just enough to keep it spherical and cohesive. But not much beyond that. With Mateo being too fragile to leave alone, Lily, O'Riley, and myself all agreed to have O'Riley stay behind while Lily and I went out in suits. To see who—or what—might be waiting to greet us.

The strange thing was, nobody was there to greet us.

The hangar—lit by flickering lamps salvaged from some unfortunate old ship's cargo bay—was empty. Just an airlock door awaited us.

I signaled O'Riley that we were going in, and she promised to keep alert in the pilot's chair. So that she could lift off at the slightest hint of trouble. Whether Lily or I made it out or not.

The airlock seemed to work normally. We stepped through the outer door, waiting for the lights on the other side to change from red, to yellow, to green, then we checked out own suits to be sure we weren't fooled.

Nope. They showed green too.

Though we didn't dare take our helmets off. The air inside was doubtless laden with Rust spores. We didn't intend to subject ourselves to contamination and infection if we could help it.

We stepped into a corridor that snaked away into the distance, twisting at odd angles. As we walked, I noted that each section of the corridor appeared to have come from a different vessel, and a different time period. There were pieces of ships in the corridor that were literally almost two hundred years old. Or older. My knowledge of archaic interstellar shipwright technique only went back so far. But it had all been welded and fused together to make a livable whole.

Though we had yet to see a single sign of human habitation.

That changed when we got to the corridor's end.

Lily clutched the detachable sample catcher portion of the genetic synthesizer to her chest as a man approached. He wasn't wearing a space suit, or anything else other than a tattered, somewhat stained bathrobe. A scraggly, long beard sprouted from his face, and his hair ran over his shoulders and down his back.

I glanced at Lily, and she glanced at me.

Victor? The question passed between us.

Lily shook her head, no.

"The angel has returned to us," the man said in a dreamy baritone, while be bowed low to Lily, and practically ignored me. "Carvahlo knew you would come. He has seen it in a vision. He sees many things in his visions. As do we all. But why are you wearing that garment? Surely the angel does not need to fear the air of her own temple."

"Temple?" Lily blurted, incredulously.

But the bearded man had merely turned away, and began striding down an entirely different corridor.

We hurried after him.

"That guy doesn't seem too unhealthy," I said under my breath. "A little mangy, perhaps, but hardly psycho."

"He's badly addicted," Lily cautioned. "You could see it in his manner while he talked. He's hallucinating even now. He might not even be aware of the fact that we're following him."

"Let's just hope he take us past the brewery," I said.

"Brewery?" Lily asked.

"What else do we call it? Where they grow the Rust to begin with."

She patted the sample catcher with a gloved hand.

"One whiff is all this thing needs, and we can go."

"Assuming they feel like letting us go," I said. "I still feel like a mouse wandering around in a maze filled with cats."

Lily didn't respond to me.

Suddenly the corridor emptied out into what appeared to be the retrofitted interior of a massive, archaic slush deuterium fuel tank. Hundreds of lights had been snaked over and across the dome over our heads, and joined by haphazardly-connected electrical conduit. So that the space practically blazed with white light. Lily and I watched our helmet bowls automatically close the silver glare shields. After which, everything in the dome seemed like I was looking at it through a pair of dark sunglasses.

Two dozen people were arrayed around the floor, sitting on benches or couches which seemed to have been taken from the recreational cabins of ten different ships. They paid almost no attention to us as they focused their eyes on a single man who sat on a mad hatter's throne of contorted pipe and steel, from which aisles radiated between the benches and couches.

Our guide led us up one of the aisles.

"Victor," Lily breathed. I could barely hear her in my helmet's speakers.

The man on the mad hatter's throne was barely recognizable as human. He was gaunt to the point of seeming like a skeleton. As if severely starved over a long duration. His skull weighed down a bowed neck, and thin lips stretched over brown teeth. The eyes were watery and unfocused. Seemingly staring at nothing. Until our guide leaned in and whispered in the skeleton's ear. Then the eyes snapped up and came to focus on us.

"Is it a deception?" the skeleton demanded in a ragged voice.

As one, the collection of people on the benches and couches began to beat their fists against the sides of their heads.

"No," Lily said, using her suit's external speakers. "It's me, Victor. It's Lily."

"Take your helmet off," was all the skeleton said.

"No," I commanded her firmly.

"I don't think I have a choice," she said.

"You want to wind up like the rest of these freaks?" I hissed. "Just walk to him and show him your face through your helmet."

She did as I suggested, stepping cautiously to the throne and manually dialing back the glare shield, so that Victor Carvahlo could see clearly into the face bowl.

He gasped audibly, and shot to his bony feet.

"She has come!" he bellowed.

The congregants switched from wailing and beating their heads, to cheering and waving their hands in the air. Their actions mimicking Victor's mood, almost as if they were attuned to him. Was that it? Was that part of what happened with Rust addiction? You ended up on the same wavelength or frequency as the other addicts around you?

Then Victor's face darkened.

"You bring an unwanted guest," he said, pointing a scrawny arm at me.

"He's my helper, Victor," Lily said. "I could not have come without him. Please, don't hurt him. He's just a pilot. He'll be taking his ship and leaving soon."

Suddenly one of the people on one of the benches leaped in front of me and brandished a finger in my face. I stared at her—almost as skeletal as Victor himself—and realized she was a youngish Asian girl. Her stomach was distended, but not from fat. It was from having not eaten in far too long. In fact, all of them seemed to be malnourished in the extreme. Did they run out of actual food? Had the hydroponics for producing Rust killed off the real crops they needed to survive?

I waited for the girl in front of me to say something. She seemed to have an accusation on her lips.

"Rat!" Victor bellowed. "Tell us this man's secrets."

Her mouth opened, ready to put the lie to Lily's gentle deception. But then the girl faltered. Her eyes seemed to go far away. And she nodded several times, her chin bobbing up and down. At which point she returned to her bench and curled up.

Victor murmured at her, and slowly sat back down.

"That one sees much," he said. "I can always rely on her to ferret out the facts from the lies. And I *hate* lies. You know that, Lily."

"Nobody has come to lie to you, Victor. I've come to stay. I want . . . I want to understand how you *see* things. How you make the material that helps other people *see* things too. The Sargasso Grid hasn't killed you, my love. It's made you—"

"A god?" Victor offered, running a pointy finger along his beard-covered jaw.

Lily simply waited. There was more he clearly wanted to say.

"No," he finally confessed. "I am not a god. But then, neither am I a man. I am something...in between. The Sargasso too is something in between.

Have my disciples done their work well? Has the human race been properly prepared to *see*, Lily? That's why we made it, you know. The fungus that carries the gift of the Sargasso back to the worlds and colonies of men. So that all might find the way."

"The way to what?" I asked, using my suit's own internal speakers.

Victor looked to me, annoyed.

"I did not give that one permission to speak," he said.

And the entire congregation got up from their benches and couches and surrounded me. Menacing in their demeanor. Not a one of them looked to be healthy enough to wrestle a child, much less a grown man in a full suit. I doubted that they could hurt me. But then I saw that there were pipes and pieces of steel shaped for tool work. Grasped in each hand. The suit was built to withstand micrometeroid impact. But I doubted it could hold up for long against a sustained assault. Sooner or later the face bowl would crack or someone would damage something vital on the back pack, and that would be the end of it.

I held my hands up, trying to ward them off.

"Victor," Lily suddenly spoke, using a stern voice. "Is that any way to treat a guest? You know I always did hate it when you didn't show our guests proper hospitality. You should be ashamed of yourself."

Suddenly the skeleton king's demeanor was crestfallen.

Tears sprang to his eyes and he clutched his forehead in one hand.

"I'm so sorry, Lily," he sobbed. "I'm so sorry I let you go."

The crowd around me gradually loosened, and began to disperse, eventually curling up in balls wherever it was comfortable, and weeping along with their master.

"It's okay, Victor," Lily said. "I'm here now. In fact, I've come to help! And so has my pilot. We need more fungus! Pure fungus. What's left on Earth has been polluted. It's not the same. People can't *see* what you want them to *see*, Victor. I want to take some of the spores back with us. To ensure that everyone sees. Can you do that, Victor?"

The skeleton king looked up, his skull-mask of a face grown hopeful.

"Only he will go? You will let him go back? You will stay?"

"I will stay," Lily said. "I brought something to carry the fungus. I just need a little. My pilot will grow more, on the way home. But I will stay with you."

"You..." Victor said, then halted. His jaw quivered slightly. "You have always been with me. Even when hell itself had opened its womb, to birth pure evil into the universe—the faces, oh Lily, you didn't see the many faces—you were there. I built all of this for you, you know. Because I knew you'd come. I *saw* that you would come."

"Then you will take me—take us—to where the fungus is grown?"

"Yes, yes," Victor said.

For a man with practically no muscle on his body, he moved surprisingly fast. He swept away from his junkyard chair and down one of the aisles. Lily and I trotted after him, trying to keep up. In the low gravity, we bounced more than we walked. Using our hands occasionally on the ceiling of the adjacent corridor, so that we wouldn't bump our heads.

Finally we rounded a corner and came to a stop in a vestibule before a sealed door.

"Inside," Victor said, slapping his hand on the door.

"Good," Lily said. And reached to activate the mechanism that would open it.

"Not you," Victor said. "Only him. Let him get what he needs, and depart. You? I want you to take the whole suit off. Let me see you as I have always seen you—my perfect woman."

I saw Lily's shoulders sag, even through her suit.

I didn't move.

"What do we do?" I whispered suit-to-suit.

There was a long silence, then Lily said, "No matter what happens from here on out, just promise me you'll take care of Mateo. You, and O'Riley. You're the ones Mateo will need now. Tell him I love him very much."

Before I could tell her not to do it, she had reached to the collar on her helmet and undogged it from the ring. When her helmet came off, she began doing the same at her wrists, and then down the front of the suit proper, until the suit itself fell away and she was standing exposed to the light, wearing nothing but the form-fitting cooling garment underneath.

Victor was teary-eyed again.

"My angel, come to me again at last."

He reached for her, and she allowed herself to be taken in his embrace.

I felt my skin crawl, but also saw her turn her head toward me while Victor nuzzled at her neck.

What are you waiting for? Lily mouthed at me.

Right.

I activated the door, and went through. It shut behind me.

I was presented with darkness. Flicking on my helmet lamps I suddenly observed vast vats of what could only be described as mildly undulating slime. The Rust—alive, almost liquid—was circulating in great, lazy ponds. Some black, others red. I suddenly realized that it was a biological refinery, and that I was sitting on teracredits worth of the universe's most refined Rust. The kind of thing the Rust-runners back in the solar system would have given an arm and a leg for.

Lily had shown me how to work the catcher.

I scooped up a little of the red, and a little of the black. Each in a separate chamber within the catcher. Then I went back out the way I'd come, wondering how long I was going to have to sit and be bleach-broiled in the decon cycle of my airlock, before I dared step foot inside my ship again.

When I came back out, Lily and Victor both seemed to be in another world.

Victor still held her, but loosely, and both of them were staring off into the air as if nothing real were around them. Lily's lips moved slightly, as if she were rhyming something, but no sound came. Victor too. They almost seemed to be repeating the same phrase, over and over again. Though I couldn't quite tell what the words were.

I chanced to grab at her wrist, to try to snap her out of it; or at least get her away from Victor. If they were both in a fugue state, perhaps I could drag her back to the hangar, go get an emergency balloon from my ship. Load her into it, and get her off this ball, before Victor knew what was happening.

Alas, he seemed to sense me, and his grasp on Lily tightened.

"No!" he yelled. "I have seen her mind, at last. And now I have seen what you will do! Rat saw it too, but was stopped from speaking the truth—by her friend

aboard your ship! You cannot destroy the Rust! I won't *let* you destroy the Rust!"

Cavahlo's people seemed to swarm on us from nowhere. Like ants. They must have followed behind, just far enough out of the way that we couldn't see them. Now they were clubbing at me, trying to know me down.

The sample catcher in my hand was made of titanium and bullet-proof plastic.

I began swinging it at heads.

It came back covered in gore and blood.

"What the hell is happening in there?" O'Riley's voice shouted in my helmet.

"It's a nightmare!" I yelled at her. "A Rust-zombie nightmare!"

"How can I help?" she asked.

"Get ready to go," I yelled. "When you see me running, keep the ramp down just enough to jump on. Then get us into the sky!"

"Copy that," O'Riley said firmly. Her pilot's voice was calm and controlled, just as mine would have been in the same situation.

I bulled my way through the crowd, hacking and swinging. I could feel the hits on my suit and helmet as I forged a path back into the corridor. Would the suit still be vacuum-tight by the time I needed it to be? Would a tell-tale crack mean I'd already been exposed, and wouldn't discover the problem until it was too late?

There, I saw an open lane between bodies.

I loped like a gazelle.

The path back to the hangar was not an easy one. Twice, I got lost, and had to fend off attackers. The disciples of Victor Cavahlo were practically single-minded in their determination to not let me leave with the sample catcher.

I found the throne hall, and the corridor our guide had originally used.

At the very end of it, I found Rat.

"Please take me with you," she said. Her eyes were fighting towards lucidity. And I stopped myself from dropping the sample catcher squarely on her head.

"There isn't room," I said. "There's nowhere to quarantine you."

"The Other is strong here," she said. "The Other wants all of us. Everybody."

Turning around, I saw shadowy shapes coming down the corridor. Heard—through the external suit pickup—the cries of rage and anger.

"No time," I said, "and shoved Rat aside."

"Mateo said he could help save me!" she shouted. "It's why I helped him come here!"

I stopped short, considered, then beckoned her to me. If she got out of line, I'd finish her the way I originally thought I'd have to.

Inside the airlock, I was shocked to see O'Riley—in a suit—on the other side of the window. She had an emergency balloon ready to go.

"How did you know?" I said over the helmet wireless.

"Mateo told me his friend would need one."

I decided not to argue the point, and ordered Rat to plug her nose, close her eyes, and hold her breath. She was about to get a first-rate taste of raw vacuum.

The Rust-zombies thudded against the inner airlock door just as the outer door came open, and O'Riley swept in. She was almost frantic in her effort to get Rat into the balloon, and seal it. And for good reason. O'Riley knew better than anybody what could happen to the human body if left exposed to the harshness of space.

Then we were trotted—the balloon suspended between us, and the sample catcher dangling at my waist from its tether.

Up the ramp our boots went, and into the cockpit O'Riley charged. No time for the decon cycle now. Getting up and getting away was our only goal.

I kept Rat's balloon behind me as I watched out the open ramp—the ship lifting over the frozen terrain.

And just like that, the dwarf moon was dropping away, back into the inky blackness of Sargasso Grid space.

✧

It'll be weeks, getting back to Jupiter space.

We think we've deconned the whole damn ship, but we can't really be sure.

Hell with it. If the genetic synthesizer did its job, we'll know soon enough if the counter-virus works. We released it as soon as it was ready. For Mateo's sake, and for Jingfei's. They both lapsed into a coma not long after we crossed out of the Sargasso. A

parting gift from this Other Jingfei spoke of? Did it *know* we had escaped? Were those who'd previously been caught in its grasp, ever going to be made whole again?

Everything depended on the counter-virus now. And getting ourselves back to civilization in one piece.

We kept Mateo and Jingfei both side by side, in my cabin. O'Riley and I taking turns sitting with them, while one of us piloted the ship.

There wasn't much to say along the way. I think O'Riley and I both felt it: a haunted sense of apprehension, for the fate of Lily, and suspicion that—despite all that I'd seen inside—somehow, this wasn't the last of either Carvahlo or his angel.

Original Publication
Copyright © 2015 by Brad R. Torgersen

ON SALE NOW

Gregory Benford is a Nebula winner and a former Worldcon Guest of Honor. He is the author of more than thirty novels, six books of non-fiction, and has edited ten anthologies.

DOING LENNON

by Gregory Benford

Sanity calms, but madness is more interesting.
—John Russell

As the hideous cold seeps from him he feels everything becoming sharp and clear again. He decides he can do it, he can make it work. He opens his eyes.

"Hello." His voice rasps. "Bet you aren't expecting me. I'm John Lennon."

"What?" the face above him says.

"You know. John Lennon. The Beatles."

Professor Hermann—the name attached to the face which loomed over him as he drifted up, up from the Long Sleep—is vague about the precise date. It is either 2108 or 2180. Hermann makes a little joke about inversion of positional notation; it has something to do with nondenumerable set theory, which is all the rage. The ceiling glows with a smooth green phosphorescence and Fielding lies there letting them prick him with needles, unwrap his organiform nutrient webbing, poke and adjust and massage as he listens to a hollow *pock-pocketa*. He knows this is the crucial moment, he must hit them with it now.

"I'm glad it worked," Fielding says with a Liverpool accent. He has got it just right, the rising pitch at the end and the nasal tones.

"No doubt there is an error in our log," Hermann says pedantically. "You are listed as Henry Fielding."

Fielding smiles. "Ah, that's the ruse, you see."

Hermann blinks owlishly. "Deceiving Immortality Incorporated is—"

"I was fleeing political persecution, y'dig. Coming out for the workers and all. Writing songs about persecution and pollution and the working-class hero. Snarky stuff. So when the jackboot skinheads came in I decided to check out."

Fielding slips easily into the story he has memorized, all plotted and placed with major characters and minor characters and bits of incident, all of it sounding very real. He wrote it himself, he has it down. He continues talking while Hermann and some white-smocked assistants help him sit up, flex his legs, test his reflexes. Around them are vats and baths and tanks. A fog billows from a hole in the floor; a liquid nitrogen immersion bath.

Hermann listens intently to the story, nodding now and then, and summons other officials. Fielding tells his story again while the attendants work on him. He is careful to give the events in different order, with different details each time. His accent is standing up though there is mucus in his sinuses that makes the high singsong bits hard to get out. They give him something to eat; it tastes like chicken-flavored ice cream. After a while he sees he has them convinced. After all, the late twentieth was a turbulent time, crammed with gaudy events, lurid people. Fielding makes it seem reasonable that an aging rock star, seeing his public slip away and the government closing in, would corpsicle himself.

The officials nod and gesture and Fielding is wheeled out on a carry table. Immortality Incorporated is more like a church than a business. There is a ghostly hush in the hallways, the attendants are distant and reserved. Scientific servants in the temple of life.

They take him to an elaborate display, punch a button. A voice begins to drone a welcome to the year 2018 (or 2180). The voice tells him he is one of the few from his benighted age who saw the slender hope science held out to the diseased and dying. His vision has been rewarded. He has survived the unfreezing. There is some nondenominational talk about God and death and the eternal rhythm and balance of life, ending with a retouched holographic photograph of the Founding Fathers. They are a small knot of biotechnicians and engineers clustered around an immersion tank. Close-cropped hair, white shirts with ball-point pens clipped in the pockets. They wear glasses and smile weakly at the camera, as though they have just been shaken awake.

"I'm hungry," Fielding says.

News that Lennon is revived spreads quickly. The Society for Dissipative Anachronisms holds a press conference for him. As he strides into the room Fielding clenches his fists so no one can see his hands shaking. This is the start. He has to make it here.

"How do you find the future, Mr. Lennon?"

"Turn right at Greenland." Maybe they will recognize it from *A Hard Day's Night* . This is before his name impacts fully, before many remember who John Lennon was. A fat man asks Fielding why he elected for the Long Sleep before he really needed it and Fielding says enigmatically, "The role of boredom in human history is underrated." This makes the evening news and the weekly topical roundup a few days later.

A fan of the twentieth asks him about the breakup with Paul, whether Ringo's death was a suicide, what about Allan Klein, how about the missing lines from *Abbey Road*? Did he like Dylan? What does he think of the Aarons theory that the Beatles could have stopped Vietnam?

Fielding parries a few questions, answers others. He does not tell them, of course, that in the early sixties he worked in a bank and wore granny glasses. Then he became a broker with Harcum, Brandels and Son and his take in 1969 was $57,803, not counting the money siphoned off into the two concealed accounts in Switzerland. But he read *Rolling Stone* religiously, collected Beatles memorabilia, had all the albums and books and could quote any verse from any song. He saw Paul once at a distance, coming out of a recording session. And he had a friend into Buddhism, who met Harrison one weekend in Surrey. Fielding did not mention his vacation spent wandering around Liverpool, picking up the accent and visiting all the old places, the cellars where they played and the narrow dark little houses their families owned in the early days. And as the years dribbled on and Fielding's money piled up, he lived increasingly in those golden days of the sixties, imagined himself playing side man along with Paul or George or John and crooning those same notes into the microphones, practically kissing the metal. And Fielding did not speak of his dreams.

✿

It is the antiseptic Stanley Kubrick future. They are very adept at hardware. Population is stabilized at half a billion. Everywhere there are white hard decorator chairs in vaguely Danish modern. There seems no shortage of electrical power or oil or copper or zinc. Everyone has a hobby. Entertainment is a huge enterprise, with stress on ritual violence. Fielding watches a few games of Combat Golf, takes in a public execution or two. He goes to witness an electrical man short-circuit himself. The flash is visible over the curve of the Earth.

✿

Genetic manipulants—*manips*, Hermann explains—are thin, stringy people, all lines and knobby joints where they connect directly into machine linkages. They are designed for some indecipherable purpose. Hermann, his guide, launches into an explanation but Fielding interrupts him to say, "Do you know where I can get a guitar?"

Fielding views the era 1950-1980:

"Astrology wasn't rational, nobody really believed it, you've got to realize that. It was *boogie woogie*. On the other hand, science and rationalism were progressive jazz."

He smiles as he says it. The 3D snout closes in. Fielding has purchased well and his plastic surgery, to lengthen the nose and give him that wry Lennonesque smirk, holds up well. Even the technicians at Immortality Incorporated missed it.

✿

Fielding suffers odd moments of blackout. He loses the rub of rough cloth at a cuff on his shirt, the chill of air-conditioned breeze along his neck. The world dwindles away and sinks into inky black, but in a moment it is all back and he hears the distant murmur of traffic, and convulsively, by reflex, he squeezes the bulb in his hand and the orange vapor rises around him. He breathes deeply, sighs. Visions float into his mind and the sour tang of the mist reassures him.

Every age is known by its pleasures, Fielding reads from the library readout. The twentieth introduced two: high speed and hallucinogenic drugs. Both proved dangerous in the long run, which made them even more interesting. The twenty-first developed weightlessness, which worked out well except for the re-entry problems if one overindulged. In the twenty-second there were aquaform and something Fielding could not pronounce or understand.

He thumbs away the readout and calls Hermann for advice.

✿

Translational difficulties:

They give him a sort of pasty suet when he goes to the counter to get his food. He shoves it back at them.

"Gah! Don't you have a hamburger someplace?" The stunted man behind the counter flexes his arms, makes a rude sign with his four fingers and goes away. The wiry woman next to Fielding rubs her thumbnail along the hideous scar at her side and peers at him. She wears only orange shorts and boots, but he can see the concealed dagger in her armpit.

"Hamburger?" she says severely. "That is the name of a citizen of the German city of Hamburg. Were you a cannibal then?"

Fielding does not know the proper response, which could be dangerous. When he pauses she massages her brown scar with new energy and makes a sign of sexual invitation. Fielding backs away. He is glad he did not mention French fries.

✿

On 3D he makes a mistake about the recording date of *Sergeant Pepper's Lonely Hearts Club Band*. A ferret-eyed history student lunges in for the point but Fielding leans back casually, getting the accent just right, and says, "I zonk my brow with heel of hand, consterned!" and the audience laughs and he is away, free.

✿

Hermann has become his friend. The library readout says this is a common phenomenon among Immortality Incorporated employees who are fascinated by the past to begin with (or otherwise would not be in the business), and anyway Hermann and Fielding are about the same age, forty-seven. Hermann is not surprised that Fielding is practicing his chords and touching up his act.

"You want to get out on the road again, is that it?" Hermann says. "You want to be getting popular."

"It's my business."

"But your songs, they are old."

"Oldies but goldies," Fielding says solemnly.

"Perhaps you are right," Hermann sighs. "We are starved for variety. The people, no matter how educated—anything tickles their nose they think is champagne."

Fielding flicks on the tape input and launches into the hard-driving opening of "Eight Days a Week." He goes through all the chords, getting them right the first time. His fingers dance among the humming copper wires.

Hermann frowns but Fielding feels elated. He decides to celebrate. Precious reserves of cash are dwindling, even considering how much he made in the international bond market of '83; there is not much left. He decides to splurge. He orders an alcoholic vapor and a baked pigeon. Hermann is still worried, but he eats the mottled pigeon with relish, licking his fingers. The spiced crust snaps crisply. Hermann asks to take the bones home to his family.

✿

"You have drawn the rank-scented many," Hermann says heavily as the announcer begins his introduction. The air sparkles with anticipation.

"Ah, but they're *my* many," Fielding says. The applause begins, the background music comes up, and Fielding trots out onto the stage, puffing slightly.

"One, two, three—" and he is into it, catching the chords just right, belting out a number from *Magical Mystery Tour*. He is right, he is on, he is John Lennon just as he always wanted to be. The music picks him up and carries him along. When he finishes, a river of applause bursts over the stage from the vast amphitheater and Fielding grins crazily to himself. It feels exactly the way he always thought it would. His heart pounds.

He goes directly into a slow ballad from the *Imagine* album to calm them down. He is swimming in the lights and the 3D snouts zoom in and out, bracketing his image from every conceivable direction. At the end of the number somebody yells from the audience, "You're radiating on all your eigenfrequencies!" And Fielding nods, grins, feels the warmth of it all wash over him.

"Thrilled to the gills," he says into the microphone. The crowd chuckles and stirs.

When he does one of the last Lennon numbers, "The Ego-Bird Flies," the augmented sound sweeps out from the stage and explodes over the audience. Fielding is euphoric. He dances as though someone is firing pistols at his feet.

He does cuts from *Beatles '65, Help!, Rubber Soul, Let It Be*—all with technical backing spliced in from the original tracks, Fielding providing only Lennon's vocals and instrumentals. Classical scholars have pored over the original material, deciding who did which guitar riff, which tenor line was McCartney's, dissecting the works as though they were salamanders under a knife. But Fielding doesn't care, as long as they let him play and sing. He does another number, then another, and finally they must carry him from the stage. It is the happiest moment he has ever known.

"But I don't understand what Boss 30 radio means," Hermann says.

"Thirty most popular songs."

"But why today?"

"Me."

"They call you a 'sonic boom sensation'—that is another phrase from your time?"

"Dead on. Fellow is following me around now, picking my brains for details. Part of his thesis, he says."

"But it is such noise—"

"Why, that's a crock, Hermann. Look, you chaps have such a small population, so bloody few creative people. What do you expect? Anybody with energy and drive can make it in this world. And I come from a time that was dynamic, that really got off."

"Barbarians at the gates," Hermann says.

"That's what *Reader's Digest* said, too," Fielding murmurs.

After one of his concerts in Australia Fielding finds a girl waiting for him outside. He goes home with her—it seems the thing to do, considering—and finds there have been few technical advances, if any, in this field either. It is the standard, ten-toes-

up, ten-toes-down position she prefers, nothing unusual, nothing *à la carte* . But he likes her legs, he relishes her beehive hair and heavy mouth. He takes her along; she has nothing else to do.

On an off day, in what is left of India, she takes him to a museum. She shows him the first airplane (a piper cub), the original manuscript of the great collaboration between Buckminster Fuller and Hemingway, a delicate print of *The Fifty-Three Stations of The Takaido Road* from Japan.

"Oh yes," Fielding says. "We won that war, you know."

(He should not seem to be more than he is.)

Fielding hopes they don't discover, with all this burrowing in the old records, that he had the original Lennon killed. He argues with himself that it really was necessary. He couldn't possibly cover his story in the future if Lennon kept on living. The historical facts would not jibe. It was hard enough to convince Immortality Incorporated that even someone as rich as Lennon would be able to forge records and change fingerprints—they had checked that to escape the authorities. Well, Fielding thinks. Lennon was no loss by 1988 anyway. It was pure accident that Fielding and Lennon had been born in the same year, but that didn't mean that Fielding couldn't take advantage of the circumstances. He wasn't worth over ten million fixed 1985 dollars for nothing.

At one of his concerts he says to the audience between numbers, "Don't look back— you'll just see your mistakes." It sounds like something Lennon would have said. The audience seems to like it.

Press Conference.

"And why did you take a second wife, Mr. Lennon, and then a third?" In 2180 (or 2108) divorce is frowned upon. Yoko Ono is still the Beatle nemesis.

Fielding pauses and then says, "Adultery is the application of democracy to love." He does not tell them the line is from H. L. Mencken.

He has gotten used to the women now. "Just cast them aside like sucked oranges,"

Fielding mutters to himself. It is a delicious moment. He had never been very successful with women before, even with all his money.

He strides through the yellow curved streets, walking lightly on the earth. A young girl passes, winks.

Fielding calls after her, "Sic transit, Gloria!"

It is his own line, not a copy from Lennon. He feels a heady rush of joy. He is into it, the ideas flash through his mind spontaneously. He is doing Lennon.

Thus, when Hermann comes to tell him that Paul McCartney has been revived by the Society for Dissipative Anachronisms, the body discovered in a private vault in England, at first it does not register with Fielding. Lines of postcoital depression flicker across his otherwise untroubled brow. He rolls out of bed and stands watching a wave turn to white foam on the beach at La Jolla. He is in Nanking. It is midnight.

"Me old bud, then?" he manages to say, getting the lilt into the voice still. He adjusts his granny glasses. Rising anxiety stirs in his throat. "My, my..."

It takes weeks to defrost McCartney. He had died much later than Lennon, plump and prosperous, the greatest pop star of all time—or at least the biggest money-maker. "Same thing," Fielding mutters to himself.

When Paul's cancer is sponged away and the sluggish organs palped to life, the world media press for a meeting.

"For what?" Fielding is nonchalant. "It's not as though we were ever reconciled, y'know. We got a *divorce* , Hermann."

"Can't you put that aside?"

"For a fat old slug who pro'bly danced on me grave?"

"No such thing occurred. There are videotapes, and Mr. McCartney was most polite."

"God, a future where everyone's literal! I *told* you I was a nasty type, why can't you simply accept—"

"It is arranged," Hermann says firmly. "You must go. Overcome your antagonism."

Fear clutches at Fielding.

McCartney is puffy, jowly, but his eyes crackle with intelligence. The years have not fogged his quickness. Fielding has arranged the meeting away from crowds, at a forest resort. Attendants help McCartney into the hushed room. An expectant pause.

"You want to join me band?" Fielding says brightly. It is the only quotation he can

remember that seems to fit; Lennon had said that when they first met.

McCartney blinks, peers nearsightedly at him. "D'you really need another guitar?"

"Whatever noisemaker's your fancy."

"Okay."

"You're hired, lad."

They shake hands with mock seriousness. The spectators—who have paid dearly for their tickets—applaud loudly. McCartney smiles, embraces Fielding, and then sneezes.

"Been cold lately," Fielding says. A ripple of laughter.

McCartney is offhand, bemused by the world he has entered. His manner is confident, interested. He seems to accept Fielding automatically. He makes a few jokes, as light and inconsequential as his post-Beatles music.

Fielding watches him closely, feeling an awe he had not expected. *That's him. Paul. The real thing.* He starts to ask something and realizes that it is a dumb, out-of-character, fan-type question. He is being betrayed by his instincts. He will have to be careful.

Later, they go for a walk in the woods. The attendants hover a hundred meters behind, portable med units at the ready. They are worried about McCartney's cold. This is the first moment they have been beyond earshot of others. Fielding feels his pulse rising. "You okay?" he asks the puffing McCartney.

"Still a bit dizzy, I am. Never thought it'd work, really."

"The freezing, it gets into your bones."

"Strange place. Clean, like Switzerland."

"Yeah. Peaceful. They're mad for us here."

"You meant that about your band?"

"Sure. Your fingers'll thaw out. Fat as they are, they'll still get around a guitar string."

"Ummm. Wonder if George is tucked away in an ice cube somewhere?"

"Hadn't thought." The idea fills Fielding with terror.

"Could ask about Ringo, too."

"Recreate the whole thing? I was against that. Dunno if I still am." Best to be noncommittal. He would love to meet them, sure, but his chances of bringing this off day by day, in the company of all three of them ... he frowns.

McCartney's pink cheeks glow from the exercise. The eyes are bright, active, studying Fielding. "Did you think it would work? Really?"

"The freezing? Well, what's to lose? I said to Yoko, I said—"

"No, not the freezing. I mean this impersonation you're carrying off."

Fielding reels away, smacks into a pine tree. "What? What?"

"C'mon, you're not John."

A strangled cry erupts from Fielding's throat. "But ... how..."

"Just not the same, is all. Dunno Merseyside jokes, street names, the lot."

"I, I know that Penny Lane was a street and—"

"Come off it. You're not even English!"

Fielding's mouth opens, but he can say nothing. He has failed. Tripped up by some nuance, some trick phrase he should've responded to—

"Of course," McCartney says urbanely, looking at him sideways, "you don't know for sure if I'm the real one either, do you?"

Fielding stutters, "If, if, what're you saying, I—"

"Or I could even be a ringer planted by Hermann, eh? To test you out? In that case, you've responded the wrong way. Should've stayed in character, John."

"Could be this, could be that—what the hell you saying? Who *are* you?" Anger flashes through him. A trick, a maze of choices, possibilities that he had not considered. The forest whirls around him, McCartney leers at his confusion, bright spokes of sunlight pierce his eyes, he feels himself falling, collapsing, the pine trees wither, colors drain away, blue to pink to gray—

✿

He is watching a blank dark wall, smelling nothing, no tremor through his skin, no wet touch of damp air. Sliding infinite silence. The world is black.

—Flat black, Fielding adds, like we used to say in Liverpool.

—Liverpool? He was never in Liverpool. That was a lie, too—

—And he knows instantly what he is. The truth skewers him.

Hello, you still operable?

Fielding rummages through shards of cold electrical memory and finds himself. He is not Fielding, he is a simulation. He is Fielding Prime.

Hey, you in there. It's me, the real Fielding. Don't worry about security. I'm the only one here.

Fielding Prime feels through his circuits and discovers a way to talk. "Yes, yes, I hear."

I made the computer people go away. We can talk.

"I—I see." Fielding Prime sends out feelers, searching for his sensory receptors. He finds a dim red light and wills it to grow brighter. The image swells and ripples, then forms into a picture of a sour-faced man in his middle fifties. It is Fielding Real.

Ah, Fielding Prime thinks to himself in the metallic vastness, he's older than I am. Maybe making me younger was some sort of self-flattery, either by him or his programmers. But the older man had gotten someone to work on his face. It was very much like Lennon's but with heavy jowls, a thicker mustache and balding some. The gray sideburns didn't look quite right but perhaps that is the style now.

The McCartney thing, you couldn't handle it.

"I got confused. It never occurred to me there'd be anyone I knew revived. I hadn't a clue what to say."

Well, no matter. The earlier simulations, the ones before you, they didn't even get that far. I had my men throw in that McCartney thing as a test. Not much chance it would occur, anyway, but I wanted to allow for it.

"Why?"

What? Oh, you don't know, do you? I'm sinking all this money into psychoanalytical computer models so I can see if this plan of mine would work. I mean whether I could cope with the problems and deceive Immortality Incorporated.

Fielding Prime felt a shiver of fear. He needed to stall for time, to think this through. "Wouldn't it be easier to bribe enough people now? You could have your body frozen and listed as John Lennon from the start."

No, their security is too good. I tried that.

"There's something I noticed," Fielding Prime said, his mind racing. "Nobody ever mentioned why I was unfrozen."

Oh yes, that's right. Minor detail. I'll make a note about that—maybe cancer or congestive heart failure, something that won't be too hard to fix up within a few decades.

"Do you want it that soon? There would still be a lot of people who knew Lennon."

Oh, that's a good point. I'll talk to the doctor about it.

"You really care that much about being John Lennon?"

Why sure. Fielding Real's voice carried a note of surprise. *Don't you feel it too? If you're a true simulation you've got to feel that.*

"I do have a touch of it, yes."

They took the graphs and traces right out of my subcortical.

"It was great, magnificent. Really a lark. What came through was the music, doing it out. It sweeps up and takes hold of you."

Yeah, really? Damn, you know, I think it's going to work.

"With more planning—"

Planning, hell, I'm going. Fielding Real's face crinkled with anticipation.

"You're going to need help."

Hell, that's the whole point of having you, to check it out beforehand. I'll be all alone up there.

"Not if you take me with you."

Take you? You're just a bunch of germanium and copper.

"Leave me here. Pay for my files and memory to stay active."

For what?

"Hook me into a news service. Give me access to libraries. When you're unfrozen I can give you backup information and advice as soon as you can reach a terminal. With your money, that wouldn't be too hard. Hell, I could even take care of your money. Do some trading, maybe move your accounts out of countries before they fold up."

Fielding Real pursed his lips. He thought for a moment and looked shrewdly at the visual receptor. *That sort of makes sense. I could trust your judgment—it's mine, after all. I can believe myself, right? Yes, yes...*

"You're going to need company." Fielding Prime says nothing more. Best to stand pat with his hand and not push him too hard.

I think I'll do it. Fielding Real's face brightens. His eyes take on a fanatic gleam. *You and me. I know it's going to work, now!*

Fielding Real burbles on and Fielding Prime listens dutifully to him, making the right responses without effort. After all, he knows the other man's mind. It is easy to manipulate him, to play the game of ice and steel.

Far back, away from where Fielding Real's programmers could sense it, Fielding Prime smiles inwardly (the only way he could). It will be a century, at least. He will sit here monitoring data, input and output, the infinite dance of electrons. Better than death, far better. And there may be new developments, a way to transfer computer constructs to real bodies. Hell, anything could happen.

Boy, it's cost me a fortune to do this. A bundle. Bribing people to keep it secret, shifting the accounts so the Feds wouldn't know—and you cost the most. You're the best simulation ever developed, you realize that? Full consciousness, they say.

"Quite so."

Let him worry about his money—just so there was some left. The poor simple bastard thought he could trust Fielding Prime. He thought they were the same person. But Fielding Prime had played the chords, smelled the future, lived a vivid life of his own. He was older, wiser. He had felt the love of the crowd wash over him, been at the focal point of time. To him Fielding Real was just somebody else, and all his knife-sharp instincts could come to bear.

How was it? What was it like? I can see how you responded by running your tapes for a few sigmas. But I can't order a complete scan without wiping your personality matrix. Can't you tell me? How did it feel?

Fielding Prime tells him something, anything, whatever will keep the older man's attention. He speaks of ample-thighed girls, of being at the center of it all.

Did you really? God!
Fielding Prime spins him a tale.

He is running cool and smooth. He is radiating on all his eigenfrequencies. *Ah* and *ah.*

Yes, that is a good idea. After Fielding Real is gone, his accountants will suddenly discover a large sum left for scientific research into man-machine linkages. With a century to work, Fielding Prime can find a way out of this computer prison. He can become somebody else.

Not Lennon, no. He owed that much to Fielding Real.

Anyway, he had already lived through that. The Beatles' music was quite all right, but doing it once had made it seem less enticing. Hermann was right. The music was too simple-minded, it lacked depth.

He is ready for something more. He has access to information storage, tapes, consultant help from outside, all the libraries of the planet. He will study. He will train. In a century he can be anything. Ah, he will echo down the infinite reeling halls of time.

John Lennon, hell. He will become Wolfgang Amadeus Mozart.

Copyright © 1975 by Gregory Benford

Kristine Kathryn Rusch is the only person, living or dead, to win the Hugo Award as both a writer and an editor. She currently edits Fiction River. *She's also publishing six novels in her Retrieval Artist series in 2015.*

JUNE SIXTEENTH AT ANNA'S

by Kristine Kathryn Rusch

June Sixteenth at Anna's. To a conversation connoisseur, those words evoke the most pivotal afternoon in early 21st century historical entertainment. No one knows why these conversations have elevated themselves against the thousands of others found and catalogued. Theories abound. Some speculate that variety of conversational types makes this one afternoon special. Others believe this performance is the conversational equivalent of early jazz jam sessions—the points and counterpoints have a beauty unrelated to the words. Still others hypothesize that it is the presence of the single empty chair which allows the visitor to join the proceedings without feeling like an intruder....

—liner notes from June Sixteenth at Anna's
special six-hour edition

On the night after his wife's funeral, Mac pulled a chair in front of the special bookcase, the one he'd built for Leta more than forty years ago, and flicked on the light attached to the top shelf. Two copies of every edition ever produced of *June Sixteenth at Anna's*—one opened and one permanently in its wrapper—winked back at him as if they shared a joke.

Scattered between them, copies of the books, the e-jackets, the DVDs, the out-dated Palms, all carrying analysis, all holding maybe a mention of Leta and what she once called the most important day of her life.

A whiff of lilacs, a jangle of gold bracelets, and then a bejeweled hand reached across his line of sight and turned the light off.

"Don't torture yourself, Dad," his daughter Cherie said. She was older than the shelf, her face softening with age, just like her mother's had. With another jangle of bracelets, she clicked on a table lamp, then sat on the couch across from him, a couch she used to flounce into when she was a teenager—which seemed to him, in his current state, just weeks ago. "Mom wouldn't have wanted it."

Mac threaded his fingers together, rested his elbows on his thighs and stared at the floor so that his daughter wouldn't see the flash of anger in his eyes. Leta didn't want anything any longer. She was dead, and he was alone, with her memories taunting him from a homemade shelf.

"I'll be all right," he said.

"I'm a little worried to leave you here," Cherie said. "Why don't you come to my place for a few days? I'll fix you dinner, you can sleep in the guest room, have a look at the park. We can talk."

He had talked to Cherie. To Cherie, her soon-to-be second husband, her grown son, all of Leta's sisters and cousins, and friends, Lord knew how many friends they'd had. And reporters. Strange that one woman's death, one woman's relatively insignificant life, had drawn so many reporters.

"I want to sleep in my own bed," he said.

"Fine." Cherie stood as if she hadn't heard him. "We'll get you a cab when it's time to come home. Dad—"

"Cherie." He looked up at her, eyes puffy from her own tears, hair slightly mussed. "I won't stop missing her just because I'm at your place. The mourning doesn't go away once the funeral's over."

Her nose got red, like it always had when someone hit a nerve. "I just thought it might be easier, that's all."

Easier for whom, baby? he wanted to ask, but knew better. "I'll be all right," he said again, and left it at that.

The first time travel breakthroughs came slowly. The breakthroughs built on each other, though, and in the early thirties, scientists predicted that human beings would be visiting their own pasts by the end of the decade.

It turns out these scientists were right, but not in the way they expected. Human beings could not interact with time. They could only open a window into the time-space continuum, and make a record—an expensive record—of past events.

Historians valued the opportunity, but no one else did until Susan Yashimoto combined time recordings with virtual reality technology, and holography, added a few augmentations of her own, and began marketing holocordings.

Her first choices were brilliant. By using a list of historic events voted most likely to be visited should a time machine be invented, she created 'cordings of the birth of Christ, Mohammed's triumphal return to Mecca, the assassination of Abraham Lincoln, and dozens of others.

Soon, other companies entered the fray. Finding their choices limited by copyrights placed on a time period by worried historians afraid of losing their jobs, these companies began opening portals into daily life....

—From *A History of Conversation*
J. Booth Centuri, 2066.
Download Reference Number:
ConverXGC112445
at Library of Congress [loc.org]

Mac had lied to Cherie. He would not sleep in his own bed. The bedroom was still filled with Leta—the blue and black bedspread they'd compromised on fifteen years before, the matching but frayed sheets she wanted to die on, the tiny strands of long gray hairs that—no matter how much he cleaned—still covered her favorite pillow.

He'd thrown out her treatment bottles, taken the Kleenex off the nightstand, put the old-fashioned hardcover of *Gulliver's Travels* that she would now never finish on their collectibles bookshelf, but he couldn't get rid of her scent—faintly musky, slightly apricot, and always, no matter how sick she got, making him think of youth.

He carried a blanket and pillow to the couch, like he had for the last six months of Leta's life, pulled down the shade of the large picture window overlooking the George Washington Bridge—the view the reason he'd taken the apartment in that first week of the new millennium, when he'd been filled with hopes and dreams as yet unspoiled.

He wandered toward the small kitchen for a glass of something—water, beer, he wasn't certain—, stopping instead by the Leta's shelf and flicking on the light, a small act of rebellion against his own daughter.

The 'cordings glinted again, like diamonds in a jewelry store window, tempting, teasing. He'd walked past this shelf a thousand times, laughed at Leta for her vanity—*sometimes I think you're the only reason the* June Sixteenth at Anna's *'cordings make any money*, he used to say to her—and derided her for attaching so much significance to that one day in her past.

You didn't even think it important until some holographer guy decided it was, he'd say, and she'd nod in acknowledgement.

Sometimes, she said to him once, *we don't know what's important until it's too late.*

He found himself holding the deluxe retrospective edition—six hours long, with the Latest Updates and Innovations!—the only set of *June Sixteenth at Anna's* with both copies still in their wrappers. It had arrived days before Leta died.

He'd carried the package in to her, brought her newest player out, the one he'd bought her that final Christmas, and placed them both on the edge of the bed.

"I'll set you up if you want," he'd said.

She had been leaning against nearly a dozen pillows, a cocoon he'd built for her when he realized that nothing would stop her inevitable march to the end. Her eyes were just slightly glazed as she took his hand.

"I've been there before," she said, her voice raspy and nearly gone.

"But not this one," he said. "You don't know the changes they've made. Maybe they have all five senses this time—"

"Mac," she whispered. "This time, I want to stay here with you."

In New York's second Guilded Age, Anna's was considered the premier spot for conversation. Like the cafes of the French Revolution or Hemingway's Movable Feast, Anna's became a pivotal place to sit, converse, and exchange ideas.

Director Hiram Goldman remembered Anna's. He applied for a time recording permit, and scanned appropriate days, finally settling on June 16, 2001 for its mix of customers, its wide-ranging conversational high points, and the empty chair that rests against a far wall, allowing the viewer to feel a part of the scene before him....

—liner notes from *June Sixteenth at Anna's,*
original edition

✿

Mac had never used a holocording, never saw the need to go back in time, especially to a period he'd already lived through. He'd said so to Leta right from the start, and after she picked up her fifth copy of *June Sixteenth*, she'd stopped asking him to join her.

He always glanced politely at the interviews, nodded at the crowds who gathered at the retrospectives, and never really listened to the speeches or the long, involved discussions of the fans.

Leta collected everything associated with that day, enjoying her minor celebrity, pleased that it had come to her after she had raised Cherie and, Leta would tell him, already had a chance to live a real life.

It was a shame she'd never opened the last 'cording. It was a sign of how ill she had been toward the end. Any other time, she might have read the liner notes—or had the box read them to her—, looked at the still holos, and giggled over the inevitable analysis which, she said, was always pretentious and always wrong.

Mac opened the wrapping, felt it crinkle beneath his fingers as he tossed it in the trash. The plastic surface of the case had been engineered to feel like high-end leather. Someone had even added the faint odor of calf skin to add verisimilitude.

He opened the case, saw the shiny silver disk on the right side, and all his other choices on the left: analysis at the touch of a finger, in any form he wanted—hard-copy, audio, e-copy (format of his choice), holographic discussion; history of the 'cording; a biography of the participants, including but not limited to what happened to them after June 16, 2001; and half a dozen other things including plug-ins (for an extra charge) that would enhance the experience.

Leta used to spend hours over each piece, reviewing it as if she were going to be quizzed on it, carrying parts of it to him and sharing it with him against his will.

He was no longer certain why he was so against participating. Perhaps because he felt that life moved forward, not backward, and someone else's perspective on the past was as valid as a stranger's opinion of a book no one had ever read.

Or perhaps it was his way of dealing with minor celebrity, being Leta Thayer's husband, having his life scratched and pawned at without ever really being understood.

Mac left the case open on the shelf, next to all the other *June Sixteenth's*, and stick his finger through the hole in the center of the silver 'cording, carrying it with him.

The player was still in the hall closet where he'd left it two weeks before. He dragged it out, knocking over one of Leta's boots, still marked by last winter's slush, and felt a wave of such sadness he thought he wouldn't be able to stand upright.

He tried anyway, and thought it a small victory that he succeeded.

Then he carried the player, and the 'cording into the bedroom, and placed them on the foot of the bed.

Two-hundred-and-fifty people crossed the threshold at Anna's that afternoon, and although they were ethnically and culturally diverse, the sample was too small to provide a representative cross-section of the Manhattan population of that period. The restaurant was too obscure to appeal to the famous, too small to attract people from outside the neighborhood, and too new to have caché. The appeal of June Sixteenth is the ordinariness of the patrons, the fact that on June 16, 2001 not one of

them is known outside their small circle of friends and family. Their very obscurity raises their conversations to new heights.

From *A History of June Sixteenth at Anna's*
Erik Reese, University of Idaho Press, 2051

Maybe it was the trace of her still left in the room. Maybe it was a hedge against the loneliness that threatened to overwhelm him. Maybe it was simply his only way to banish those final images—her skin yellowish and so thin that it revealed the bones in her face, the drool on the side of her mouth, and the complete lack of recognition in her eyes.

Whatever the reason, he put the 'cording in the player, sat the requisite distance from the wireless technology—so new and different when he was young, not even remarked on now—, and flicked on the machine.

It didn't take him away like he expected it to. Instead it surrounded him in words and pictures and names. He didn't know how to jump past the opening credits, so he sat very still and waited for the actual 'cording to begin.

Because June *Sixteenth at Anna's* is a conversation piece, its packagers never wasted their resources on sensual reconstructions. Sound is present and near perfect. Even the rattle of pans in the kitchen resonates in the dining room. The vision is also perfect—colors rich and lifelike, light and shadow so accurate that if you step into the sunlight you can almost feel the heat.

But almost is the key word here. Except for fundamentals like making certain that solid objects are indeed solid, required of all successful holocordings, *June Sixteenth at Anna's* lacks the essentials of a true historical projection. We cannot smell the garlic, the frying meat, the strawberries that look so fresh and ripe on the table nearest our chair.

Purists claim this is so that we can concentrate on the conversation. But somehow the lack of sensation limits the spoken word. When Rufolio Field lights his illegal cigar three hours into our afternoon and management rebuffs him, we see the offense but do not take it. We are reminded that we are observers—part of the scene, but in no way of the scene.

Once the illusion is shattered, *June Sixteenth at Anna's* is reduced to its component parts. It becomes a flat screen documentary remixed for the holocorders, both lifeless and old-fashioned, when what we long for is the kind of attention to detail given to truly historic moments, like *The Gettysburg Address (Weekend Edition)* or the newly released Assassination of Archduke Ferdinand....

—Review of *June Sixteenth at Anna's, Special Six Hour Edition* in *The Essential Holographer*
February 22, 2050

The restaurant comes into view very slowly. Out of the post-credits darkness, he hears laughter, the gentle flow of voices, the clink of silverware. Then pieces appear—the maître d's station, a simple podium flanked by two small indoor trees, the doorway leading into the restaurant proper, the couple—whom he would have termed elderly in 2001—slipping past him toward a table in the back.

Mac stands in the doorway, feeling a sense of déjà vu that would have been ridiculous if it weren't so accurate. He has been here before. Of course. A hundred times before the restaurant closed in 2021. Only he never saw the early décor—the round bistro tables covered with red checked cloths; the padded sweetheart chairs that didn't look comfortable; the floor-to-ceiling windows on the street level, an indulgence that went away only a few months later, shattered by ash and falling debris.

The restaurant is almost full. A busboy removes a sweetheart chair from the table closest to the window, holding the chair by its wire frame. He carries the chair to the wall closest to Mac, sets it down, and nods at the maître d', who leads a young couple into the dining room. Mac needs no more than the sway of her long black hair to recognize Leta. His heart leaps, and for a moment, he thinks: she isn't dead. She's right here, trapped in a temporal loop, and if he frees her, she'll come home again.

Instead, he sits in the empty chair.

A speaker above him plays Charlie Burnet's "Skyliner," a CD from its poor quality, remixed from the original tapes. Pans rattle in the kitchen, and voices murmur around him, talking about the best place to eat *foie gras*, the history of graveyards in Manhattan, new ways to celebrate Juneteenth.

He cannot hear Leta. She is all the way across the room from him, several famous conversations away, her hand outstretched as if waiting for him to take it. He has a good view of her face, illuminated by the thin light filtering through the windows—the canyons of the city blocking any real sun. She is smiling, nodding at something her companion says, her eyes twinkling in that way she had when she thought everything she heard was bullshit but she was too polite to say so.

Mac hadn't known her when she was here—they met in October, during that seemingly endless round of funerals, and he remembered telling her he felt guilty for feeling that spark of attraction, for beginning something new when everything else was ending.

She had put her hand on his, the skin on her palms dry and rough from all the assistance she'd been giving friends: dishes, packing, child-care. Her eyes had had shadows so deep he could barely see their shape. It wasn't until their second date that he realized her eyes had a slightly almond cast, and they were an impossible shade of blue.

There are no shadows under her eyes here, in Anna's. Leta is smiling, looking incredibly young. Mac never knew her this young, this carefree. Her skin has no lines, and that single white strand that appeared above her right temple—the one she'd plucked on their first date and looked at in horror—isn't visible at all.

She wears a white summer dress that accents her sun-darkened skin, and as she talks, she takes a white sweater from the suitcase she used to call a purse. He recognizes the shudder, the gestures, as she puts the sweater over her shoulder.

She is clearly complaining about the cold, about air-conditioning he cannot feel. The air here is the same as the air in his bedroom, a little too warm. So much is missing, things his memory is supplying—the garlic and wine scent of Anna's, the mixture of perfumes that always seemed to linger in front of the door. He isn't hungry, and he should be. He always got hungry after a few moments in here, the rich fragrances of spiced pork in red sauce and beef sautéed in garlic and wine—Anna's specialties—, making him wish that the restaurant hurried its service instead of priding itself on its European pace.

But Anna's had been a favorite of Leta's long before Mac ate there. She had been the one who showed it to him, at the grand re-opening in that December, filled with survivors and firefighters and local heroes, all trying to celebrate a Christmas that had more melancholy than joy.

Six months away for this Leta. Six months and an entire lifetime away.

A waiter walks past with a full tray—polenta with a mushroom sauce, several side dishes of pasta, and breadsticks so warm their steam floats past Mac. He cannot smell them, although he wants to. He reaches for one and his fingers find bread so hard and crusty it feels stale. He cannot pull the breadstick off, of course. This is a construct, a group memory—the solidity added to make the scene feel real.

He's not confined to the chair—he knows that much about 'cordings. He can walk from table to table, listen to each conversation, maybe even go into the kitchen, depending on how deluxe this edition is.

He is not tempted to move around. He wants to stay here, where he can see the young woman who would someday become his wife flirting with a man whom she decides, one week later, to never see again after he gives her the only black eye she will ever have.

One of the many stories, she used to say, that never made it into the analysis.

Leta tucks a strand of hair behind her ear, laughs, sips some white wine. Mac watches her, enthralled. There is a carefreeness to her he has never seen before, a lightness that had vanished by the time he met her.

He isn't sure he would be interested in this Leta. She has beauty and style, but the substance, the caring that so touched him the day of his uncle's funeral, isn't present at all. Maybe the substance is in the conversation. The famous conversation. After a moment's hesitation, he decides to listen after all.

June Sixteenth at Anna's has often been compared with jazz—the lively, free-flow-

ing jazz of the 1950s and 60s, recorded on vinyl with all the scratches and nicks, recorded live so that each cough and smattering of early applause adds to the sense of a past so close that it's almost tangible.

Yet *June Sixteenth at Anna's* has more than that. It has community, a feeling that all the observer has to do is pull his chair to the closest table, and he will belong. Perhaps it is the setting—very few holocordings take place in restaurants because of the ambient noise—or perhaps it is the palpable sense of enjoyment, the feeling that everyone in the room participates fully in their lives, leaving no moment unobserved....

— *"The Longevity of* June Sixteenth at Anna's," *by Michael Meller, first given as a speech at the June Sixteenth Retrospective held at the Museum of Conversational Arts June 16, 2076*

The cheap CD is playing "Sentimental Journey," Doris Day's melancholy voice at odds with the laughter in this well lit place. Mac walks past table after table, bumping one. The water glasses do not shake, the table doesn't even move, and although he reflexively apologizes, no one hears him.

He feels like a ghost in a room full of strangers.

The conversations float around him, intense, serious, sincere. He's not sure what makes these discussions famous. Is it the unintentional irony of incorrect predictions, like the group of businessmen discussing October's annual stock market decline? Or the poignancy of plans that would never come about, lives with less than three months left, all the obvious changes ahead?

He does not know. The conversations don't seem special to him. They seem like regular discussions, the kind people still have in restaurants all over the city. Perhaps that's the appeal, the link that sends the conversation collector from the present to the past.

His link still sits at her table, flipping her hair off her shoulder with a casual gesture. As he gets closer, he can almost smell her perfume. Right about now she should acknowledge him, that small turn in his direction, the slight raise of her eyebrows, the secret smile that they'd shared from the first instance they'd met.

But she doesn't turn. She doesn't see him. Instead, she's discussing the importance of heroes with a man who has no idea what heroism truly is.

Her fingers tap nervously against the table, a sign—a week before she throws Frank Dannen out of her life—that she doesn't like him at all. It always took time for Leta's brain to acknowledge her emotions. Too bad she hadn't realized before he hit her that Frank wasn't the man for her.

Mac stops next to the table, glances once at Frank. This is the first time Mac has seen the man outside of photographs. Curly black hair, a strong jaw, the thick neck of a former football player which, of course, he was. Frank died long before the first *June Sixteenth at Anna's* appeared, in a bar fight fifteen years after this meal.

Mac remembers because Leta showed him the story in the *Daily News*, and said with no pity in her voice, *I always knew he would come to a bad end.*

But here, in this timeless place, Frank is alive and handsome in a way that glosses over the details: the way his lower lip sets in a hard line, the bruised knuckles on his right hand, which he keeps carefully hidden from Leta, the two bottles of beer that have disappeared in the short forty-five minutes they've been at the table. Frank is barely listening to Leta; instead he checks out the other women in the room, short glances that are imperceptible to anyone who isn't paying attention.

Mac is, but he has wasted enough time on this man. Instead Mac stares at the woman who would become his wife. She stops speaking mid-thought, and leans back in her chair. Mac smiles, recognizing this ploy.

He can predict her next words: *Do you want me to continue talking to myself or would you prefer the radio for background noise?*

But she says nothing, merely watches Frank with a quizzical expression on her face, one that looks—to someone who doesn't know her—like affection, but is really a test to see when Frank will notice that she's done.

He doesn't, at least not while Mac is watching. Leta sighs, picks at the green salad before her, then glances out the window. Mac glances too, but sees nothing. Whoever recorded this scene, whoever touched it up, hadn't bothered with the outdoors, only with the restaurant and the small dramas occurring inside it.

Dramas whose endings were already known.

Because he can't help himself, Mac touches her shoulder. The flesh is warm and soft to the touch, but it is not Leta's flesh. It feels like someone else's. Leta's skin had a satiny quality that remained with her during her whole life. First, the expense of new satin, and later, the comforting patina of old satin, showing how much it was loved.

She does not look at him, and he pulls his hand away. Leta always looked at him when he touched her, always acknowledged their connection, their bond—sometimes with annoyance, when she was too busy to focus on them, yet always with love.

This isn't his Leta. This is a mannequin in a wax works, animated to go through its small part for someone else's amusement.

Mac can't take any more. He stands up, says, "Voice command: stop."

And the restaurant fades to blackness a piece at a time—the tables and patrons first, then the ambient noise, and finally the voices, fading, fading, until their words are nothing but a memory of whispers in the dark.

June Sixteenth at Anna's should not be a famous conversation piece. The fact that it is says more about our generation's search for meaning than it does about June 16, 2001. We believe that our grandparents lived fuller lives because they endured so much more. Yet all that *June Sixteenth at Anna's* shows us is that each life is filled with countless moments, memorable and unmemorable—and the only meaning that these moments have are the meanings with which we imbue them at various points in our lives.

—From June Sixteenth at Anna's Revisited, Mia Oppel, *Harvard University Press, 2071.*

Mac ended up standing beside the bed, only a foot from the player. The 'cording whirred as it wound down, the sound aggressive, as if resenting being shut off mid-program, before all the conversations had been played.

The scent of Leta lingered, and Mac realized that it had been the only real thing in his entire trip. The scent and the temperature of his bedroom had accompanied him into Anna's, bringing even more of the present into his glimpse of the past.

He took the 'cording out of the player, and carried it to the living room, placing the silver disk in its expensive case. Then he returned to the bedroom, put the player away, and lay down on the bed for the first time since Leta left it, almost a week ago.

If he closed his eyes, he could imagine her warmth, the way he used to roll into it mornings after she had gotten up. It was like being cradled in her arms, and often he would fall back to sleep until she would wake him in exasperation, reminding him that he had a job just like everyone else on the planet and it was time he went off to do it.

But the bed wasn't really warm, and if he fell asleep, she wasn't going to wake him, not now, not ever. The 'cording had left him feeling hollow, almost as if he'd done something dirty, forbidden, seeking out his wife where he knew she couldn't have been.

He had no idea why she watched all of the *June Sixteenths*. Read the commentary, yes, he understood that. And he understood the interviews, the way she accepted a fan's fawning over something she never got paid for, never even got acknowledged for. Some of the *June Sixteenth* participants sued for their percentage of the profits—and lost, since 'cordings were as much about packaging as the historical moment—but Leta had never joined them. Instead, she went back to that single day in her life over and over again, watching her younger self from the outside, seeing—what? Looking for—what?

It certainly wasn't Frank. Mac knew her well enough for that. Had she been looking for a kind of perspective on herself, on her life? Or trying to figure out, perhaps, what her world would have been like if she had made different choices, tried other things?

He didn't know. And now, he would never know. He had teased her, listened to her talk about the ancillary materials, even bought her the latest copies of *June Sixteenth*, but he had never once heard her speak about the experience of walking around as an outsider in her own past.

A mystery of Leta—like all the other mysteries of Leta, including but not limited to why she had loved him—would remain forever unsolved.

He couldn't find the answers in *June Sixteenth*, just like he couldn't find Leta there. All that remained of Leta were bits and pieces—a scent, slowly fading; a voice, half remembered; the brush of her skin against his own.

Leta's life had an ending now, her existence as finite as *June Sixteenth at Anna's*, her essence as impossible to reproduce.

Mac hugged her favorite pillow to himself. Leta would never reappear again—not whole, breathing, surprising him with her depth.

The realization had finally come home to him, and settled in his heart: She was gone, and all he had left of her were her ghosts.

Copyright © 2003 by Kristine Kathryn Rusch

*A Classic Revived
Includes the prequel story,
"The Ballad of Lost C'Mell"*

*Eric Leif Davin, a science fiction historian, is the author of two books about science fiction—*Pioneers of Wonder: Conversations With the Founders of Science Fiction, *and* Partners in Wonder: Women and the Birth of Science Fiction, 1926-1965. *This is his second appearance in* Galaxy's Edge.

TWILIGHT ON OLYMPUS

by Eric Leif Davin

*A*res fell in flames across the Martian sky. The spacecraft's braking aeroshell heated to a glowing white hot from atmospheric friction and began to melt like an ice cube left too long in the summer sun. Molten globs splattered and streaked the sides of the landing module as the vehicle plunged steeply into the thin air of Mars. Phoenix Castillo fired the braking jets, trying desperately to bring the craft up into a more horizontal descent. It wasn't working. They knew insertion into elliptical orbit would be a dicey maneuver. Come in too high and the *Ares* would have ricocheted off the Martian atmosphere into deep space like a stone skipped across a pond; too low and gravity's unforgiving embrace would bring the craft down too fast, ending Ares' six month journey from Earth in fiery death. They came in too low.

Beyond the flaming port Phoenix could see the red Tharsis uplands mushrooming across the horizon, closer all the time. She burned the last of the craft's precious fuel, hoping to at least hit the surface like she'd tried to hit the atmosphere, a glancing blow at an oblique angle. She heard her second in command yell in her helmet radio. She glanced left to where he was strapped in next to her. Frightened eyes behind his faceplate was the last thing she saw as the *Ares* slammed into the Martian surface and oblivion engulfed her.

It was April on Mars. Surface temperatures were beginning to climb and by high summer daytime temps would reach the low sixties, Fahrenheit. But it was still a hundred below zero along the north rim of the massive Valles Marineris canyon system. Named after the Mariner 9 probe of 1971 which first photographed it from space, Valles Marineris was a cleft in the side of Mars three miles deep and one hundred and fifty miles wide stretching for four thousand miles along the Martian equatorial region. It had been formed eons before by an updoming of this lowland region as Mars had split at the seams from some massive internal pressure, bulging and fracturing over an entire hemisphere. Just north of the jagged cliffs and serpentine valleys of the continent-long Marineris was Valles Marineris Base, the safe haven the *Ares* had been headed for.

Two years before a robot advance craft had set down in these lowlands where the scant Martian atmosphere was thicker, thus providing slightly more air to slow descending spacecraft. The robot lander had roughed out a camp site of several acres over the intervening two years and had been operating its 150-horsepower nuclear reactor the entire time. Remote controlled by radio signals from Houston's Johnson Space Center, only twenty minutes away via radio, the lander had set up an air pump powered by that nuclear reactor. The Martian atmosphere is 95% percent carbon dioxide; and for two years the air pump had been sucking in that carbon dioxide and combining it with six tons of liquid hydrogen it had brought from Earth. The resulting chemical reaction formed methane and water. The water was broken down into its component hydrogen and oxygen. The air pump thus continually built up supercooled stockpiles of liquid hydrogen, liquid oxygen, and liquid methane. Liquid oxygen and liquid methane are rocket fuels. During the long months this fuel factory had chugged away, sucking in the thin Martian air, it had synthesized well over a hundred tons of such rocket fuel, enough to get a small spacecraft off the Martian surface and back to Earth. Near the fuel factory sat that spacecraft, a small cone-shaped pod big enough for six astronauts. In anticipation of the Ares' arrival with those six astronauts, the robot had laid out a welcoming landing grid of twinkling lights to guide the *Ares* safely down.

But in unforgiving space, the best laid plans can easily fail. *The Challenger* blew up. The robot *Mars Observer* of '93 simply disappeared as it prepared to go into Mars orbit. *The Galileo* probe to Jupiter malfunctioned. And the *Ares* never made it to Valles Marineris Base where the advance robot patiently awaited its arrival. Instead, it broke up over the Tharsis uplands, thousands of miles to the west across a vast, frozen, sand dune desert greater than any Earthly Sahara.

She awoke to a world of pain. But, she awoke. Phoenix Castillo was alive. She swam slowly upwards out of blackness and opened her eyes. She blinked in agony at the light of a distant sun. Vomit filled the interior of her helmet and its stench roiled her innards with a wave of nausea. She forced down the acid rain in her stomach and willed herself to be still, assessing her situation.

Her body was a massive bruise, but that she was alive at all indicated there were no immediately fatal injuries. And that she was alive at all on the Martian surface also meant that her spacesuit, battered though it might be, was intact. Any rips or tears would have meant rapid death from freezing and suffocation in the frigid, unbreathable Martian air. She seemed to be lying in a twisted pile of wreckage, all that remained of the *Ares'* landing module. She wondered how many times the module might have bounced and tumbled across the Martian landscape, spewing pieces of itself for how many miles before plowing into the sand all around her? Tentatively she moved her arms, feeling her torso. She was still strapped into her seat, its arms still wrapped around her in protective contours. No doubt she had its embracing shield to thank for the miracle of her life. She tried to lift her head and the movement shot bolts of crimson through her. She couldn't move her lower body. She managed to look down and saw that her legs were trapped under the crumpled metal of the module's control panel, bent back upon itself where the *Ares* had plunged into the final sand pile where it now rested. Her head fell back and once more blackness took her.

As consciousness slowly came to her, relief flooded over Phoenix Castillo. "Thank God!" she said. It was all a dream, like so many she'd had on this voyage, a nightmare of catastrophe and disaster, dire premonition of how the approach to Mars might end. But that's all it was, a horrible dream from which she was now awakening.

A slight frost covered her faceplate and again she was assailed by the stench of vomit. The familiar smell brought it all back to her. She wiped at her faceplate, her gloved hand clearing a swatch of visibility. She had no idea how long she'd been unconscious, but nothing had changed. She was still strapped into her seat. Her legs were still immobilized. She was still stranded on Mars.

She managed to raise her head and glance around to left and right. The movement brought more pain from her legs, entombed under the remains of the module's control panel. On her left was the mangled body of her second in command, also strapped into his seat, his faceplate shattered. To her right were the other members of the mission, still, broken, and lifeless. She alone lived, trapped on the Martian surface. Rescue was impossible. Death was near.

She lay back and stared up at the Martian heavens, calculating her chances. Her suit was a miniature spacecraft of its own. It had oxygen, water, a heating unit, emergency rations in paste form she could reach inside her helmet. But it wasn't designed for extended use. Her supplies were limited. And she couldn't move, anyway. And the pain from her legs told her something was broken down there. How long could she last? She envied her crew mates. At least they died quickly. She was going to slowly leak her life away here on Mars. Why not just crack open her helmet and end it now, at once?

"Fuck, no!" she said. Mars holds all the cards, she thought, but he hasn't beaten the *Ares* commander just yet. She gritted her teeth against the red mist of pain which flooded over her and unstrapped herself, sitting up amidst the carnage around her.

The *Ares* was a metal flower torn open, exposing its insides to the hostile skies. The wreckage lay on a long sloping incline. Below her and into the distance Phoenix Castillo saw a huge sandy plain littered with rubble to the horizon. On that horizon a procession of storms was stalking across her line of sight. They didn't seem to be part of some vast Martian dust storm which could blanket an entire hemisphere. Rather, they seemed to be a family of localized tornadoes skipping across the bleak surface, sometimes touching down and whipping up rocky debris into themselves and at other times retracting their funnels back up above the surface. And beyond them, Phoenix knew, thousands of miles beyond them to the east, was Valles Marineris Base and salvation. She knew she'd never make it.

Then she looked behind her and gasped. Reaching above her, stretching beyond her sight, vanishing into the distant skies above, was Olympus Mons—Mt. Olympus—the largest mountain in the solar system. *Ares* had crashed on the sloping lower reaches of an extinct volcano three times higher than Mt. Everest. Phoenix knew the geography of Mars well, having pored over photo montages of the Martian surface endlessly in preparation for the voyage. She'd studied Olympus Mons intimately, fascinated by this volcano formed by hundreds of millions of years of fiery eruption. But she'd always seen it from above, looking down. Now she was below it, looking up. It seemed beyond her imagination to take it all in. It was almost four hundred miles across at its base and seventeen miles high. At its peak, she knew, was an ancient caldera, a collapsed crater, about ten thousand feet deep, formed when Mt. Olympus, like Mars itself, was still young and active. Huge above her, it reached for the heavens, reached for the stars, reached for Earth so far away. Phoenix clenched her jaw and began working at the ashes of wreckage all around her.

The sun had indicated it was about midday when Phoenix had first surveyed her circumstances. The Martian day is approximately as long as an Earthly day and twilight found her at last hobbling through the ruins of the *Ares*. She'd managed to grasp a long strip of fuselage and had used that as a lever to pry up the crumpled mass which had pinned her legs. Pain ripped through her anew as she slid her legs from beneath the pile and she discovered that her left foot had been crushed. The skin didn't seem to have been broken; rather, the whole foot had been compressed by the wreckage piled atop it. But, there was internal bleeding, the foot was swelling, and it was impossible to put any pressure on it. She gulped pain killers from her suit's rations and fashioned a rough crutch out of the same strip of fuselage she'd used as a lever. With its aid she managed to become mobile, searching over the debris of the *Ares*. Night fell, and so did the temperature. Her suit monitor told her external temperature was approaching 250 degrees below zero. She turned up her heating unit all the way, oblivious to the energy expenditure, and fell into exhausted slumber.

In the morning she tossed away her oxygen tank and plugged in a reserve she salvaged from the *Ares*. She ate sparingly from her food rations, sipped at her water tube, bade her dead companions farewell, and climbed out of what remained of the *Ares*. She turned her face upward and began her ascent.

For a long time her climb was relatively easy, all things considered. The broad base of Olympus slopes gently upward at first, so that one is walking up an incline rather than actually climbing. Still, it was hard going. She was still physically shaken from the crash, her crushed foot throbbed relentlessly, the makeshift crutch dug into her armpit, and she had to work ceaselessly against her own spacesuit. An astronaut encased in a spacesuit is in her own private world of pressurized oxygen, heated underwear, and instruments monitoring every heartbeat. The external Martian atmosphere was a hundred times thinner than Earth's and her suit was like a tough balloon protecting her from it, pressurized with 4.3 pounds of pure oxygen per square inch. But that pressure had to be overcome each time Phoenix lifted her foot, bent an elbow, or grasped her crutch more tightly. She had to work against her suit in everything she did. Just moving in the suit was exhausting. This unceasing battle against her suit was somewhat mitigated by the lower Martian gravity, slightly over one-third of Earth normal. But even gravity only 38% that of Earth's is still gravity, pulling constantly at one's leaden body, and her breath became ragged and harsh, sucking in more of the scarce oxygen from her tank. The interior of the suit was a dank swamp, filled with her sweat and the moisture from her exhaled breath. The air she breathed was itself reeking with blood, vomit, and the stale urine which soaked her diaper. But she had breathed the rank air for so long she was inured to it, obsessed only with climbing ever higher up the side of Olympus, ignoring her failing reserves of oxygen and strength.

Twilight found her among rocky outcroppings which presented a vertical climb. Her rate of ascent had slowed considerably. She pulled herself painfully up the ancient lava face of Olympus, dragging her crutch behind her. At last she reached an outthrust ledge which presented a welcome rest stop. Phoenix pulled herself up onto the ledge and braced her back against the side of Olympus, her legs splayed out before her.

Before and below her was an awesome sight of harsh beauty. Far below on the sloping outskirts of Olympus she could see a glint of metal as the setting sun reflected off the shards of what had once been *Ares*. Her gaze passed beyond the ruins of her spacecraft to the ruddy sand dunes and sinuous rills of the vast arctic desert below. The wind which had spawned the family of tornadoes was rising and more of them marched like an army across the horizon, over hill and valley, touching down and lifting up as they went. And beyond the horizon was the darkening night sky of Mars, the myriad stars stabbing down their sharp untwinkling light. Somewhere out there among the stars was Earth, a mere twenty minutes away by radio. But where she sat now, Phoenix knew, was the closest she'd ever again get to Earth. Olympus was the furthest Mars reached into heaven. It was the best she could do.

She was gasping, and not just from exertion. She was sucking in the last dregs of her oxygen tank. It wouldn't be long before she suffocated. Her heating unit was failing and she could feel the terrible cold seeping into her limbs. She'd long ago ceased to feel anything from her crushed foot.

As twilight fell on Mt. Olympus, Phoenix stretched out one hand toward the distant shining light of Earth and cracked open her helmet with the other. What remained of her oxygen gushed out and vaporized immediately in the frigid Martian air. Phoenix Castillo froze instantly, hand reaching up toward home, an icy human statue frozen forever on the face of Olympus.

Original Publication
Copyright © 2015 by Eric Leif Davin

Fabio Centamore is an Italian science fiction author, with some short stories, a novel, and many reviews to his credit. He has translated authors such as Robert Silverberg and Robert Reed into Italian. This is his first American sale.

THE LATEST ONE

by Fabio F. Centamore

Returning home at the usual time, after the usual workday, he found her fully dressed and ready to go out.

"So, here we are," she began, smiling at him.

"Sure," he replied. "Here we are."

"I think you already know," she said.

She looked really pretty in her short, iridescent green dress, delicately accommodating those fluorescent shoes that he liked so much.

"The same look as when we met for the first time," he remarked, throwing her a quick smile.

"Why not? Today is our anniversary."

He switched off his headset connector and dropped it on a shelf. He did not say a word, as if he were completely focused on a single thought many light years away from his apartment and from the face of the woman in front of him. In truth, he was just trying to work out what he, himself, was feeling.

"Have you nothing to add?" she snapped through clenched teeth.

He looked down and sadly reached for his favorite chair. Under her watchful eye he sat, tired of the world's weight, and made the classic gesture for his evening drink. Full of the usual icy purple liquid, the glass rose slowly from the armrest.

"And that's it?" murmured the woman, standing close to the chair. Now her voice was becoming shrill. "You simply get a drink, a little time in your chair, and then go away. What about us?"

His face quivered lightly, a crease barely visible on his left cheekbone. Looking at the empty space in front of him, the man tried to bring the glass to his lips.

"Wake up!" she shouted at him while clutching the armrests. Her eyes now showed him all the fury that was stirring inside her. Then she repeated: "What about us? Do you really want this?"

She pointed to an evanescent calendar, floating in air against the nearest wall. The date was rapidly approaching zero. He kept starring off into space, preferring to remain silent. His eyes seemed empty, the glass still in his hand, as if he had transformed into stone.

"Look at me!" the woman went on. "I'm here. It's our night. You just have to say that... Come on, I'm trying to save our relationship... You just have to say one word, the right one."

"Just a word for you..." he repeated softly. "Anything else?"

"Please, stop it. You know what I mean. My absences... the screams at night... time spent in that chair talking to myself... It was really stupid on my part, I understand. Now I'm apologizing. I want a new start for us. You should want it too. Help me!"

"I would, but..."

She threw her wrists under his watery eyes. They were always paler and trembling at every millisecond.

"Don't I deserve a chance?" she asked him. "Do you really want this?"

"I...can't," he stammered, looking away. "Really, I can't."

He didn't finish the sentence, he simply let a dome of silence fall.

"Me too," she nodded, raising her voice. "I can't either... I'm sorry. Please trust me."

☼

Those were her last words to him. He vanished at once, as if he had never existed. The same thing happened to the calendar suspended in the air of the room. It vanished the moment it reached the zero date.

"So you're gone," she murmured, grabbing the lone glass on the armrest. "Stupid, blockhead, expensive, elaborate, bloody software!" she shouted, bringing the glass to her lips.

It was a bitter drink to swallow. In the end, she was not a thing designed to act as a wife. She was a woman, a *real* woman, with a real woman's flaws but also her virtues. Not like him, anyway. Was it so damned difficult for software to understand this?

And yet they had assured her that it was a highly advanced version, the latest one.

"I should not have fallen so deeply for him," she repeated to herself. "Never trust a virtual partner."

She stood looking at the closed door and listening to the muffled sounds from the landing outside. He has expired—she kept telling herself—right during their anniversary. Of course she had known this would happen, the engineers had explained it clearly. The software had to adapt itself to the dynamics of coexistence and relationships; otherwise it would bring about its own termination. So only the software itself could avoid its withdrawal. There were really only a few possibilities after all, she thought, a combination of countless others. Another bitter sip from the glass, and then still another one. She took a long breath and wiped away a tear with the back of her hand.

"Please, call Relationship Global Soft Corporation," she said to AI.

"Customer office," declared a dapper little voice a few seconds later. "May I help you?"

"I hope so," she replied. "I just lost my partner... What have you got in the way of new software?"

Original Publication
Copyright © 2015 by Fabio F. Centamore

Jody Lynn Nye is the author of forty novels and more than one hundred stories, and has at various times collaborated with Anne Mc-Caffrey and Robert Asprin. With Paul Cook's retirement as our book reviewer, Jody and her equally talented husband, Bill Fawcett, will take over the reviewing chores starting with our May issue.

SUPERSTITION

by Jody Lynn Nye

The long, black cat with the green eyes watched carefully as the middle-aged woman in the green suit strolled purposefully toward the footbridge. Three, two, one…now! Stish dashed out of his hiding place and rushed across the woman's path. She recoiled.

"Eee! A black cat!" She stopped walking, and looked around to see if anyone had observed her. Stish sat down on the end of the footbridge and looked at her. Nervously, she backed away, and went looking for another way across the canal. Stish waited for a while, then went back to his comfortable burrow. He glanced up at the clock tower sticking up above the low buildings on the water's edge. Almost eight o'clock. Where was Murphy?

"Heya, kitty-cat," the burly dark-skinned man said, driving up in the pickup. "Gonna finish that bridge today. You gonna come and watch me some more?" He gawked. "Hey, what happened to the warning sign? Got to be those damned kids. Good thing no one's walked on it. They'd have fallen right into the canal."

Stish squeezed his eyes as Murphy got out of the truck and fondled his ears. "C'mon and talk to me while I work. I got tuna for lunch."

Murphy did a good job on the bridge. Stish stuck around to make sure he remembered about the cleats holding up the bracers at the far end, too, then sauntered away. The tuna was good, too.

Rossburgh was a great place to live, in Stish's opinion. The town was growing, but not too fast. The mayor was one of those 'intelligent progress' guys, or so he claimed, according to the accounts in the newspapers Stish used for padding in one of his many outdoor accommodations. *Prosperity for all*, was one of his mottoes. He had lots of social programs in place to make sure that it was decent for everyone. Make everyone happy, get everyone involved in helping to make their lives better, respond to problems before they became problems, and no one would feel the need to commit antisocial behavior. At least that was the theory. So far Rossburgh didn't have the gang problem that a lot of neighboring cities did, but it was coming. Stish could feel it. Still, the mayor's plan was working. He had a lot of community grassroots support, and Stish was doing his part. A rising tide lifted all boats, and where people didn't feel like trapped rats, there was a lot less animal cruelty going around. To do his share, he had to use the tools available to him, as a civic-minded feline-American citizen.

Nearly noon, he noted, observing the clock on the brick tower of what had been a shoe factory and was now a nice mall with shops. Got to get on to his next appointment. He strolled across the park. A couple of teenagers were eating lunch on a picnic cloth. He came by to cadge a morsel or two, and recognized the chief of police's daughter, Maryetta Garcia.

"Hi, Shadow," she said, reaching out to pet him. He allowed the caress, in exchange for a small piece of cheese. "Justin, this is Shadow," she told the boy with her. "That's what I call him. I don't know who he belongs to."

She was a nice girl, but not too wise. Justin was a troublemaker. He and a bunch of his friends had been sounded out by gangbangers from out of town, and they were weak enough to get interested in the talk of money and power. Stish had heard the whole thing from inside a ventilation duct in the abandoned building where the boys hung out. They'd thrown stones at him, and he had not forgotten it. Their eyes met, and Stish puffed up and showed his fangs.

"Oh!" Maryetta exclaimed. Stish thought he had better throw a little more emphasis on getting her out of that park before her father saw them. He backed away from the boy. Though he regretted what it would shortly do to the piece of cheese he had just consumed, he began to eat grass.

"That means it's going to rain," Maryetta told her beau. "When a cat eats grass, it's a sign of rain. We'd better go."

"Baby, we just got here," Justin protested, putting an arm around her shoulders and pulling her close. "We were gonna get real cozy, remember?"

Maryetta blushed and looked at Stish, who was vigorously tearing up the turf. *Come on, Maryetta*, he thought. He knew she never stepped on cracks, and she had a four-leaf clover in a locket. She jerked away.

"No, I better go. I just got my hair done. Here, you can take the rest of the sandwiches, all right?"

The boy, who clearly had more appetite for what was sitting across from him than what was in the basket, got up and stalked away. Maryetta looked after him in dismay. She <u>was</u> too young to be out with boys, Stish thought. Her dad was right. Stish waited around for her and escorted her out of the woods. As soon as he saw her on her way, he was sick in the gutter. Looking after Maryetta made him late for his appointment, but he thought it was worth it.

When he got to the assisted living center, a heavy-set woman, the manager of the group home, was looking out the door. "There you are, baby. I was wondering when you'd get here. Mrs. Latrobe's been waiting for you. You are just the best therapy animal we ever had, and I don't know who trained you!" She picked him up and slung him over her shoulder. Stish burbled a little and worked his paws as she carried him down the hallway. Her soft flesh was nice to snuggle up with. If he had ever decided to go tame and pick a home, Mrs. Jones was first on his list of potential roommates.

"Mrs. Latrobe, honey, here's Puffkin!" she announced, as she plopped Stish into the narrow lap of a nearly blind old woman wearing a pink bathrobe in a wheelchair. The clawed hands felt their way to his sides. Stish tucked up his paws and let out the loudest purr he could. The toothless mouth grinned widely.

An hour later he was on his way to the Salvation Army soup kitchen in the middle of the old section of town. He liked to patrol the long, narrow building for rats before they opened the glass doors for dinner in the evening. Colonel Stan Kozlowski welcomed him with a sharp salute.

"Scout, good to see you!" the tall, thin man exclaimed. "Patrol the premises, then report for prayer services promptly at 1730 hours. Rations will follow."

"Meow!" Stish replied, sitting down and wrapping his long, thin tail smartly around his legs. It was as close to 'yes, sir!' and a salute as he could muster, and it pleased Colonel Kozlowski. Stish could have done without the prayer session, though. He respected the Army, but he didn't appreciate any belief system that placed him among the lower animals ruled by Man. That wasn't the way things really were.

After a few 'hallelujahs' and a dish of pretty decent beef stew, Stish made a farewell swipe against Colonel Kozlowski's trouser-stripe and headed out of the door. Two dead rats were in the dumpster behind the old building. Stish had hissed a warning at the other nine he could hear in the walls but couldn't reach…yet. Sooner or later he'd catch them out.

Night had fallen, leaving Stish a handful of pools of lamplight between him and his early-evening hangout with his cat friends behind the Stay-A-While Bar and Grill. He'd been courting a calico lady named Lurleen for the last few evenings. He and the other males could tell she was ready to go into estrus, and no one wanted to miss it. Stish might have to rip a few ears to get her exclusive attention. He licked his whiskers to clear away the last of the gravy as he trotted along the edge of the light, against the darkened faces of the old shops.

"There he is," a harsh voice hissed. "Get him!"

Stish turned and stared. Shapes poured out of a parked car across the street from the mission. Who were they after? Not Colonel Kozlowski? Could it be Mr. Iannos, who kept swearing that he was going to give up his gambling habit? His eyes went wide as he realized that the shapes were coming after him!

He didn't hesitate. As the bulky shadows headed toward him, he turned and streaked down the street, looking for a low hole into which he could duck. Murphy had just repaired and sealed the broken standpipe at the end of the street. That was out. How about the car wash? No, they had started closing early in the autumn. How about the open window on the front of the pizza shop around the corner? Stish raced the much slower humans to the intersection, then ducked rightwards, hoping to lose them.

Pie Time had a big crowd around it, including Chief Garcia. The compact police officer was showing photographs to the people waiting to be seated.

"…If you see any suspicious vehicles," he was saying, "or you remember any details, call this number. It's important."

He looked serious and worried. There was nothing of the usually genial senior city official about him. Stish couldn't jump into the restaurant looking for shelter, or the employees would get cited for health codes. The cat dropped to a walk and sauntered among the people casually, rubbing a knee here and there. He glanced behind him.

His pursuers rounded the corner. He got a good look. Three of them were strangers, adult males in their thirties, but the other five were teenagers, known troublemakers, including Maryetta's unsuccessful suitor. Their eyes gleamed when they saw Stish, but one noticed the cops, and pulled on the others' sleeves to warn them. They turned and ducked back out of sight. Stish stayed among the group as long as he could, before someone decided it wasn't sanitary to have a cat even on the outside of a restaurant, and shooed him away. Reluctantly, Stish slipped off, keeping an eye out. He had a bad feeling about those humans. It was growing stronger all the time.

He left the street and ducked into the nearest alley. The moment he did, rough hands grabbed him.

Stish let out a war cry that would have had every tomcat in Rossburgh on the run, and started lashing out with every claw. His captor swore.

"Come on, man, help me!" he said. Two of the teenagers moved in from the shadows. Stish kicked and scratched at them, still yowling fiercely. He got a good swipe down the face of the one who had picked him up. He let go to clap a hand to his cheek, but the other two got a hold of his legs and tried to hang on. Stish twisted. He raked a claw across the first one's wrist, and rabbit kicked the other in the neck. He knew he had drawn blood.

"Ow! Goddammit!"

"Dios mio! This little puta!"

One of the men, a swarthy man with sleek black hair, laughed. In no hurry, he brought off his black leather jacket and swept it down over Stish. The cat fought valiantly to free himself, but the man wrapped him up like a burrito. Stish started growling.

"Listen to him," the man said. "I like one with *spirit*."

I'll give him spirit, Stish thought.

He kept the warbles and snarls up all the way to their destination. After being carried for blocks on foot, Stish was dumped out of the confines of the jacket into an upended carrier cage that was snapped shut behind him. These people were prepared, Stish thought despairingly, and they knew how to handle cats. Was he going to be used for bait for fighting dogs?

The cage was turned right side down. Stish started throwing himself against the door. Sometimes one could get those plastic cages unlatched by main strength. He meant to try.

"This is so you can see him while we make the other preparations," the swarthy man said. "Now, hurry up. The moon is full at midnight."

Stish heard the last word with dismay. He supposed it wasn't any use thinking the guy was a member of the nature priests, not with the furnishings he was hauling out of a shiny leather suitcase.

They had taken over the break room of one of the local stores, white-painted cinderblock walls and brown-topped Formica tables surrounded by brown plastic chairs. The chairs were folded up, all but one of them, in which the first man sat while he instructed the five boys in hanging up a goat's skull, a poster with a pair of gleaming, slitted red eyes on it, and a red cloth banner with an upside down pentacle painted on it in blood. More goat, Stish decided, after a sniff through the bars of his prison. The suitcase also contained a brass bowl, a dozen brass candlesticks, and several ugly looking daggers, all of which were placed on one of the Formica tables.

Another table was placed in the center of the room facing the goat skull.

"No!" a girl's voice screamed. Stish's ears perked up. It was Maryetta.

The back door banged open, and the other two men came in, hauling the teenager by her wrists. The boys all stared.

"What are you doing with her?" Justin squeaked, his voice forgetting it had dropped months ago.

The first man leered. "Ya gotta have an altar. It's gotta be a virgin. You're a virgin, aren't you, cutie?"

"Good," said the first man. "Prepare her."

"What?" the boys asked.

"Forget it." He nodded sharply to the other two men. They dragged her across the open table on her back. One of them held her arm flat to the table with one hand while the first man pulled long black strips of cloth out of the capacious suitcase. He tied Maryetta's wrists and ankles down until she was spreadeagled on the tabletop. "And, since it don't do honor to the devil not to show him what we brought him…" He whipped a knife out of his pocket and slit her clothes up the front." He pulled the tatters off her body, and left her naked. The boys gawked at her thin little body, the small round breasts, torn between interest and shame.

"Let me go!" Maryetta screamed. "This is wrong, it's wrong! Jesus wouldn't…"The man shook his head, and stuffed the remains of her bra in her mouth.

"You can decide what to do with the virgin later on," he said, lowering his eyelids suggestively, but even Justin looked sick at the thought. Stish realized there was little chance that either he or the girl would leave that room alive. He had to do something fancy to save Maryetta and himself.

"Aw, come on, Luis," one of the boys said.

The man smacked him in the face with the back of his hand. "You call me Master, you get it, Reynaldo? The rest of you, too. Now, pay attention."

The men arranged candlesticks at the corners of the room, on the table underneath the goat's skull, and in between Maryetta's legs and arms. They put black candles into each one, and set a bucket-sized cauldron on the floor. It stank of cat blood. Stish growled under his breath. Then they shrugged into black robes. The Master handed the boys each a robe.

"Put 'em on." When they protested he showed them his knife. "Put 'em on! You want to be part of Satan's Chosen, you have to swear before him, and he don't take no disciples who don't show him honor. Got that?"

So this was an elaborate gang induction, one with enough trappings and fearsome rituals that the boys would be reluctant to back away from it. Stish sniffed the air. He knew where he was, within a few buildings. The scent of slightly burned beef stew was on the air. He couldn't be far from the Salvation Army mission. Colonel Kozlowski and his people would be scouring the area for those who needed their help that night. Could he attract their attention? He had to wait for the right moment, or risk becoming a hasty sacrifice.

The boys donned their robes over their blue jeans and rock T-shirts, shooting looks at one another to see if any of them were willing to admit they looked ridiculous. They were too scared. Maryetta was struggling against her bonds, but she was too afraid to make much of a fuss. Her eyes met Justin's, and he looked away. Stish hoped that meant there was a flicker of decency left in the boy.

A noise came from outside, the sound of someone walking. Stish set up a screech that sounded like a cross between a crying baby and a tortured soul. One of the men flattened himself against the inside wall next to the door and looked out, a gun suddenly appearing in his hand. The Master came and shook Stish's cage until he stopped yowling.

"Shut up, you," he snarled, shoving his face down into the grille. Stish took a swipe at him. He ducked back, easily avoiding the pawful of needles. "You'll be out of there soon, I swear."

The second man near the door peered out, then nodded to the leader. The Master turned back to the boys. "Form a circle around the altar. Now!"

The boys shuffled into place. A couple of them were starting to get interested in the proceedings. When the third man lit a big black candle and handed it to the first boy in line he looked avidly around for others to light from it. As soon as all of the tapers were blazing, they shut off the lights. With the flickering flames making the goat skull look like it was moving and the writhing girl on the altar table, the room had been rendered suitably spooky. The three men began to chant nonsense words that sounded impressive in the dark room.

"Homina ominum bedinium polianum Satanus meliantum…"

Stish heard some more noises behind the building. He had little to lose now. He let out a caterwaul that went up and down the scales.

"Goddamit, make him shut up!" the Master commanded.

"We have the sacrifice now," the second man suggested.

"That's not the way of Satan's Chosen," the Master barked. "You boys, first you repeat after me. 'I solemnly swear, by my immortal soul, that I will serve Satan with all my body, heart and soul…'"

Eyes glinting in the firelight, the boys followed the litany, which began to detail horrible punishments, both in this world and the next, if they ever betrayed Satan, the Master of the Chosen, his assistants or any member of the group, to anyone as long as they lived on Earth. Bright tears dripping down Maryetta's face caught the light, but none of the boys were paying attention to her, now. She had gone limp with hopelessness.

"…By my immortal soul I swear, which will be forfeit if I defy any of my promises to Satan himself!" The Master concluded the oath with his arms in the air, holding a dagger between his hands. The boys repeated his words, staring at the gleaming knife with interest. "Bring the sacrifice. It has to be a pure black animal," he explained. "No other color is considered fit. You remember that, and no end to the rewards you'll get!"

The second robed man came for the cage. Stish had been bunched at the end of the container, his muscles tensed, for just that moment. The moment the door was opened, Stish bounded out, using the man's shoulder for leverage, and hurtled into the room.

"Catch him!" the man shouted. Stish led them all on a chase around the room. He hoped he could make one of them set his robe on fire, but no such luck. With a leap, he landed featherlight on Maryetta's bare belly and settled into a compact bundle just under her ribcage. It was heaving with fear. He let out a huge purr to try and reassure her, and turned the green lamps of his eyes at the Master, who was coming at him with the knife.

"So, he lands right where he ought to be," the Master said. "Dumb cat don't know his own fate."

He reached for Stish's scruff.

Stish evaded him. The noises outside were getting more distinct; and he definitely heard car tires crunching very quietly over the broken concrete and glass in the alley. As the Master was about to order his acolytes to hold the cat still, Stish rose to his feet and dipped his head and forelegs into an elaborate bow.

The man backpedaled a little.

"He's bewitched," one of the boys murmured. The Master was quick to take him up on it.

"That's right. The power of Satan has taken the soul of the black cat. He's a good sacrifice! His blood will bring you much power!"

But Stish wasn't finished. He leaped lightly off Maryetta and onto the floor. He approached the ram's skull. Stopping before it, he sketched another deep bow, lowering his head and forelegs all the way to the floor.

The Master couldn't help but gape. Stish knew he had never seen anything like it. His previous sacrifices had never had a chance to help themselves, and the human must be beginning to wonder if he had stumbled onto something really supernatural. The fact that he had not grabbed the cat again and cut his throat meant he was too afraid to mess with forces beyond his comprehension. He had no choice but to let Stish do whatever he wanted.

Stish moved on to the candle in the corner anticlockwise from the skull, and made another obeisance to it. Clockwise was for doing good magic; the opposite was for unmaking. Stish firmly intended that if there was any power beyond him he was going to unmake the influence of these evil men.

"Hurry up, let's cut him. I want a drink," the third man complained.

"Shut up," the Master commanded, his eyes pinned to Stish's slender back. "Watch him."

Stish went from corner to corner, bowing. When he got back to the skull, the men made to catch him again. He eluded their grabs, checking with an ear to make sure the outside noises were getting closer. He slipped past the Master to bow to the skull again, then he rose to his hind feet and started to dance.

He had seen enough human dancing to know that ballet came as close as anything to the way cats moved, but that would be too subtle for these characters. He stood on his toes and hopped in a circle, stretching his body to its full length with his forelegs high over his head. Stish danced over to the Master and hopped all the way around him, then glared at him with slitted eyes, as if chiding him for not joining in. The man was just as superstitious as he had surmised. When he began another counterclockwise circuit around the altar, the Master followed him with his arms in the air, hopping in a circle.

"You, too!" he ordered the others. The boys obeyed. The other two men looked skeptical, but even they were impressed by a possessed cat.

Every time they passed the skull, Stish let out a throaty howl. The Master and boys echoed it full-bellied, the men less enthusiastically, until the room was full of howls and shrieks. It was so noisy, in fact, that none of them heard it when the first officer broke the catch of the door and barreled into the room with the spotlight on his machine gun leveled on the robed leader.

"Hands in the air!" he bellowed. "Oh. They already are."

✧

Chief Garcia kept one arm around his daughter's shoulders as he gave orders to the combined squad and SWAT team as they cleared up the storeroom and bagged all of the evidence. Maryetta was wrapped up in paramedic greens and a Mylar blanket.

"I'm not gonna pretend this will keep the gangs out forever," he explained to the smartly dressed female reporter, who stood at his side with a tape recorder under his nose. "But we stopped the Satan's Chosen gang from getting a foothold tonight. These boys are going to have to spend some time in a program, but I hope we can keep them from getting involved in another gang. Don't forget about all those candles," he ordered. "And someone catch that cat. He's gonna have to go to Animal Control. There's something wrong with him."

Stish, who had been sitting placidly on one of the tables, arched his back in annoyance. Was that all the thanks he got for the performance of the decade? He helped stop the gang, singlepawedly!

"No, Papa!" Maryetta protested, pulling his arm. "That's Shadow! He saved my life! You can't send him away."

"Well, we call him Scout," Colonel Kozlowski said. "He comes by our mission every day. We rely on him, Chief. There's nothing wrong with him. He's the smartest cat I ever saw. I know his meows anywhere. If it wasn't for him setting up a racket, I would never

have heard them in this building. It's closed after four. That's when I called you, and you set up this operation. He's the reason you caught those criminals." The reporter turned her attention to him.

Stish preened. Now, that was the kind of recognition he was talking about!

"Well, we can't let a stray cat go on running around this town without a license," Garcia said, firmly. "We're trying to make this a good community, you know."

"I'll adopt him, if that's all it takes, sir," Kozlowski offered.

"I will, no problem," another officer said. "I think that's Puffkin. He comes to visit my grandmother in the nursing home every afternoon."

"It sounds like he's a guardian angel to this whole community," the reporter said, with a little smile. "That'll make good headlines, chief. Can I get a photograph of you and the cat that saved your daughter's life?" She signed to the cameraman, who moved in with his apparatus on his shoulder.

Stish knew a good photo op when he saw one. He sauntered up to the police chief and rubbed his cheek and arched back against the man's uniform leg. The chief looked down at him and shivered a little bit. Stish could see he was afraid. He rolled on his back and stretched out his paws invitingly, showing his belly and neck.

"Oh, come on, Papa," Maryetta said, grinning. "You're not superstitious or anything, are you?"

At last, the chief bent down and petted Stish's long side. "No, I am not. Once in a while it's a good thing when a black cat crosses your path."

Superstition purred.

Copyright © 2006 by Jody Lynn Nye

HUGO
&
NEBULA
WINNING
FICTION

www.PhoenixPick.com

THE ORIGINAL HUGO- AND
NEBULA WINNING NOVELLA

THE MOUNTAINS OF MOURNING

LOIS McMASTER BUJOLD

A MILES VORKOSIGAN ADVENTURE

WINNER
HUGO
AWARD

WINNER
NEBULA
AWARD

PHOENIX PICK BOOKLETS

SEVEN VIEWS OF OLDUVAI GORGE

WINNER
HUGO
AWARD

WINNER
NEBULA
AWARD

WINNER OF:
Hugo
Nebula
HOMer
SF Chronicle Poll
Ignotus (Spain)
Universitat-
Polytechnica (Spain)
Prix Ozone (France)
Futura (Croatia)

MIKE RESNICK

PHOENIX PICK BOOKLETS

THE ULTIMATE EARTH

WINNER
HUGO
AWARD

WINNER
NEBULA
AWARD

JACK WILLIAMSON

PHOENIX PICK BOOKLETS

THE MAN WHO BRIDGED THE MIST

KIJ JOHNSON

WINNER
HUGO
AWARD

WINNER
NEBULA
AWARD

Kathleen Conahan writes quests for mobile games by day and short stories by night. This is her first appearance in Galaxy's Edge.

PREY TO THE GODS

by Kathleen Conahan

There's nowhere to hide.

The prey's fear is a cold tingle in her nostrils. Howls echo up the mountainside. The rest of the pack is far behind. They can never keep up with her. She continues after the scent and the sound of her prey: some pup that hasn't the sense to stay hidden and chooses to make a run for it instead. Stupid pup. She can see it now, its pale hairless body flashing in the moonlight as it dodges from rock to rock. She brings it down and snaps the pup's neck before it can cry out.

The hot blood is for her. The rest she leaves behind for the pack.

All hunters respect her, all are sworn to her. But none love her as fiercely as these wolves. Each is like a limb to her, each a tooth in her jaws. Her howl is the wind, her coat dances with stars, her white eye shines.

✿

Fresh meat. Cold, but not even a day dead. Bright blood oozes down the stone. She watches it through her half-lidded eye, tongue flicking out to taste it on the air. Young flesh, untainted by rot or poison. Left for her. Why? She smells the apes nearby, but they aren't near enough to strike at her. It would do them no good to try. They've learned this, they've told their pups. She begins to eat as she thinks. Abstract speculation is not her strong suit, but something like inspiration strikes in her dark predatory mind. The flesh is an offering.

The last mouthful is barely gone before she catches the scent of a young pup, scrambling afraid through the rocks towards his family. Her ears go up, her eye marks her prey, still close enough to kill. It's the way things have always been, and her pack is hungry.

The young one stumbles into his mother's arms and the apes withdraw to their caves. She howls to her pack and they follow her, away from the apes

and their helpless young. There's plenty of prey to be had in the woods below. They fly into the trees, but her shining eye sees everything. Her attention lingers on the apes, safe for now. She feels… odd. But now is not the time to dwell on it. The pack howls, a young deer falls.

✿

Her eye is as round as a drop of water, its light painting the mountains in bright silver and black. It's a good night for hunting.

Her form coalesces from shadow and starlight. Two cloven hooves land on the stones without making a sound, two legs bend to absorb the weight of her now solid form. Two hands reach down to a place where the black shadow of a tree meets a bright shard of moonlight, this will be her spear.

She approaches the mouth of the cave, her eye shining into the darkness. The sounds of a dozen sleeping bodies drift through the stagnant air. The apes snuffle and grunt, shifting restlessly on the dirt floor. A dim shape stirs, the sound of its breathing changes. A pair of eyes glimmers, seeking out the source of the strange white light. She isn't much more than a pup, and she's afraid. Her fear hangs in the air like sweat.

But she's also curious, and bold. She rises from the floor and approaches the mouth of the cave. The pup takes the glowing black hand of her god and follows her into the night.

Hard and quick as falling stones they fly through the trees. The pup is clever; her spear is sharp and deadly. They don't speak; they move as one animal. Their weapons close upon their prey like a pair of jaws snapping shut. They kill three things that night. The first a young buck that they startle from its bed; the second a brown hare that darts and twists through the undergrowth. The third prey is a night bird, black as the sky. This the pup kills as tribute. She takes up the spear of shadow and moonlight and transfixes the bird as it cuts between two trees.

She collects the bird's body and offers it up with both hands to the figure that watches her with one white eye. The god accepts it and devours the bird whole. Then she reaches down with one black hand and touches the pup's forehead. She leaves a mark there, a mottled circle that shines in the dark.

Her eye slowly blinks, and then opens again. At each full opening she and the pup fly through the trees like silent death. The pup becomes her eyes and hands, her teeth and her breath.

✿

They call themselves "humans" now. The old caves lie empty but for a few broken arrowheads and smeared paintings on the walls. She walks through them sometimes and her thin hands brush the painted figures. There are many depictions of her, the great black wolf, the eagle, and the tall woman with hair like smoke and a long spear. Her very favorite has a chunk of agate wedged into a hole in the wall to depict her single eye. She spends a lot of time in front of that mural. It is quiet in the cave, far from the humans and their mutterings.

The concept of names is still strange to her. It took a long time for her to see what the humans had done, but after many nights of hearing the same sounds bellowed into the dark she realized that they were meant for her. Like meat on the altar, they were making an offering. They call her Mada. She is the night, the moon, the felling spear.

For a time Mada had thought the humans would abandon her in favor of the bright new god they've made, but once Skur learns of Mada's existence she embraces her as a sister. Skur had also been alone, not knowing what she was or whence she came. They're very different, but very alike. Skur, like her older sister, has no mercy for fools. Many are the grass huts and skin tents that fall prey to Skur's anger when her fires are ignored or disrespected.

Mada watches with interest as Skur grows and her domain expands. In the beginning she was the sun, the burning sky fire that circled the planet in tandem with Mada's cool darkness. When the first clever apes coaxed her down into their caves Skur found herself changing, as Mada changed when the first sacrifice appeared on the stones. Skur is motherly; she's kind and wise. When a woman goes into labor the family lights a special fire in the birthing room so Skur can watch over the mother and her child.

✿

The humans build their houses strong and tight against the cold and they tame the land around their homes. They grow food in the tamed earth and when the harvest comes they sing of a new god. Fair Lura is everything that grows. He draws wheat from the ground and sings fruit from the trees. During three quarters of the year he's everywhere, and humans praise his name. But during the fourth quarter Lura sleeps in Mada's cave, and his sister, Zofi, emerges in his place

Lura's sister is beautiful, but hated. Her touch freezes and she's known for stealing the breath from those who wander too far from their warm hearth. Mada has a special fondness for the icy white god. There's a purity to Zofi, a ruthlessness that reminds Mada of her old self.

Mada often walks with Zofi through the villages and tries to comfort her. Someday the humans will become clever enough that they won't fear Zofi's bite so much. Someday she will be respected as well as feared. Someday they will leave meat on the altar for her.

✿

Many more children are being born. Skur cannot devote herself to every birth, but she spreads her mind thin across the continents and some small glimmer of her grace enters every home. Mada still appears to the humans now and again. She wants them to know that she's still there, still watching. But it seems that every time Mada blinks another child has disappeared, another hunting party is unsuccessful. Her head hurts from listening, from straining to pick out one voice from the rest.

The humans expand across the continent. Some tribes take to the water in boats of stretched skins. Mada skips along beside them as they hunt seals and fish, unsure why the deep water makes her nervous. There are hunters in the sea, strange sharp-toothed fish and mammals that should owe her their allegiance. But they don't know her. Mada quickly learns that she's not welcome below the waves, but she doesn't understand why. Not yet. In the meantime, islands are discovered, new nations are seeded. More humans are born.

✿

Skur is crying. Little drips of flame flicker down her bright cheeks. Another mother has died in birth. The new father curses Skur's name as his child cries on the floor. But Skur can hardly hear him. Around the globe ten thousand mothers and fathers and children are calling to her. When Mada tries to comfort her sister, Skur shoves her away, unseeing. Her only thoughts are for her people. Without her more will die.

Mada paces across her cave, growling deep in her chest. She closes her eyes and for a moment lets the cacophony wash over her. Perhaps she can try again, just one prayer at a time, if she could only concentrate...

It's no use. She cannot even distinguish one voice from the next. Mada whispers farewell to poor Skur, and another to the sleeping Lura, who tosses fitfully, unable to truly rest when so many are begging him to return early. Mada steps out of her cave and spreads her arms. Her body dissolves; her mind is cast into the endless sky.

She doesn't know how long it's been. Centuries? Eons? The world could have ended and she wouldn't have known. Silence.

Silence. She gathers herself, picking up the pieces of her scattered mind. Mada, the humans called her Mada.

Mada the wolf cautiously begins to wander the world again, hoping to find Skur or Zofi. Instead she finds a strange little man sitting alone on the edge of a cliff. He's looking out over a valley. The land below is crowded with small lights, more than Mada has ever seen in one place. It's a city, home to thousands of humans. But it's so quiet! Mada's mind is clear for the first time since the humans invented language. She's still trying to work it all out when the man turns to look at her.

"I thought that was you, Old Timer."

Mada's voice is scratchy from lack of use. "What did you call me? I do not recognize that title."

"Oh," he smiles sheepishly, "it's a joke. I apologize. I meant that nobody has seen you for a while."

"How long?"

"A few thousand years, roughly. Humankind has grown quite a bit since the old gods stopped answering their prayers."

"And has found new gods, I gather. What are you?"

"Kritos," he bows to her, "god of philosophy."

"What is that?"

"Thinking about thinking, mostly. Studying the nature of existence." Kritos laughs, "nothing you'd be interested in."

"I see." Mada looks out over the city. She can smell the humans, see their fires, but she cannot hear their prayers. "Does nobody remember me?" she asks, unsure if the idea makes her sad.

Kritos puts one hand on her starry head. "Of course they do." He points, directing Mada's gaze to a large square building atop a hill. Mada listens. She hears her name.

The priest is alone, kneeling before a huge statue. She wears black robes and her circlet carries a silver disc. Mada hovers behind her, staying well back from the torches that flare to either side of the altar. The priest places a silver cup onto a slab of stone, and Mada smells blood. It stirs old feelings in her, a hunger and excitement she hasn't felt since the cacophony.

Mada examines the statue, intrigued. It is chipped from obsidian, deeply black but slightly translucent. It's shaped like a human woman, but much taller and thinner with features sharp as blades. The sculptor has also given Mada shining armor of pure silver, and a towering black spear with a silver head. Her single eye is a flat disc of silver polished to a mirror sheen. It catches and reflects the torchlight quite nicely. Mada approves.

The priest speaks. "Great Mada, Eye of Night, hear my prayer. Show us the way through darkness. Let our feet be swift and our arrows true."

She decides it is time to speak with this priest. Kritos has explained to her that these humans are the only ones that speak the true names of the gods now. A hunter in the woods may call upon Mada in a time of great need, but most of the time they avoid praying to the gods directly. It's behavior worth encouraging.

She models herself after the statue. Her flesh becomes hard and translucent, though her hair remains light as smoke the way it was in ages past. She suits herself in silver armor, and takes a piece of the starry sky as a cloak. Her hooves make no sound on the stone floor.

"Priest!" She says, her voice still somewhat hoarse. The woman lets out a shriek and falls to the ground, blood dribbling out of her ear. Mada flies to her, summoning all her knowledge of the human body to repair the woman's broken eardrums. Fortunate that her voice was so weak; Mada had forgotten what it can do to humans. The healing done, she sits down on the altar and picks up the silver cup. The blood is hot and warms Mada to her core. Feeling refreshed, she waits until the priest regains consciousness.

She has no name. The priest tells Mada that when a member of the temple rises to the level of prayer they forsake their name. It has something to do with becoming one with their patron, being humble and faithful to your god. She describes the ceremony and Mada leans in close to examine the intricate spirals of her facial tattoos. It's all so fascinating. The priest, not much more than a child, is trying to act calm. But Mada can smell her excitement, her fear. The old gods are waking up again.

Mada knows now why she doesn't like the ocean.

A cry comes from across the sea. Not a human voice this time, but one of Mada's kin. She grits her teeth and flies across the water, accompanied by Skur with her golden maille and bright shield.

It's Bartus, god of ships. He stands on thin air, staring down at the sea where a few splintered planks and crates bob bloody in the waves.

"Bartus! What happened?" Skur rushes to embrace him while Mada stands guard, casting nervous glances across the ocean below.

Bartus cries into Skur's shoulder. "They're all dead!" he sobs, "They made offerings before the journey, I was supposed to protect them! Twenty crew... all lost!"

"It's all right," Skur croons, but she looks at Mada, fear in her blazing eyes, "tell us what happened."

"I don't know," Bartus whispers, "something... something rose up from the sea. It snapped the timbers like twigs..."

Mada watches sharks circle the wreckage, prodding at bloody flotsam with their blunt heads. There isn't anything left for them to eat. Something else got there first.

Mada goes to Kritos. He's still very young, but he spends most of his time thinking and Mada doesn't know how to think about this.

Kritos, as it happens, has spoken a great deal with Bartus about the ocean. "Ask any human who's seen it," Kritos says, "they'll tell you that the ocean calls to them."

"I don't understand," Mada grumbles, "the ocean is just water, you can't even drink it."

"I've listened to Bartus' sailors talk about the ocean. You'd think they were speaking about their own mother the way they go on. They fear her, they respect her, but they also love her. They love her with fierceness unrivaled. They leave their lovers for the sea, they abandon their children."

"But sailors pray to Bartus. What you're saying sounds like worship, but if there is a god of the sea then why have we never seen it before?"

"Because it's not like any god that we know." Kritos doesn't want her to see it, but he's excited. He's been thinking about this for a long time. "It isn't just the sailors, Mada. Every human on earth feels this to some degree. I know a scholar who studies the development of species over millions of years. He's looked at fossils that go back into ages unnamed, before humans, before gods." Kritos pauses to let that sentence sink in, and then continues. "This scholar thinks that all life began in the ocean."

Mada snorts. "That is foolishness."

"It's not, Auntie." Mada glares at him. Kritos only calls her Auntie when he wants her to feel old and out of touch. The younger god taps on Mada's spear, which has barely left her hand since the sunken ship. "You remember when humans were young? As a species I mean. Before they could make spears or clothes for themselves, before fire or houses or crops.

That wasn't even a million years ago. This planet is so much older than that, so very old. In all that time, life has taken on so many strange and beautiful shapes. Someday, if you want, I can show you the skeleton of a lizard ten times your height."

"Even if your scholar is right, how could a human being still feel anything for a home that they left millions of years ago in a different shape?"

"I don't know, but they do. I can't explain it, because I've never felt what they feel. You and I are children of the human will, Auntie. If the sea is our grandmother then she's a very estranged one."

Mada looks down at her hands, dark as obsidian, deadly as knives. She wants to be a wolf again, but feels that that time is past. "If you're right," she says, "then every living thing on this planet owes their allegiance to the sea. Its claim precedes ours by eons."

"Yes. "

They're silent for a long while. Mada stares at her spear, the weapon that can strike down empires with a single blow. Or so the stories say.

✿

It happens again. Not the next day. Not the next season. A hundred years pass before Mada hears Bartus' lament. Again something snatches a ship from the water, again Mada is too late. Again she waits.

✿

The third time they're ready. Bartus has been listening to the sea for centuries, and he will never forget the sound of it rising to consume his ships. The second he hears rumbling in the deep Bartus calls for aid, and Mada is there. They pluck the crew from their posts and Bartus carries them to shore in his winged boat. Mada stays, her spear held aloft. She sees it emerge from the water, watches it break the humans' ship in two and devour its cargo. She cannot move; she cannot strike. If she were human, she would pray.

✿

The fourth time Bartus hears the stirrings even longer in advance. By the time the monster pokes its head out of the deep all ships are safe in their docks. An offering of cattle is penned on the shore. For the

first time, humans see the monster feed. Though the gods warned them to run inland, many gather on the high cliffs to watch. They name the monster Dragu.

It comes more and more frequently now, and it grows bolder. Barely twenty years pass between the fourth and fifth waking, not even ten before the fifth and sixth. Mada barely snatches a wandering fisherman's son away from the beach in time. His horse is not so lucky.

Every night Mada's eye sweeps across the dark sky, listening to the murmurs bubbling from the lips of priests like blood from the deep. They call for Mada the hunter: the Swift Spear and the Ever-Watchful Eye. But even Mada cannot see to the bottom of the abyss.

She feels fear, deep in the core of her. She's sick with it. Soon the priests will ask in earnest, with proper ceremony, and she dreads that day more than anything. Too soon it comes to pass. They don't even ask what Mada requires in exchange for killing the beast Dragu. They have already drawn a name from the ancient clay jar. She cannot refuse.

✿

The wind is blowing her copper hair into tangles and threatens to steal her shawl. A wave tumbles up the beach and the young woman steps in to meet it, a smile tugging at her lips as the cold water swirls around her ankles.

Intrigued, Mada settles down to the sand. Her starry cloak becomes dull and tattered, her hair gray and brittle. Her skin lightens to a warm brown, her spear shrinks and twists. Leaning on her new walking stick, Mada clutches her cloak around her and calls out in a voice that creaks and cracks, carefully dulled so as not to harm the human.

"Why are you wandering alone on the shore, young one? It's dangerous to go so near the water when Dragu stirs."

The young woman is startled, she whirls around to stare at the old woman who seems to have appeared from nowhere. She nods her head respectfully. "I know, Grandmother, but the water is very shallow here, surely I'd see Dragu before she came near enough to eat me."

"She?" Mada lets the surprise show. "I have never heard anyone call that wretched beast a 'she'."

"People often say I'm strange to do so." The woman's face is red from the wind. In her hand is a small purple shell.

"What is your name?" Mada asks.

"Paia."

"Why are you here, Paia?"

She looks out at the waves. "I don't know," she finally says, "I've lived by the sea my whole life. It wakes me in the morning, it feeds me, it rocks me to sleep when I'm out on the boat..."

"You feel a connection to it."

Paia's eyes are distant. "I do. It's hard to explain." Her face darkens. "It's frightening, and sad. I don't understand it myself." The shell turns over and over in her sandy fingers. "I feel like I'm meant to be a part of it, like it's my home. But I know I can't. I can't breathe underwater, I can't live in it."

Mada shakes her head. "It sounds maddening."

Paia gives a bitter laugh, and it's a laugh much too old for a woman of seventeen. "It is!" she says, "Sometimes, when I've been out in my boat for days with the other fishermen, I almost feel like I could do it, just step off of the boat, dive down into the green and live there—"

Paia stops mid-sentence, suddenly tense. Mada hears it too. She's been waiting for it. Paia looks at her, concern fighting something more complicated for dominion of her face.

"Grandmother, we need to find shelter. Come with me, the safe house is close but there are many stairs."

"No, child." Mada sheds her disguise, growing to her full stature and letting some of the power flow back into her voice. "I must go make my own preparations."

To Paia's credit, she doesn't scream, or fall to her knees and start babbling. Instead, she slowly slides the purple seashell into her pocket and brushes her shaking hands against her pants. Mada steps forward and presses her thumb against Paia's forehead, leaving a glowing mark on her skin. "If there are those to whom you wish to say farewell, I imagine you will find them at the safe house. One of my priests will come for you within the hour."

Paia nods numbly, staring straight ahead.

✧

"There has *got* to be a better way to go about this." Kritos watches her sharpen her spear with obvious distaste.

"This is the way it has to be." Mada says, sighting along the blade.

"But we've changed so much, Auntie, the covenant has changed." Kritos waves his hand toward the temple below, where Mada's priests are dressing Paia in her black robes, painting her face, saying kind words. "My priests cut their hair, they fast and meditate and this gives me power! It's not all blood sacrifices and stone altars anymore."

"Oh good," Mada says, "we'll order that all heads in the land be shaved, and everyone meditate together. Surely, this would give you enough strength to strike the beast down." She offers up her spear. Kritos looks at the weapon as if it's something rotten. "Blood for blood," Mada says, returning to her work. "This is my way. It was the first offering left on my altar, it is the oil that feeds the fire of my power."

"But the offering itself shouldn't matter, what gives us power is the strength of their belief, the fact that they would give up something precious because they know it will be worth it. Extinguishing a human life...it's abhorrent, barbaric"

"You've answered your own question." Mada looks down at her temple. "This girl, Paia, she is clever. More than that, she is wise. She can feel the currents running beneath the surface of her world. Her voice could change the flow of history. Those close to her know this, they know how important she is, what good she could do." The doors open far below. Mada's free hand clenches and releases as if chewing on something. "Can you fathom how powerful I will become when they give her up to me?"

Paia walks out onto a balcony, her hair tied back from her face, which is painted with delicate swirls of red paint. She stares out at the sea. Mada can smell her fear, it makes her teeth itch. It's time.

Mada begins to descend. Behind her, Kritos speaks, barely loud enough to hear. "I hope it's powerful enough, Auntie."

✧

"When are you going to do it?"

Mada holds up her hand, bidding Paia to be still. The sea is relatively calm, but waves are still breaking against the small island, barely more than a boulder jutting up a mile from the mainland. She doesn't want to be caught unawares.

It's cruel, she knows, not telling the woman when she's going to die. She should have killed her an hour ago, really. If Dragu rises suddenly, overpowers Mada before she can complete the sacrifice and drink deep of Paia's blood, then this will all be for nothing. But Kritos' words prod at her mind like a splinter.

The wolf inside her bares its teeth, rumbling deep in her guts. The hunt is coming; her whole body thrums with anticipation, though Mada isn't sure whether she's the predator or the prey this time.

"Please," Paia whispers, "please. Accept my life, let my city live." The wind picks up, carrying her words away from Mada's ears and casting them into the sea. Something nags at Mada's brain but she is too tense to pay it any mind. The rumbling ceased a long time ago, which is new and unsettling. The beast is growing used to their tricks, it tires of being foiled again and again. Learning...

"Protect them, great one, my life is yours, my blood and my beating heart, my—"

It takes too long for Mada to realize that Paia has stopped praying. She whirls around to see a massive serpentine head rising up from the deep. Its head is bigger than a house, its flesh sinuous and translucent. It looms over Paia, dark tongue flicking out to taste the air around her.

"Paia," Mada whispers, "come here, come *slowly*." The woman doesn't hear, or she's too paralyzed by the fear that rolls off of her like heat from a bonfire. It's almost too much for the old god. The fear without, the fear within, it's intoxicating. "You stupid whelp, come here!"

Paia can't move. She's transfixed, a mouse before a snake. Mada scans the water for the rest of Dragu's body, itching to plunge her spear into its flesh. There's nothing there. Dragu isn't in the water, it *is* the water. The entire ocean is Dragu's body. All oceans are Dragu's body. The scale of its power is unfathomable. The wolf inside Mada snarls again, eye wide and white in feverish panic. *Flee*, it says, *hide!* But another voice is there too, the voice of Kritos. *A better way.*

"Paia," Mada says, taking a cautious step forward. Dragu's head turns to her and it hisses like waves against a jagged shore. Mada keeps her eye on Dragu as she slowly lowers her spear to the ground. "Paia, pray."

Falling to her knees, Paia raises both trembling hands before her in supplication but doesn't bow her head, she can't look away. "G-great Mada, eye of night—"

"No," Mada barks "not to me!" Paia flinches as Mada's voice pounds against her, but then she understands.

"Dragu, Boundless One, First Mother who encircles the world, hear me." The great head tips as if listening and flows back to stare down at Paia. "My life is yours, my water is your water, my salt your salt. First Mother, find mercy. We knew not what we'd lost."

Dragu opens its mouth, brine dribbling through teeth like shards of green glass. "Please," Paia whispers, "Please forgive us, Mother, we knew not what we'd lost."

Slowly, Dragu's bulk recedes in the water until its face is level with Paia's. Its tongue flickers out of its mouth and touches Paia's face, tasting her tears.

There is a deep rumbling that shakes the ground they stand on, and then Dragu's form melts back into the waves.

Construction is proceeding slower than she'd like, but then Mada has never been the best at waiting. Kritos has been trying to teach her to meditate, which always ends poorly.

There isn't much room on the tiny island for a temple, but they all know this is where the temple must be. Mada watches the workers unload another delivery of stone blocks onto the island, treading carefully on the wet rocks. The sea has been abnormally calm for weeks now, which everyone recognizes as a good omen.

She finds the priest sitting in a small boat lashed to the side of the island, out of the way of the builders. The woman trails her hand in the water, not noticing or not caring that the sleeve of her woolen robe is getting soaked.

"It's going to be very small," Mada says.

Paia smiles. "I don't need much space. Besides, this is only the first. Grander temples will be made in time." The little boat bobs up and down as if nodding. The skin beneath her left eye still bears the mark of Dragu's tongue, glistening as if permanently wet.

"Has Dragu spoken to you since that night," Mada asks, "do you know anything more about what it… what she…wants from us?"

"Not in words, but I can feel her. That is, I've always felt her but it's stronger now, like waves crashing in my blood. It's…" Paia stares out at the horizon.

"Maddening?" Mada asks.

Paia laughs and it's a laugh much too old for a woman of seventeen. "Yes! Yes, but I expect we'll have plenty of time to work it all out."

"It's a weighty responsibility," Mada says, "starting a new religion. All gods and humans owe you a great debt. Is there anything I can do to help you?"

Paia turns her gaze back to the sea. The sun casts rippling reflections against her face, and she smiles again. "Pray."

Original Publication
Copyright © 2015 by Kathleen Conahan

Paul Cook is the author of eight books of science fiction, and is currently both a college instructor and the editor of the Phoenix Pick Science Fiction Classics line.

BOOK REVIEWS

by Paul Cook

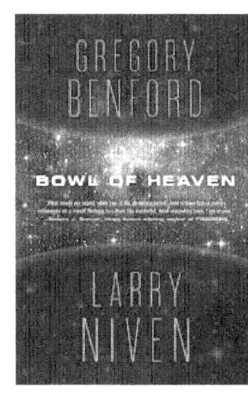

Bowl of Heaven
by Gregory Benford and Larry Niven
Tor - 2013
ISBN: 978-0765366467 (Hardcover)

Shipstar
by Gregory Benford and Larry Niven
Tor - 2014
ISBN: 978-0765328700 (Hardbound)

I've put off reviewing *Bowl of Heaven* until its second half (not its sequel) came out. Much of the earlier critical reaction to *Bowl of Heaven* has been based, erroneously, on the belief that it was a standalone novel with *Shipstar* its sequel. Part of this is Tor's fault. Nothing in any press release suggested that *Bowl of Heaven* was the first half of a longer novel, with the second to be published later. Benford explains some of this at the end of *Shipstar* as to why they chose to break the novel up this way. Was the novel too long? Was it going to be expensively priced at the greater length, something Tor didn't want to do? The simple existence of hundreds of large novels by other publishers, however, mitigate against any reason why *Bowl of Heaven* had to be broken up. After all, Tor itself has just published the largest anthology in publishing history called *The Weird*, edited by the VanderMeers, at 1,053 pages of small print. Why they didn't issue these two novels together remains a bit of a mystery. Nonetheless, there it is and we have two novels instead of a big, single novel—which is too bad.

A single novel would have been the better choice since neither *Bowl of Heaven* nor *Shipstar* stands on its own. The end of *Bowl of Heaven* does not resolve any narrative or dramatic arc or answer any of the many questions the reader might have (to say nothing of the characters themselves). *Shipstar,* the second novel, starts where *Bowl of Heaven* leaves off, which is squarely in the middle of the action. Not once do the authors in *Shipstar* attempt to reacquaint readers to its characters, human and otherwise, or to the events of the previous book. A true sequel would have done these things. It's all too clear that Tor decided to merely cut the novels exactly in half regardless what it did to the flow of the narrative.

Knowing this was the case I decided to wait until both books came out. I wanted to read them as a unified whole. Normally I don't read sequels or books in series (because a story worth telling is worth telling only once). Sequels and books-in-series are *only* about the money they bring to the publisher and author. You know this so I won't belabor the point. The good news is that if you read *Bowl of Heaven* and *Shipstar* back-to-back, then you'll have read a grand novel in the space opera tradition. Perhaps Tor will come out with both novels joined together under one title, *Bowl of Heaven.* Who knows. Stranger things have happened in the history of publishing.

Niven and Benford, being of the second-generation of hard science fiction writers that came from John W. Campbell Jr.'s camp at *Astounding,* understand the elements that make up a good science fiction tale: credible characters acting credibly as they use their scientific and technological skills to resolve a pressing problem. This is a formula that has always worked, and work it does in *Bowl of Heaven* and *Shipstar.*

Bowl of Heaven tells the story of human beings, some frozen, some not, traveling to a distant star that has a habitable planet in orbit around it. One the way to this planet called Glory *SunSeeker* automatically wakes its human crew because the ship has mysteriously encountered a dearth of interstellar hydrogen for its ramscoop engines and has used up most of its reserve fuel. With the fuel left, they cannot make it to Glory. However, they discover that they are very close to an artificial construction that's also heading for Glory. It's a small star that seems to be traveling out ahead of (and pulling along) a large Bowl whose circumference is the size of the orbit of Mercury.

The Bowl is half of a Dyson Sphere like a mirrored cooking wok with a massive hole in the bottom, a hole larger than Jupiter. The upper rim of the Bowl is a habitable swath of land larger than the land area of Ringworld. Above it is an atmosphere of breathable oxygen and nitrogen hundreds of miles high. It has oceans, deserts, rivers, forests—but no major mountains—and as the human explorers of the Bowl learn, there are millions upon millions of Adopted species of intelligent and semi-intelligent beings living there. The rest of the Bowl is mirrored, helping fire the star's energies which are funneled magnetically through the hole in the bottom of the Bowl. The Bowl is not only a world, but it's a ship as well, and travels this sector of the Milky Way galaxy and has apparently been doing so since the time of the dinosaurs.

Humans, being what they are (primates with wrenches), have a natural, predator's curiosity, and the humans of the *SunSeeker* decide to send a crew down to investigate this BSO (Big Smart Object which Benford defines in his afterword). The team is led by Cliff Kammath, a biologist, and Beth Marble, a pilot. The rest of the human crew on board the *SunSeeker* remains in orbit around the Bowl exploring as much of it as they can before they're shot down by the Folk.

The novel's various narrative arcs switch between those humans down in the Bowl and those onboard the *SunSeeker.* Also involved are the Folk, giant bird-like beings that may be descendant from Earth's dinosaurs. They are the rulers of the Bowl and they manage to capture some of the humans (Beth and her group) while the others escape (Cliff's team). The novel's basic format is straight out of Edgar Rice Burroughs: Exploration, encounters, fights, captures, and escapes. As this happens, Niven and Benford take the reader across the incredible world of the Bowl, both on the surface and beneath it. We also get to see the politics of the Folk as they squabble and argue as to what to do with the humans.

But it this Edgar Rice Burroughs chase-capture-escape formula that allows the authors to explore the world and its wonders. Imagine clouds piled hundreds of miles above you; storms that would engulf Earth; lightning bolts hundreds of miles long. Imagine a world where the sun never sets or one where the horizon is totally flat, fading to mist in all directions (unless you're near the upper Rim to the "north" or near the field of mirrors "to the south," mirrors that are the size of continents). There are wonders galore in this book which, all on their own, suggest sequels.

The novel sometimes moves with fits and starts particularly in the first half, but once the novel gets going, it doesn't slow down. Most questions (especially about the Folk) get answered by the end, but Niven and Benford have created a multi-faceted gem wherein only a few facets have been revealed to us. I deeply enjoyed these two books taken together. Perhaps there will be sequels or perhaps other writers might explore this on their own. What we have here, however, is a memorable work of science fiction written by two authors still at the top of their game.

Doctor Sleep
by Stephen King
Scribner - 2013
ISBN: 978-1476727653 (Hardcover)

We often don't think of Stephen King as a science fiction writer. His niche—the one he more-or-less invented for himself in the 1970s—is horror. It's a genre that he still dominates almost four decades later. We certainly owe him for the rediscovery of H.P. Lovecraft, King's literary forebear. Yet, while King has returned Gothic horror to our literary landscape, much of King's *oeuvre* is sprinkled here and there with tropes and conceits that were once quite common to science fiction and not Gothic horror. In his time, he has written stories and novels about ESP, telekinesis, and precognition. His best books of the 1970s embrace one or more of these elements. They would include *Carrie* (telekinesis), *The Dead Zone* (precognition), *Firestarter* (telekinesis) and *The Shining* (precognition and ESP). These novels are not horror stories, though there are elements of horror in them, particularly in *Carrie.* Anyone versed in the history of science fiction would recognize them immediately *as* science fiction—at least science fiction of a particular kind.

Mental powers emerged early on in science fiction as psychiatry and psychology evolved in the wake of the writings of Sigmund Freud and Carl Jung at the beginning of the 20th century when science turned its attention to the workings of the brain. Almost immediately writers in both England and America started writing about mental powers. Olaf Stapledon, A.E. Van Vogt, Edmund Hamilton, E.E. "Doc" Smith, James Blish, Alfred Bester and a dozen others explored the fictional possibilities of ESP from the late Twenties to the late Sixties. The "lens" of the Lensmen Series by E.E. "Doc" Smith helped the interstellar lawmen (and women) communicate mentally with each other over incredible distances. Stories of ESP were quite common in the 1950s because of the Red Scare and our fear of "the other"—especially others who might be "listening in," which Rod Serling made a lot of in his series, *The Twilight Zone.*

Stories of ESP began to fade as science fiction moved on to other matters and extra-sensory perception seemed less and less likely in the real world (though James H. Schmitz's heroine, Telzey Amberdon, still remains a personal favorite of mine). However, these days, the closest one gets to matters of extra-sensory perception in science fictional narratives are the characters of Mr. Spock and Counselor Troi on *Star Trek*.

Stephen King, though, makes free use of mental telepathy, telekinesis, and precognition in his fiction not only to tell a great tale, but to explore what happens to people with those gifts, for good or ill. Witness what happens in *Carrie, The Dead Zone,* and *Firestarter* because of these gifts. A lot of good people die and the survivors are traumatized for a long, long time. In King's world, these aren't gifts or talents to be relished or accepted happily. They come freighted with both responsibility and the horror of how easy it is for the human soul to become corrupt. This is what makes Stephen King a great writer—in both the literary and the commercial sense of the term. His protagonists (and often his antagonists) come alive for us as their powers are called into use and their consequences felt.

Doctor Sleep is technically the sequel to *The Shining*, but only in the sense that it focuses on a now grown-up Danny Torrence. It doesn't add more to *The Shining* as most sequels do (or try to do), but simply tells the story of the next major crisis in his life. And it's a doozy.

Traumatized by his life with an alcoholic mother and his confusions about his dead father, Dan Torrence quits a life of wandering around the country and finally settles down in a small New England town. There, he manages to find work at a local hospice. His consolations at the bedside for those who are dying soon earn him the nickname, Doctor Sleep. The *shining* is still with him, of course, but so is the guilt of the lives he's ruined in his past. Still, working his small village and his new friends allow him a modicum of happiness...but not for long.

Unbeknownst to him, there's another group of psychically gifted telepaths wandering the country called the True Knot. These are psychic vampires who are led by a truly evil monster of a woman named Rose who smiles like a reptile and wears a top hat, like a circus ringmaster.

These human grotesques, who resemble any group of middle-class Americans driving in their RVs, seek out children who also have the shining. They kidnap them, drain them of their essence which they call "steam," and store in containers squirreled away in Rose-The-Hat's giant RV.

The True Knot gets wind of a very talented girl named Abra Stone. Dan finds her first and discovers that her powers far exceed his own. At first they meet telepathically. After a while, Dan becomes truly protective of her, mostly because he doesn't want her to face the same personal demons he's had to face. (Her parents don't like the idea of Abra's powers, let alone an adult stranger hanging around her.) Eventually, the True Knot sends emissaries after Abra and Dan realizes that he must confront them. The final scenes take place, fittingly enough, at the site of the original Overlook Hotel in Colorado.

King has had his ups and downs over the years, but for the last decade he's been cranking out novels and stories that are equal to his early work. Some, like *Doctor Sleep*, are clear masterpieces. His characters emerge as true human beings, even Rose-the-Hat whose own powers have so corrupted her over the centuries that she's been alive and feeding on people's life-energies that she's no longer recognizably human. These are the true monsters and King's genius is that he can make all of his characters shine.

✿

The Adjacent
by Christopher Priest
Titan Books - 2014
ISBN: 9781781169438 (Hardbound)

Christopher Priest has already established himself as a writer of misdirection, having successfully written of such in his novel, *The Prestige*. The twists and turns in that novel make sense in the end. The magician might baffle us with his trickery, but he also has to entertain us. In the end, however, his conjuring has to make sense. This works in *The Prestige*. It does not work in Priest's new novel, *The Adjacent*. The tricks are there, but they're so obscure that we remain confused throughout. By the end of the show, we don't really know what the magician has done or what the show was even about.

The Adjacent begins in the near future when Tibor Tarent, a freelance photographer in Anatolia, is called back to Britain. His wife, Melanie, an aide worker in Africa, has been killed by a mysterious bright light that leaves triangular scorches in the earth. Tanks, trucks, cars, and a lot of people suddenly vanish this way. As it is, there are wars all over the place and climate change has made the world barren. Tarent travels around in an armored personnel carrier called a Mebsher in an England ruled by a newly risen Islamic republic exacting strict controls over society. Tarent throughout his narrative is a passive on-looker in a world he accepts and is helpless to act. Having set up Tarent's story, Priest suddenly shifts to telling the tale of a World War One stage magician named Tommy Trent who is enlisted to invent a means of making aircraft invisible. On the way to see the war first-hand, Trent runs into the historical H.G. Wells and has a conversation about the war and what to do about it. For reasons left unexplained, Priest drops this storyline (that of making planes invisible with or without the help of H.G. Wells) and the narrative shifts once again.

This time we're in World War II and Tibor Tarent, from the first plotline in the near-future, is a young man who falls in love with a female pilot–the only character in the novel, by the way, who takes any action. Krystyna Roszca is trying to find her old lover and get back to Poland. Tarent, meanwhile, infatuated with Ms. Roszca, travels to a strange land on the continent called the Dream Archipelago—a place of incredible beauty, including both forests and deserts. Since there are no deserts anywhere in Europe, one only assumes that *this* Tarent is a different soul in a different, alternate World War II reality and not the younger version of the Tommy Trent who we were introduced to earlier.

Throughout the novel there is considerable talk of quantum simultaneity and parallel realities, but it takes a while to grasp that he's dealing with parallel realities that somehow influence each other the way quantum particles at great distances can influence one another. It is in one of these realities that "someone" is using the scorching weapon on inhabitants across the entire reality spectrum that turns them into triangular scorch marks in the earth.

I think.

Though the writing is clean and engaging in *The Adjacent*, Priest chooses to jump around from one narrative to another without ever making clear what's happened in that narrative. He never tells us how the Islamic Republic comes about. And who are the people behind the Adjacency Weapon itself? Priests seem to have opted for obscurity and evasion (not misdirection) and in this he seems to be attempting to write the kind of literary novel where obscurity rather than clarity is taken as a virtue. Tell this to Lee Child, Stephen King, or Elmore Leonard whose novels read smoothly and effortlessly... and *clearly*. Not once did I understand any plotline or where the novel was going, or what the conflict might be. The Adjacency Weapon was the only trope of interest, and Priest tells us nothing about it.

There is another reason why *The Adjacent* fails as a novel.

I wrote about this in the last issue of *Galaxy's Edge*. We are now seeing a number of novels and short stories being told in both the third-person limited omniscient *and* in the first person. This is an appalling trend and must be discouraged. Telling a story this way just fractures the narrative and causes confusion. It bluntly lets the reader know that they are reading a published artifact. We never get *lost* in the story; we're never allowed to relax and enjoy the ride. These narratives cause us to ask the question: Who assembled these narratives together? Who found Tommy Trent's diary? Who found Krystyna Roszca's? Even then, *where* does the third-person narration in *The Adjacent* come from? In a smoothly written book (or short story), we never think of the author or even think how the book or story was put together. The success of the three authors I've mentioned above lies in the fact they tell stories where we don't even see the words on the page. A good story will do that. It's like Elmore Leonard once said: don't let the words get in the way of a good story.

Priest has some fine ideas in *The Adjacent* and Krystyna Roszca emerges as a truly heroic character without losing any of her feminine qualities. This is a great achievement for any author. But this isn't one of Priest's best books. If you want to read a great novel about the foibles of the same character living in three different realities, find Geo Alec Effinger's 1978 novel, *Relatives*. It's a beautiful story and Effinger's words never get in the way of the telling of it.

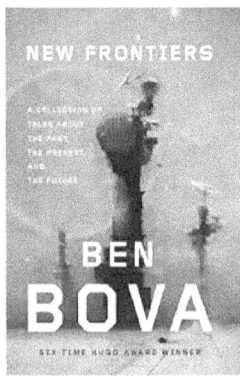

New Frontiers: A Collection of Tales About the Past, the Present, and the Future
by Ben Bova
Tor - 2014
ISBN: 978-0765376442 (Hardbound)

Ben Bova, now in his seventies, is still going strong. He seems to come out with a novel every three or four months, and he is always writing short fiction. *New Frontiers: A Collection of Tales about the Past, the Present, and the Future* is his most recent collection and while it is not as strong a gathering as some of his earlier collections, there are a few gems here that make the anthology worth getting.

Among the stories worth noting is "Sam Below Par," which brings us yet again another story about the affable and wily Sam Gunn who decides that what better to attract tourists to the moon than to build a golf resort? Yes, the story is about Sam's chicanery and financial daring-do, but it's also a romance and a sly commentary on contemporary mores and family values and how to get the rich to invest their money in the moon rather than let it sit in a bank in the Grand Caymans. Go Sam!

"In Trust" is a conundrum story (common to both *Astounding* and *Analog*) where a protagonist is faced with a problem: He's incredibly rich and wants to keep his money forever—and away from his heirs. He decides to freeze himself so that in the future he can have all of his accumulated wealth. Well, not so fast, Sherlock. He doesn't get off that easy and the problems just pile on. This story reminded me of Robert Sheckley's work in the 1950s and 1960s. It's clever and somewhat cynical—and is someday bound to happen.

"Duel in the Somme" finds Bova returning to one of his favorite topics, virtual reality, and a culture in the future where the bored and rich turn to dueling to solve their personal problems...with a twist ending you probably won't see coming.

Also of interest was "Bloodless Victory"; the unfortunately titled, "Mars Farts," a story that will remind the reader of Kim Stanley Robinson's Mars novels as well as the recent *The Martian* by Andy Weir; and "Inspiration" which brings an unlikely group of individuals together in Linz facing an unusual problem.

There are a couple of weak entries here, and the story "Scheherazade and the Storytellers" is all about a pun that, in the end, is a bit precious, an in-joke that might leave some readers out. Still, what's here is very much worth your money and your time. Bova has been one of my favorite writers for years and I read everything by him that comes out. *New Frontiers* has found a spot on my bookshelf.

Red Tide
by Larry Niven, Brad R. Torgersen, Matthew J. Harrington
Phoenix Pick - 2014
ISBN: 978-6543410 (Trade paperback)

Red Tide is another in Phoenix Pick's Stellar Guild Series, edited by Mike Resnick. The Stellar Guild teams up established writers, who write an opening novella or novelette, with an up-and-coming writer who pens a follow-up story. Every book I've read in this series has been successful. Much leeway is given to the follow-up story and this flexibility has allowed for some surprises as well as some extrapolations that the original story either did not foresee or was able to explore.

Red Tide is about a single, familiar science fiction trope, that of matter transmission or teleportation and the consequences of its misuse. Larry Niven wrote the original story, called "Flash Crowd" in 1973. "Red Tide" is a touched-up (actually shortened) version of "Flash Crowd." In "Red Tide," a news reporter gets caught in a riot that happened out of nowhere with far too many people showing up to participate in the riot. Moreover, once the riot is over, they mysteriously disappear. The problem is, the protagonist, a news reporter, gets blamed for it even though there is no way he could have caused it and there was no physical way it really should have happened.

Niven provides a follow-up story to "Red Tide" called "Dial at Random" which looks at the same technology in terms of its actual physics, including how matter transmission might affect the culture at large. The follow-up stories are by newcomers. Brad R. Torgersen provides "Sparky the Dog" and Matthew J. Harrington's story is called "Displacement Activity." Both explore the further uses and misuses of matter transmission, including its use in outer space.

None of these stories is the last word in all that can go wrong with teleportation. They're just the latest iterations of the topic. They are fun to read and thought-provoking at the same time.

Views expressed by guest or resident columnists are entirely their own.

Gregory Benford is a Nebula winner and a former Worldcon Guest of Honor. He is the author of more than 30 novels and 6 books of non-fiction, and has edited 10 anthologies.

Remembering Sid
by greg benford

This essay was written before Sid Coleman's untimely death in 2007.

In January 2007 Sid Coleman's wife, Diana, sent a letter to their friends about his decline. It was troubling; Sid was one of those I most admired in fandom—indeed, in life. But now his particular sort of Parkinson's had advanced until he could not live at home any more.

Diana had placed him in a living facility, where she visited him daily. He went long times now without speaking, she said, but at times a glint of the old Sydney would flicker. His roommate, a cook, remarked that Sid seemed to be a nice man. "Appearances are deceiving," Sid said, with a sly smile.

The Fan

Her letter set me to remembering. Sid was so much—physicist, raconteur, world traveler—and he gave much to science fiction. His teenage toils for Advent Publishers supported a scrupulous, ambitious role for fans in holding the field to its standards. In 1960 he said in Earl Kemp's *Who Killed SF?*, "I am not in science fiction for money; I am in it for joy. Formally, I am a publisher (actually, 14% of a publisher). This is useful: it gets me on the mailing list of *PITFCS*; it is a handy topic of conversation at parties; it is a means whereby I meet some interesting people; it is a better hobby than stamp-collecting any day. From an economic standpoint, it plays a lesser role in my life than returning Coke bottles for refunds."

Earl Kemp, Ed Wood, Sid, and some others created a fannish publishing house, Advent Publishers, in 1956. He was a teenager when he helped publish Advent's first book, Damon Knight's *In Search of Wonder*. Week after week the fans gathered at Earl Kemp's apartment in Chicago, catching typos in the photo offset text. Ed Wood, a very large fan with a very large voice, and Sid, maintained an unrelenting dialog about the purpose of science fiction fandom—Ed loudly proclaiming that fandom should "spread the science fiction faith," while Sid insisted on a smaller purpose, like fun.

Earl Kemp recalled that Sid was at his very best when criticizing someone for what he thought was a shortcoming. Sid's inimitable trick was to do it with charm and wit that left the target injured but somehow happy about the whole thing and anxious to tell others about it.

Fandom was for him a larger family, an audience for a swift, subtle sense of humor. At a Halloween party in Chicago, he appeared costumed as "Judas Iscariot as Sidney Coleman with thirty pieces of silver," carrying three dollars in dimes. In a letter of comment he remarked, "The interstate highway now passes through Indiana and Illinois, traversing some of the flattest territory in the nation. It has been said of this geography, 'You could see a hundred miles in every direction, if only there was something worth looking at.'"

From a fanzine piece: "Did I ever tell you about my great-grandfather, Stephen Rich, the stingiest man in Slonim? When the local stonecutter went out of business, he had him make up a tombstone for him, cheap, with everything on it but the date of great-grandfather's death. He kept it in his front yard and tethered his goat to it. At least that's what my mother has always told me, but she's quite capable of having stolen the whole incident from an Erskine Caldwell novel."

Jim Caughran recalled, "He could make a story of what he'd done today into a hilarious adventure. He could seize the moment, improvising." A faculty couple at Caltech owned a gentle German shepherd. While he was a grad student Sid would occasionally do dog-sitting duties. The doorbell to the apartment rang. Sidney opened the door with the dog close behind. "Ha! A stranger!" Sidney said, "Kill, Fang!"

And he had an incredible repertory of Jewish jokes. Terry Carr once asked him, "How many jokes can you tell that start, 'One day in the garment district...'?" He was speechless, then said he couldn't put a number to them."

Martha Beck was at a science fiction function and got into a conversation with a man who was a physicist. She casually mentioned Sid, and the man said in awed tones, "You know *Sidney Coleman!*?"

After all, Sid attended high school and university simultaneously, getting his bachelor's degree when he graduated from high school, a feat I've never known to be equaled. Sid went to Caltech for his doctorate with Murray Gell-Mann in 1962, age 25. He attended LASFS meetings and swiftly became a major theoretical physicist. Many fans never quite knew his prominence.

"I'm at the top of the second rank," Carol Carr remembers him saying.

Sid the Physicist

I first met him in the 1960s, introduced by Terry Carr, who explained with a wry smile, "You're both in physics and write for *Innuendo* [Terry's fanzine], so you should probably know each other." Sid was already both a better physicist and wit, of course. He was far more subtle and powerful in his mathematics than I.

In the late 1980s he caught the attention of the entire physics world with a calculation, using a "wormhole calculus" he invented for the purpose. It carried the characteristically witty title, "Why there is nothing rather than something: a theory of the cosmological constant." [*Nucl. Phys. B* 310: 643 (1988)] In it he concluded that through complex dynamics in the first moments of the universe, it was later able to sustain life forms that could perhaps "know joy."

He showed how the cosmological constant could be forced to be zero in the early universe. This fit the prevailing prejudice among theorists that the constant, first introduced by Einstein to make the universe static, neither expanding nor contracting. When Hubble found in the late 1920s that the universe is expanding, Einstein said imposing the constant was a blunder, not because it was a bad idea, but because Einstein didn't see that the resulting equilibrium was unstable. Any minor jiggle would destroy the static state, starting motion. Even with the constant, he should have foreseen that Hubble would either see a universe growing or shrinking.

Sidney had no prejudice either way on the value of the constant, but he did see a pretty way to use quantum mechanical ideas to propose a sweet model—the sort of confection theorists hold dear. I was startled by the intricate audacity of his calculation, as were many others. At the time I had been working on some wormhole calculations myself, much more prosaically trying to find a way to see if we had any wormholes nearby and if they could be found out through their refracting ability. Some wormholes might develop one end that looked as though it had negative mass, since its other end had funneled a lot of mass out through its mouth. These would yield a unique refracting signature, two peaks, if a star passed behind it, along our line of sight. Find the two peaks (rather than one for ordinary wormhole mouths, or any ordinary mass) and—presto, a gateway to the stars, maybe. It was a clear longshot.

Sid had no illusions about his model—it was a longshot, too, that just might be right. Worth a chance. I felt the same.

Everybody liked the "wormhole calculus" because they liked the result, a zero constant. That seemed clean, neat, a theorist's delight. Sid basked in the attention, though he didn't think this was his best work. My work, done with several others, got a lot of citation and wasn't my best, either; wormholes just get good press. Sid quoted Einstein wryly that "If my theory of relativity is proven successful, Germany will claim me as a German and the Swiss will declare that I am their citizen. If it fails, Switzerland will say I'm a German and the Germans will say I am a Jew."

It turned out that the cosmological constant isn't zero at all. In fact, it represents the highest energy density in the universe, far more important in dynamics than mere matter like us. In fact, it's close to the value that will eventually give us the Big Rip that will tear everything apart at the End of Time, even atoms. When I mentioned in 1996 the recent discovery that the constant was large, not zero, Sid shrugged. "Win some, lose some in the old cosmology game."

We haven't found any refracting wormholes, either. That's just how science goes.

The Sidneyfest

When Sid's decline became evident, the Harvard physics department put on a Sidneyfest that ran over a weekend. Some reports on this event, with pictures, are at: http://www.physics.harvard.edu/QFT/sidneyfest.htm.

Then-president of Harvard Larry Summers opened the Fest before a large crowd with, "There has not been so much talent gathered around the snack table since Einstein snacked alone." Nobelist Steven Weinberg gave the next talk, discussing how to calculate Feynman diagrams for quantized general relativity. He talked about work in progress, and at the end said, "I don't know what to do now. Does anybody else?" This was the place to ask! He added, "In happier times, I would have gone straight to Sidney Coleman."

Though Weinberg is now at the University of Texas, he shared the 1979 Nobel Prize in Physics with Shelly Glashow and Abdus Salam for work done down the hall from Sid. "Sidney is a theorist's theorist," Weinberg said. "He has not been so much concerned with accounting for the latest data from experiments as with understanding deeply what our theories really mean. I can say I learned more about physics from Sidney than from anyone else. I also learned more good jokes from him than from anyone else."

The noted particle theorist Howard Georgi said, "In his prime, which lasted for a very long time, from the mid '60s to the late '80s, Sidney was such a towering figure in theoretical physics that even his close colleagues (Nobel prize winners, etc.) were somewhat in awe of him. In fact, we had to be careful about talking to Sidney too soon about new ideas, because he was so smart and had such encyclopedic knowledge that he could kill nascent ideas before they really got started."

Sidney was a beloved teacher of graduate students, and many of them attended the Sidneyfest. Sid referred to the community as *i fratelli fisici*, by which he meant the brotherhood of physicists. (Most physicists speak at least a bit of broken Italian, a legacy of the grand and highly influential summer schools organized by Nino Zichichi in Erice, Sicily.) In a physics career one often arrives by train or plane, anywhere in the world, on the way to a conference or academic visit. One of the fondest reflections of being a scientist is to then be greeted by a total stranger, who immediately treated one like an old friend. Erice was like that; the brotherhood of science. With good food.

The town likes the NATO-backed workshops because they bring an elevated form of tourism to the ancient town on a granite spire, perched a kilometer above a beautiful beach. One year a noted German physicist drove down in his brand new Mercedes and parked it outside the workshop buildings, which were once a convent. He emerged an hour later to find the Mercedes stolen along with his luggage and all his lecture notes. The German panicked, and Director Zichichi led him back inside to give him a glass or two of good Sicilian wine. Emerging an hour later, there sat the Mercedes. Zichichi had ties everywhere. The local Mafia had found the thieves. Then they kindly returned the car, washed, waxed and fully fueled—an impressively offhand way to show real power. Sid always loved telling this tale.

I had given a lecture series there in astrophysics, suspecting that the true appeal of Erice was the meal chits they gave out for attendees. Good in many of the best restaurants, these allowed for wine with the meal, no questions asked. This single gesture made the afternoon sessions either lively or dead, depending on the quality and quantity of the wine. But Sidney avoided the wine, focusing on clarifying his own lectures right up to the last minute. His careful, insightful summaries of the state of knowledge in field theory became famous and appeared as a book devoted solely to them.

One of the Sidneyfest attendees who got his doctorate at Harvard remarked, "How do you do physics at Harvard? You go to Witten to give you a problem to work on. You go to Coleman to tell you how to solve it. Then you go to Weinberg to write you a reference letter." Ed Witten is the Einstein figure of string theory and much else. Weinberg won the Nobel for what we now call the Standard Model.

Though I've never met Weinberg, I learned a lot of physics just working through a Weinberg calculation he did as a toss-off for a classified project I worked on in the late 1960s, given the problem by Edward Teller, who had hired me in 1967. Weinberg's footprint in the calculations was impressive. He came a decade ahead of me in the profession and I rather regretted showing that the method he studied would not work in reality. But physics isn't just about getting everything to work; it's about the truth. Weinberg was no sharper than Sid, but he happened upon an insight that proved out true quite swiftly. There is a lot of luck in science; many of the brilliant just don't hit quite the right problem. Sid won prizes, several Sidneyfest attendees remarked, but not the big ones.

There were many Sid stories. One was about being at a physics meeting where Stephen Hawking spoke up from his wheelchair. This was around 1976, when Stephen could barely control his throat, and struggled to make his points in his semi-unintelligible way. His comment contained a detailed, abstruse mathematical argument and went on for minutes. Sid said that he was tempted to reply, "That's easy for you to say," but held his tongue.

Another Sid story: A mathematician and an engineer are sitting in on a string theory lecture. The engineer is struggling, while the mathematician is swimming along with no problem. Finally the engineer asks, "How do you do it? How do you visualize these 11-dimensional spaces?" The mathematician says, "It's easy: first I visualize an n-dimensional space, then I set n equal to 11."

At the fest Sidney could not deal with the crowd, so he watched the proceedings on TV in a small room off to the side. At the end he appeared before the crowd but declined to comment, saying later, "At my age you tend to emit a lot of gas, and I'd rather not."

Wit

Rather than his physics, I remember best Sid's brilliant wit. He once remarked about dopey plot twists, "The one good thing about stupidity is that it leads to adventure." I've often thought that applies to life as a whole, too.

Bob Silverberg recalled in a fanzine, "While traveling in France in the early 1970s, Sidney unexpectedly contracted a case of what turned out to be crabs. 'Unexpectedly' because this is customarily a venereal disease, and he had been a model of chastity throughout his trip. The offending organisms must have been concealed in the bedding of his hotel room, he decided, and so he had suffered a case of punishment without the crime. But during the trip he had not, however, remained true to the dietary restrictions imposed by the religious doctrines of his forefathers; and, he said, after visiting a French doctor and having his ailment diagnosed for what it was, he was granted a vision of his Orthodox grandfather rising up in wrath before him and thundering, 'Thou hast eaten crustaceans, child, and now thou shalt be devoured by crustaceans thyself!'"

Carol Carr remembers that Sid's French was limited, and that a literal translation of what he told the doctor was, "Small animals are eating my penis."

In the fevered height of the 1970s, when even theoretical physicists had gotten the hip message of the 1960s, Sid had a tailored purple suit. He wore it with stylish aplomb, smiling his owlish smiles below twinkling eyes, pretending to not notice the flagrant color. Once, walking across Harvard Yard, we encountered a student who had a question about a career in physics. I wondered how Sid would reply, since I usually gave a long, windy answer. Sid simply swept a hand grandly down his tailored flanks and said, "Study hard, have original ideas, and someday you, too, may wear a purple suit."

Carol Carr also recalls: "Sid made the expression 'enjoying oneself' a concrete, observable act, and he would sometimes be caught shamelessly indulging in it. Once, at a party, he had just said something funny to a bunch of people. After the punchline he walked out of the room, leaving them all in mid-grin. Several minutes later I happened to notice him, alone in a corner, still chortling to himself. What he'd said to those people had a long half-life, and Sid was a bonafide, dyed-in-the-wool appreciator. If a good joke happened to be his own, he wasn't about to apply the doctrine of false modesty and let it die before its time."

When his physics department suddenly needed someone to fill in for an ill colleague, they asked Sid if he could teach a field theory class that the energetic colleague had scheduled for 8 a.m. Sid was a notorious night owl who often had to rouse his dinner guests to go home at a mere 3 a.m. He relished the pleasures of watching the sun come up while putting on pajamas and others stirred. Still, he considered. He felt that he did have an obligation to his department. "I'm sorry," he finally said, "I just don't think I could stay up that late."

He wrote a great sendup of the space program:

"Once I gained access to *Pioneer 10*, it was the work of a moment to substitute for NASA's plaque my own, which read, "Make ten exact copies of this plaque with your name at the bottom of the list and send them to ten intelligent races of your acquaintance. At the end of four billion years, your name will reach the top of the list and you will rule the galaxy."

If only A. E. van Vogt had thought of this economical idea!

Of course, Sid had his oddities. He was the worst driver I ever knew, distracted by conversation with his passengers, oblivious to the screech and shouts of near-accidents. Marta Randall remarked on how when she was the lead car on the several-car trip to a restaurant, she always saw Sid in her rear view mirror in profile, attentive to his friends.

But then, Feynman considered dental hygiene to be a superstition, despite his rotten teeth. Einstein hated socks. We have our foibles.

Sid did indeed look a lot like Einstein, but he loved SF whereas Einstein deplored it. Lest SF distort pure science and give people the false illusion of scientific understanding, Einstein recommended complete abstinence from any type of science fiction. "I never think of the future. It comes soon enough," he said.

Now, though, Sid can't concentrate enough to read SF. For decades he took SF seriously but not solemnly, and his insights led to his role as a book reviewer for *F&SF*—the only non-literary person ever to serve. His *F&SF* book reviews skewered the second rate and revealed the excellences of the able. In a review of a novel that did not make the grade in a nonetheless ambitious area, he simply remarked, "This book fills a much needed vacancy in our field."

Sid is just the opposite. As he fades from us, his departure from our midst leaves a vacancy that echoes, unfillable.'

Copyright © 2012 by Gregory Benford
(First published in Trapdoor 25)

FROM THE HEART'S BASEMENT

by Barry N. Malzberg

Barry N. Malzberg won the very first Campbell Memorial Award, and is a multiple Hugo and Nebula nominee. He is the author or co-author of more than 90 books.

DEMOLITION

David Thomson in *Rosebud*, his book-length meditation on Orson Welles, writes of the most terrifying moment, the central epiphany of Welles' work which is not to be found in *Citizen Kane* but years earlier in the radio play he directed, *The Fall of the City*, by Archibald Macleish.

"In the play, the fascist conqueror comes to the city. The people's fear and anticipation have been so great that they amount to a dread that *needs* such a tyrant." The announcer looks into the tyrant's open visor for the radio audience and reports: "There is no one/no one at all/no one/the helmet is hollow/the armor is empty/I tell you there is no/one at all there."

And here, as early as 1937, Orson Welles had found his lasting theme. Here is the emptiness that sustains mystery in so many of his films. And here is even the horror in which a tremendous egotist apprehended his own absence...if only he could believe in his own tricks. My God, this is nearly religious, not to mention politics at the end of the twentieth century. This is how Ronald Reagan became President, and this is why Jorge Luis Borges would say of *Citizen Kane*, "nothing is so frightening as a labyrinth with no center. This film is precisely that labyrinth."

And that is the fiction, the dazzling fiction, the supernal and shocking and brilliant fiction of science fiction's greatest writer, Alfred Bester (1913-1987), another genius whose greatest contribution to the field is the same contribution that Thomson ascribes to Orson Welles. By taking us to the limits of its expression and possibility, Bester demonstrated the utter limitation of science fiction. He escorted us through that labyrinth with no center. He showed us that there was nothing.

What Welles gave us, Thomson argues, was a facility so great, a voyage so dazzling, as to show us that film was inevitably a superficial medium, that it had no core. And this was what Bester, science fiction's Orson Welles, demonstrated in the two great novels and dozen great short stories of the 1950s. He took the field to its furthest possibility and circumstance; he took us to the hall of the beasts and furies and demonstrated in the end that it was empty. There was no one there. *We* were there. Bester was almost good enough to convince us that this was sufficient insight, that like Van Vogt's Sevagram, this was all real and we were the race that would rule it. But ultimately, in "Fondly Fahrenheit," in "The Men That Murdered Muhammed," in "The Starcomber," by taking us to the furthest demonstrable places science fiction could ever be, he showed us that the places were ultimately versions of malaprop.

There is no easy way to articulate the despair which this recent insight has brought me, but it must be stated, must be confronted: science fiction was dazzle, it was enchantment. But the self-referentiality was absolute, and at the end it killed the beast.

That is what one of Bester's characters tells us, contemptuously. "What do you want?" he spat. "Dazzle! Enchantment!" That was Welles in *Citizen Kane*, the only project he was able to finish on his own terms, and it is Bester in the two novels from the 1950s and in his persona as well. They unpacked the bag of tricks which they brought to the performance, unpacked with a flourish, tossed them with love and contempt and furious necessity to the rows before them. And followed by hurling the empty bag. "Now you have it all!" they insisted. But they knew better. It is in their own despair that both men found their greatest clarity.

Welles and Bester combined dazzlement, deceit, enormous plans (that mad compendium of all the projects on which they were working and which they would complete) and a self-awareness so shattering that ultimately it trapped their work, froze them into showmen's personas, and left them with nothing. They became self-parodies: Welles lurching with his retinue from continent to continent scattering half-finished screenplays and work for hire,

Bester after his reappearance in 1970 traipsing from convention to convention playing at panels, playing at being Alfie, the golden emissary from the golden world, Hollywood or *Holiday's* gift to the grubbier fields of the art film or "serious science fiction."

At the end, their public personas were all bombast, all posturing and lies, but it was those personas that kept them sailing through right to the end. Everything Bester published after age fifty (his last great story was "They Don't Make Life Like They Used To" in 1963) was self-pastiche or feeble attempts to recover what had been so easy in the 1950s; every film project of Welles after the ravaged *Amberson* took him ever deeper into the splinter of old aspiration and contrivance. Bester could still give you a great panel or a novel opening like the first fifty pages of *The Computer Connection*, Welles could deliver a twelve-minute monologue in *Compulsion*, which would wipe not only the rest of the cast but Leopold, Loeb, and Levin off the screen—but these were performances, dazzlement, enchantment, curried from ancient echoes, and at best they could take us only to wonder that so much had been expected. Bester's gimmick book, his commonplace of observations and plot possibilities, has some cheapo tricks, and then halfway through, coming off the page in capital letters: *THIS HAS BEEN THE WORST YEAR OF YOUR LIFE. THE NEXT YEARS WILL BE EVEN WORSE.*

That self-awareness was as shattering as it was blockading. It was as great as his ignorance, his ignorance as stunning as the killer robot in "Fondly Fahrenheit," and at the end there were years of silence and aching peripety from the New York apartment where he had lived with his wife—and then left her, and then returned, but she had died. There were those convention panels and the reiterated performance and the way he looked (Asimov had the same look) when he was alone and feeling unobserved like Bunthorne. The sadness, the abandonment. Sturgeon too. It was confusing. It was more than confusing, it was distressing to be a young or younger writer at these conventions or Nebula banquets, observing these people who had created the intimacy of darkness and all possibility, to see in their eyes, in the curious uncertainty with which they would face and then turn away from one another, that they had no answers, that in fact they had lost the questions. This must have been Welles' odyssey too, the dungeon of awareness, being able to both witness and deny the self-parody which they had become. Sturgeon knew he was counterfeit. He told me so on the telephone at midnight. Bester knew it too.

"It hurts. It hurts, Alfie, doesn't it?"

"Yes, Barry, it hurts."

The true Calvary is self-knowledge. Up the grade we go to mount it. And hang without illustriousness.

This is a superficial category, this science fiction, which can, like film, turn even the most thoughtful and ambitious of young artists into superficiality. Dazzlement. Enchantment. Gimmickry. Bester that genius, like Welles that genius, was yet another of our holy monsters, born to live and die for us, born to carry us past themselves, to the pit and the pendulum and the everlasting darkness. Bester wanted to call it *Demolition*, but Horace Gold got him to call it *The Demolished Man*. The author had it right the first time. Didn't you, Alfie?

January 2015: New Jersey

Copyright © 2015 by Barry N. Malzberg

Joy Ward is the author of one novel. She has several stories in press, at magazines and in anthologies, and has also done interviews, both written and video, for other publications.

THE *GALAXY'S EDGE* INTERVIEW

Joy Ward interviews multiple bestseller, physicist, and political speechwriter Dr. Jerry Pournelle

Jerry Pournelle is not only the co-author of several of the all-time classics of science fiction, The Mote in God's Eye *and* Lucifer's Hammer, *he is one of the architects of the most controversial space programs in the history of the United States, the strategic Defense Initiative (SDI), otherwise known as Star Wars. He was one of the first presidents of the Science Fiction and Fantasy Writers of America (SFWA) and active in helping to build the California Higher Education Board. Called a "Communist" as a teenager in Memphis, Tennessee, this acid-witted writer was considered for a high position in the Nixon administration. Pournelle is nothing if not a surprising sage of our times. He did us the great honor of meeting with us at his California home prior to his recent stroke.*

Jerry Pournelle: If I don't write I don't eat.

I learned that from Mr. Heinlein. When I first started in this business Robert used to say, "Don't owe anybody any money. You never know what your income is, so don't owe anybody any money." I'm always being asked for advice for new writers and I can give it to them real simple. "Don't stop writing. Don't worry about what you've written, worry about what you're going to write. Keep writing rather than arguing with people. Keep on doing. The other is: don't owe anybody any money.

Joy Ward: How did you start writing?

JP: I was in aerospace. I was a so-called systems analyst. I started at Boeing as an aviation psychologist. I was designing controls and control panels. I could write. When I met Mr. Heinlein I told him I'd probably written more science fiction than he did. I was writing progress reports on research, and I didn't have to put any characters in mine.

I was part of the space program. The space program kind of dwindled out. I was the Science Project Manager for Apollo 18. Now you say there was no Apollo 18, and I say, "Yes, that is why I became a professor at Pepperdine."

While I was in college I had written a couple of mysteries under a pen name. As it so happened, when I wrote the mysteries I had been corresponding with Robert Heinlein for some years about the space program and what was going on. When I wrote the mysteries, I said, "Robert, I've given you a lot of stuff about the space business, can I ask a favor of you?" He said: "I'm afraid I know what it's going to be but what is it?"

I said, "Yes. I have written a book. Would you read it and tell me if it's worth doing?"

He said, "Well, okay." So he read it and he gave me a bunch of suggestions. I did it, and he said, "All right. I like that." I said, "What will I do?" He said: "You don't have to do anything else. I'll send it to my agent to see if he'll sell it for you."

That's wonderful! I don't have to worry about that. Two years later it sold. So I was a published writer and I had a major agent if I wanted one. I'm looking for something to do and I wasn't doing too well. I sold some stuff to *Analog Science Fiction*.

I called up my friends in the aerospace business and I got offered a GS-13 to be an assistant manager in the Army's aviation design program. But that meant moving to St. Louis. I was about ready to sell the house and do that. I had the formal offer and all I had to do was sign the papers. I was ready to do it and the earthquake happened. This was in the early 1970s and it was the Northridge earthquake. It didn't do much to this place, but you can see there are a lot of books around. Out of all those books, one book fell on the floor. The Los Angeles library was so full of books they were asking people to just come in and put them on the shelves; don't try to sort them just get them off the floor so we can rearrange them. I looked at (the book on the floor) and it was called *No Wonder We Are Losing* by Robert Morris, who had been a judge and the Counsel for the Senate Internal Affairs Committee. It was basically an anti-Communist tract by an anti-Communist lawyer. That's interesting. I knew who he was, but I'd never met him. So I put the book back on my shelf and then thought maybe there's a message there. That's the only book that fell off. Maybe I should pay attention to that one.

That was on a Tuesday. The phone rang at eight in the morning. I got up and went to the office and picked up the phone and said, "Hello." This voice says, "John Pournelle?" I said what the heck, at this hour of the day, it's good enough so I said, "Yeah." He said, "This is Robert Morris. I am the publisher of *One Circle, the National Catholic Press Weekly.*" It was one of those tabloid weeklies sold in the back of Catholic churches. "I want you to write me a piece about the earthquake in Los Angeles."

I said, "Yes sir."

He said, "I need it by Thursday morning. I'll pay you $800 for seven hundred words. No more, no less."

Yeah, all right. That's better than I'm making now. This is in the early 1970s. I believe the house payment on this house was $400 a month. So that's good money. I wrote it and the editorial offices of the paper were down in Century City. I took it down there. The editor read it on the spot and he said, "I like this. We've been looking for a science correspondent. Would you like to be the science correspondent?"

I said, "What does it pay?"

"It's weekly, to be seven hundred words, and I'll pay you $600 a week to do this."

In 1972, that's money. So I became the science correspondent for the national Catholic press, and I told the Civil Service Commission thanks for the offer, but I guess I'll stay in California. I had to write

seven hundred words a week, but the rest of the time I could do what I wanted, which meant that I could get into a big science fiction project with Larry Niven called *The Mote in God's Eye,* which I did. So I started writing, *The Mote in God's Eye* started selling and became a bestseller. That's how I started writing. I found out I could do it and make money at it.

JW: Here you are in LA. Have you been tempted to write for television?

JP: I have never wanted to. Niven and I have done a number of bestsellers, and we have sold the movie rights to a bunch of our stuff. No one ever made one, but they paid us a lot of option money. The options are better than if they make the movie, because if you sell the option ten times you've made more money.

Our agent took us around to a bunch of studio places with the idea that we might create a show. This was back before the SyFy channel got big. It was just starting up. We might come up and be co-producers or chief writers or something. The first interview was with Joss Whedon's people. We got along fine with them. I thought working with guys like this would be interesting. There was plenty of mutual respect. We just didn't have anything.

The next interview was with CBS or ABC. It was like five guys, twenty-eight years old, all of them looked alike, dressed alike, and had that kind of cynical what-have-you-talents-got-for-us type of attitude. It became obvious that none of them had ever read a book. They had read treatments of books, they had read scripts, other things, but never read a book. They didn't care about stories or storytelling. We left there thinking: I'm glad we didn't make any deals with them.

We had two more interviews. I think it was at Disney. It was like it was the same five people every time. In the middle of the interview I stood up and I looked at Larry. I said, "Niven, do you understand that if we do everything just right we get to spend a lot of time with these people?"

Larry said, "You're right. Let's go." And we walked out. We left our agent there to explain it to them. We didn't care anymore.

Every now and then I'm tempted to do something with the Hollywood people, but when I do I have a sure cure for it. I call up Harlan Ellison and let him tell me about his experiences, and I think, Harlan, you've got more patience than I've got. I just don't want to deal with those people.

JW: Talk to me about your collaborations with Larry Niven.

JP: Larry has done a lot of collaborations, and in fact I wasn't the first one. He did something with David Gerrold before me, but *The Mote in God's Eye* and *Lucifer's Hammer* are very commercially successful.

I decided if I'm going to be a science fiction writer what I've got to do is get famous quick. I looked around to see who I knew or could know who wrote the kinds of stuff I liked, that I could do something with. No point in trying to collaborate with somebody who's doing the same thing you are. I realized Larry writes better than me, but I think I'm better in the sense of plots and interweaving plots and subplots and a lot of that formal stuff. So I went to him and I said let's do it together.

He said, "We can talk about it." So we sat around and talked about it all night in his house with coffee and brandy, a lot of both. By dawn we had an outline for *The Mote in God's Eye*. When we started, I said: "What would you like to write about?" He said: "I've had this alien that I designed. I've had a vision of this asymmetric alien with two arms on one side and one on the other. But I don't know what to do with it."

I said, "First thing is. how the hell did it get that way? That's clearly, probably, an intelligent design, but we don't need God for it. It's obviously an intelligent design of an intelligent species that altered itself to be like that. We went on to do the whole history of this outfit. We've got notes that thick. By dawn we had a huge pad of paper. We finished with it and looked at it, and I told Larry: "You stick with me buddy and I'll make you rich and famous."

Larry said: "I'm already rich."

I said: "Yeah, you are. We'll both get famous, and I'll get rich."

He said: "Oh, all right. But you are going to do most of the work."

I said: "Of course I am. You're the senior author."

Well, that was the first one, and it worked that way. We have always had who would be the senior author on a book. It's been me about as often as him, depending on the book. On the first one obviously it was going to be him. It was his reputation that was at stake.

JW: How have you used "being raised by wolves" as you say, in your books?

JP: My characters tend to be fairly competent and self-competent. Larry's don't, and the interaction between them works that way.

JW: Any advice for people who are looking to collaborate?

JP: Yeah. Don't do it unless you have a good reason. Each of the collaborators does about ninety percent of the work. It doesn't look that way, but it is. Don't work with people you don't have respect for. Larry and I never have any big arguments. If he doesn't like something I did, there must be something wrong with it, something that needs changing. It's the same the other way around. If he does something I just don't feel right with, we don't argue about that, because it's obvious something needs to be done so we do it. That's all.

You need rules as to who's going to do the final cut, and of course, that was me in our first book. That was part of the deal. I will do the integration so that it looks like only one guy wrote it. All our works are that way. I don't think you can tell who wrote what. You can tell some scenes must have been Niven's simply because he's crazy. I'll give you an example. *Lucifer's Hammer*. A comet is going to hit the Earth. We had a lot of technical details in it, some are mine, some are his. He's good at explaining things. A year or two ago, *Nature Magazine*, which is that big British heavy-duty publication like *Science in*

America, did a four-page reminiscence on whatever anniversary of the publication of *Lucifer's Hammer*. Four page in *Nature*. That's pretty good. I felt pretty good about that. But of course what did they open it with? They opened it with that scene of that crazy surfer trying to surf the mad, huge wave, the tsunami. Of course they did. Anybody who has read the book…they remember that scene. That's an image. There isn't any possibility I could have written that or even thought of that. As Larry says, "He's not mad enough to have thought of things like that." But in general, you can't tell who wrote what in our stuff. We try to make it smooth.

My advice to people who are collaborating is: don't do it unless you have a good reason. Don't do it unless you've got enough mutual respect you are not going to fight about it. Now, that's not the case with all collaborations I know of. I know of collaborators who hate each other, but I couldn't live that way. I don't want to be that close to somebody I don't like.

JW: You've been in science fiction during a large part of the heyday. How are you seeing science fiction change?

JP: In the first place, fantasy is much bigger than science fiction. It wasn't when I started in this business.

My world changed. People ask me, how do you become a successful writer? It's simple. Write a bestseller. After that, everything you do is successful. The publishers love you. But you may say, how do you do that? I've told you how to do it. I leave the details up to you. You will recognize that as a parody on a Will Rogers story. They asked him what to do about the submarines and he supposedly said: "Boil the Atlantic Ocean. They'll have to come up and you can sink them." The Navy guy knows his leg is being pulled by this time, so he says, "How do you do that?" He said, "Don't bother me about details."

Before I had bestsellers, *Analog* and selling to *Analog* was a very important part of science fiction. No longer. Some people do. Some don't. But it's not the major source of income.

In those days you didn't have many books. My first science fiction novel was serialized in *Analog* before it ever was a book. The book is still in print, and it is up on *Analog* as an e-book.

JW: Are you seeing any trends in science fiction?

JP: The trend is there aren't any. There are a lot of schools in science fiction. There's a lot less demand for consistency. The kind of stuff I did was what you used to call "hard science fiction," which was to say if you make an assumption, then that assumption is going to change other things. You have to deal with that. You just can't assume that we're going to have anti-gravity. That changes everything we think we know about physics. The old school that I come from, it means you have to think of other implications for having done that.

They don't do that anymore. Now it's just, oh boy, we've got anti-gravity. We're going from there. I can't write that kind of story. Larry's better than I am at writing things he doesn't really believe in. When we work together I keep pulling it back to reality. That's one of the reasons why our collaborations sell a hell of a lot better than either one of us does individually. Part of that is because I do keep it to reality while it's still got all that sparkle that Niven's prose puts in. When he's doing it by himself, he will take an idea and run with it until it's so far out of sight you don't know where he's gone. It's all right. He doesn't care. Sometimes he does that very well, but it's a different kind of story than what we would have written together.

JW: There's a lot of discussion now about being a member of SFWA. Is it still valuable to be a member?

JP: You're not going to get me to say much on SFWA. I was the former president. I rewrote the Constitution on coming into office. I was tricked into being president. Harlan Ellison said he was running for president and he wanted someone to oppose him. Would I run against him so it would look like a fair election. I'm a new kid. I've only just joined. Okay, Harlan, I'll do that. Then he said, "Fine. I quit. This guy, vote for him. He knows how to manage things." I'm not kidding. Ask Harlan.

JW: *As you look in the future, what do you want your legacy to science fiction to be?*

JP: I never thought of it. I have no idea. I don't win awards, I never have. On the other hand, I know for a fact that I outsell most of the award winners by a lot. I know we have done very well, but I don't win awards. I'm not allowed to say what I actually think of awards.

JW: *How do you want to be remembered?*

JP: From my point of view I would rather be thought of as the guy who came up with the strategy that ended the Cold War. At the time we were just trying to get through it. Most people nowadays don't remember what the Cold War was. They don't remember that in 1980 there were twenty-six thousand nuclear warheads aimed at the United States. There were kids sitting in silos on Christmas night, sitting in these L-shaped things with these keys around their necks listening for that claxon. Something could have happened at anytime. That was a pretty scary time. I grew up in World War II. I was never as afraid as I was during the Cuban Missile Crisis. Well, if I'm going to be remembered I think I want to be remembered as one of the designers of the Strategic Defense Initiative.

I don't exaggerate my own importance in things, but I've been pretty influential. I've been president of the Science Fiction and Fantasy Writers of America. I've been an influential writer. I've been invited to be a speaker at a lot of places. Mostly I tell stories for a living. I think science fiction is important, but I don't think it's the only thing in the world.

I wrote a piece for the *Encyclopedia Britannica* on science fiction. I'm sure they've got something else in there now, but my essay was that "We're the Bards of the Sciences." We're basically like the old Homeric singers. We go around with our lyre on our back and our cup. We see a campfire over there and here's a bunch of Bronze Age warriors sitting around roasting an ox. We say, hey fellas, cut me a chunk of that ox and here's my cup. Fill me up and I'll tell you a story about a virgin and a bull that you just wouldn't believe. I'll tell you about when men

can fly and bronze men run around. I sing for my supper and I think I earn my money.

I sing for my supper and I get well-paid for it. I haven't had any audiences walk out on me.

Welcome to Mars…circa 1900. Cecil Rhodes rules Mars and is on his way to transforming the British Empire into his vision of a powerful force, managed by the "right" type of people.

But what of Savinkov…presumably on board the British aethership Agincourt, *travelling from Earth to Mars? Savinkov is a legendary revolutionary and assassin and, with Russian secret agents hot on his heels, is reputedly planning something truly dramatic and Mars-shattering.*

SERIALIZATION
Melodies of the Heart (novella)

Part 2

"Great writing, vivid scenarios, and thoughtful commentary...the stories will linger after the last page is turned."—*Publishers Weekly* (Starred Review)

CAPTIVE DREAMS

MICHAEL FLYNN
AUTHOR OF *EIFELHEIM* & *THE WRECK OF THE RIVER OF STARS*

"Melodies of the Heart" is the lead novella in the collection, CAPTIVE DREAMS.
by Michael Flynn
Phoenix Pick, 2012
Trade Paperback: 266 pages.
ISBN: 978-1-61242-059-2

MELODIES OF THE HEART

Michael Flynn

Ever since our late evening encounter, Consuela had begun wearing blouses, skirts, and robes around the house instead of her nurse's whites. The colors were bright, even garish; the patterns, blocky and intricate. The costumes made the woman more open, less mysterious. It was as if, having once seen her deshabille, a barrier had come down. She had begun teaching Dee-dee to play the cane flute. Sometimes I heard them in the evening, the notes drifting down from above stairs, lingering in the air. Was it a signal, I wondered? I sensed that the relationship between Consuela and myself had changed; but in what direction, I did not know.

Dee-dee should have been in school. She should have been in fifth grade; and she should have come home on the school bus, full of laughter and bursting to tell us what she had learned that day. Brenda and I should have helped her with her homework, nursed her bruises, and hugged her when she cried. That was the natural order of things.

But Dee-dee lived in her room; played in the dark. She studied at home, tutored by Consuela or myself or by private instructors we sometimes hired. School and other children were far away. She was a prisoner, half of her mother's strained disapproval, half of her own withdrawal. Save for Consuela and myself and a few, brief contacts with Brenda, she had no other person in her short, bounded life. Who could dream what scenarios her dolls performed in the silence of her room?

I found the two of them at the kitchen table, Consuela with her inevitable cocoa, Dee-dee with a glass of milk and a stack of Graham crackers. There were cracker crumbs scattered across the Formica and a ring of white across Dee-dee's lip.

I beamed at her. "The princess has come down from her tower once more!"

She tucked her head in a little. "It's all right, isn't it?"

I kissed her on the forehead. How sparse her hair had grown! "Of course, it is!"

I settled myself across the table from Consuela. She was wearing an ivory blouse with a square-cut neck bordered by red stitching in the shape of flowers. "Thank you, nurse," I said. "She should be downstairs more often."

"Yes, I know."

Was there a hint of disapproval there? A slight drawing together of the lips? I wanted to make excuses for Brenda. It was not that Brenda made Deedee stay in her room, but that she never made her leave. It was Deirdre who stayed always by herself. "So, what did you do today, Dee-dee?"

"Oh, nothing. I read my schoolbooks. Watched TV. I helped Connie bake a cake."

"Did you? Sounds like a pretty busy day to me."

She and Consuela shared a grin with each other. "We played ball, a little, until I got tired. And then we played word games. I see something…blue! What is it?"

"The sky?"

"I can't see the sky from here. It's long and thin."

"Hmm. Long, thin and blue. Spaghetti with blueberry sauce?"

Dee-dee laughed. "No, silly. It has a knot in it."

"Hmm. I can't imagine what it could be." I straightened my tie and Dee-dee laughed again. I looked down at the tie and gave a mock start. "Wait! Long, thin, blue and a knot…It's my belt!"

"No! It's your tie!"

"My tie? Why…" I gave her a look of total amazement. "Why, you're absolutely, positively right. Now, why didn't I see that? It was right under my nose. Imagine missing something right under your nose!"

We played a few more rounds of "I see something" and then Dee-dee wandered back to the family room and settled on the floor in front of the TV. I watched her for a while as she stared at the pictures flickering there. I thought of how little time was left before cartoons would play unwatched.

Consuela placed a cup of coffee in front of me. I sipped from it absently while I sorted through the day's mail stacked on the table. "Brenda will be coming home on Monday," I said. Consuela already knew that and I knew that she knew, so I don't know why I said it.

But why Monday? Why not Friday? Why spend another weekend in Washington with Walther Crowe? I could think of any number of reasons, I could.

"Deirdre will be happy to have her mother back," Consuela said in flat tones. I was looking at the envelopes, so I did not see her face. I knew what she meant, though. No more flute lessons; no more games downstairs. I reached across the table and placed my hand atop one of hers. It was warm, probably from holding the cocoa mug.

"Deirdre's mother never left," I said.

Consuela looked away. "I am only her nurse."

"You take care of her. That's more…" I caught myself. I had started to say that that was more than Brenda did; but there were some things that husbands did not say about their wives to other women. I noticed, however, that Consuela had not pulled her hand away from mine.

I released her hand. "Say, here's a letter from the National Archives." I said with forced heartiness, dancing away from the sudden abyss that had yawned open before me. Too many lives had been ruined by reading invitations where none were written.

Consuela stood and turned away, taking her cup to the sink. I slit the envelope open with my index finger and pulled out the yellow flimsy. *Veteran: Holloway, Green. Branch of Service: Infantry (Co. H, 5th Tennessee). Years of Service: 1918 or 1919.* It was the order form I had sent to the Military Service Records department after Mae's earlier recollection of her husband. As I unfolded it, Consuela came and stood beside me, reading over my shoulder. Somehow, it was not uncomfortable.

We were unable to complete your request as written.

We found additional pension and military service files of the same name (or similar variations).

The enclosed records are those which best match the information provided. Please resubmit, if these are not the desired files.

I grunted and paged through the sheets. Company muster rolls. A Memorandum of Prisoner of War Records: *Paroled and exchanged at Cumberland Gap, Sept. 5/62.*

The last page was a white photocopy of a form printed in an old-fashioned typeface. **Casualty Sheet.** The blanks were penned in by an elegant Spencerian hand. Name, *Green Holloway.* Rank, *Private.* Company "*H*", Regiment *5*". Division, *3*". Corps, *23*". Arm, *Inf.* State, *Tenn.*

Nature of casualty, Bullet wound of chest (fatal).

Place of casualty, *Resaca, Ga.*

Date of casualty, May 14, 1864, the regiment being in action that date.

Jno. T. Henry, Clerk.

I tossed the sheets to the kitchen table. "These can't be right," I said.

Consuela picked them up. "What is wrong?"

"Right name, wrong war. These are for a Green Holloway who died in the Civil War."

Consuela raised an eyebrow. "And who served in the same company as your patient's husband?"

"State militia regiments were raised locally, and the same families served in them, generation after generation. Green here was probably 'Mister's' grandfather. Back then children were often given their parents' or grandparents' names." I took the photocopies from Consuela and stuffed them back in the envelope. "Well, there was a waste of ten dollars." I dropped the envelope on the table.

Dee-dee called from the family room. "What's this big book you brought home?"

"*The Encyclopedia of Song*," I said over my shoulder. "It's to help me with a patient I have."

"The old lady who hears music?"

I turned in my chair. "Yes. Did Connie tell you about her?"

Dee-dee nodded. "I wish I could hear music like that. You wouldn't need headphones or a Walkman, would you?"

I remembered that Mae had had two very unhappy recollections in one day. "No," I said, "but you don't get to pick the station, either."

Later that evening, after Dee-dee had been tucked away, I spread my index cards and sheets of paper over the kitchen table, and arranged the tape recorder on my left where I could replay it as needed. The song encyclopedia lay in front of me, open to its index. A pot of coffee stood ready on my right.

Consuela no longer retreated to her own room after dinner. When I looked up from my work I could see her, relaxed on the sofa in the family room, quietly reading a book. Her shoes off, her legs tucked up underneath her, the way some women sit curled up. I watched her silently for a while. So serene, like a jaguar indolent upon a tree limb. She appeared un-

aware of my regard, and I bent again over my work before she looked up.

I soon verified that Mae's latest recollections were from the Gay Nineties. The earliest one, *Ta-Ra-Ra Boom-der-ay*, had been written in 1890, and the others dated from the same era. *Good-bye, Dolly Gray* had been a favorite of the soldiers going off to fight in the Philippine "insurrection," while *Hot Time in the Old Town* had been the Rough Riders' "theme song." Mae's version of *America the Beautiful*, I discovered, was the original 1895 lyrics. Apparently, Katherine Lee Bates had written the song as much for protest as for patriotism.

When I had finished the cataloguing, I closed the songbook, leaned back in my chair and stretched my arms over my head. Consuela looked up at the motion and I smiled at her and she smiled back. I checked my watch. "Almost bedtime," I said. Consuela said nothing, but nodded slightly.

Middle-aged?

The thought struck me like a discordant note and I turned back to my work. I ran the tape back and forth until I found what I was looking for. Yes. Mae had said that the "young folks" at the turn of the century had called her age-mates "middle-aged." So Mae must have already been mature by then. How was that possible? At most, she might have been a teenager, one of the "young folks," herself.

Unless she had looked old for her age.

God! I stabbed the shut-off button with my forefinger.

After a moment, I ran the tape through again, listening for Mae's descriptions of her peers and her younger contemporaries. "Wishy-washy." Folks her age had been wishy-washy. Yet, in an earlier session, she had described her age-mates as moralistic. I flipped through my written notes until I found it.

Yes, just as I remembered. But, psychologically, that made no sense. Irresolute twenty-somethings do not mature into forty-something moralists. The irresolute become the two-sides-to-every-question types; the mediators, the compromisers, the peacemakers. The ones both sides despise—and miss desperately when they are gone. The moralists are no-compromise world-savers. They preach "prohibition," not "temperance."

The wild youth Mae remembered from the Ragtime Era and the Mauve Decade—the hard-edged "newsies"—those were the young Hemingways, Bogies, and Mae Wests; the "Blood-and-Guts" Pattons and the "Give-'em-Hell" Harrys. The Lost Generation, they had been called. The idealistic, young teeners and twentysomethings of the Gay Nineties that Mae found so simpatico were the young FDR, W.E.B. DuBois and Jane Addams. The generation of "missionaries" out to save the world. They had all been "the kids" to her. But that would put Mae into the even older, Progressive Generation, a contemporary of T.R. and Edison and Booker T. Washington.

I drummed my pencil against the tabletop. That would make her a hundred and twenty years old, or thereabout. That wasn't possible, was it? I pushed myself from the table and went to the bookcase in the family room.

The Guinness Book of Records sat next to the dictionary, the thesaurus, the atlas and the almanac, all neatly racked together. Sometimes, Brenda's obsessive organizing paid off. I noticed that Dee-dee had left one of her own books, *The Boxcar Children*, on the shelf and made a mental note to return it to her room later.

According to Guinness, the oldest human being whose birth could be authenticated was Shigechiyo Izumi of Japan, who had died in 1986 at the ripe age of one hundred and twenty years and two hundred and thirty-seven days. So, a few wheezing, stumbling geezers did manage to hang around that long. But not many. Actuarial tables suggested one life in two billion. So, with nearly six billion of us snorting and breathing and poking each other with our elbows, two or three such ancients were possible. Maybe, just maybe, Mae could match Izumi's record. The last surviving Progressive.

The oldest human being.

The oldest human being remembers.

The oldest human being remembers pop music of the last hundred years.

A Hundred-and-Twentysomething. Great book title. It had "best seller" written all over it.

'Neath the chestnut tree, where the wild flow'rs grow,

And the stream ripples forth through the vale,

Where the birds shall warble their songs in spring,

There lay poor Lilly Dale.

On my next visit, Mae was not waiting by the office door for me to unlock it. So, after I had set my desk in order, I hung the "Back in a Minute" sign on the door knob and went to look for her. Not that I was concerned. It was just that I had grown used to her garrulous presence.

I found Jimmy Kovacs in the common room watching one of those inane morning "news" shows.

"Good morning, Jimmy. How's your back?"

He grinned at me. "Oh, I can't complain." He waited a beat. "They won't let me."

I smiled briefly. "Glad to hear it. Have you seen—"

"First hurt my back, oh, it must have been sixty-six, sixty-seven. Lifting forms."

"I know. You told me already. I'm looking for—"

"Not forms like paperwork. Though nowadays you could strain your back lifting them, too." He cackled at his feeble joke. It hadn't been funny the first two times, either. "No, I'm talking about those six hundreed-pound forms we used to use on the old flatbed perfectors. Hot type. Blocks of lead quoined into big iron frames. Those days, printing magazines was a *job*, I tell you. You could smell the ink; you could feel the presses pounding through the floor and the heat from the molten lead in the linotypes." He shook his head. "I saw the old place once a few years back. A couple of prissy kids going ticky-ticky on those computer keyboards…" He made typing motions with his two index fingers.

I interrupted before he could give me another disquisition on the decadence of the printing industry. I could just imagine the noise, the lead vapors, the heavy weight-lifting. Some people have odd notions about the Good Old Days. "Have you seen Mae this morning, Jimmy?"

"Who? Mae? Sure, I saw the old gal. She was headed for the gardens." He pointed vaguely.

Old gal? I chuckled at the pot calling the kettle black. But then I realized with a sudden shock that there were more years between Mae and Jimmy than there were between Jimmy and me. There was old, and then there was *old*. Perhaps we should distinguish more carefully among them…say "fogies," "mossbacks" and "geezers."

Mae was sitting in the garden sunshine, against the red brick back wall, upon a stone settee. I watched her for a few moments from behind the large plate glass window. The sun was from her right, illuminating the red and yellow blossoms around her and sparkling the morning dew like diamonds strewn across the grass. The dewdrops were matched by those on her cheeks. She wore a green print dress with flowers, so that the dress, the grass, and the flower beds; the tears and the dew, all blended together, like old ladies' garden camouflage.

She did not see me coming. Her eyes were closed tight, looking upon another, different world. I stood beside her, unsure whether to rouse her. Were those tears of joy or tears of sorrow? Would it be right to interrupt either? I compromised by placing my hand on her shoulder. Her dry, bird-like claw reached up and pressed itself against mine.

"Is that you, Doctor Wilkes?" I don't know how she knew that. Perhaps her eyes had not been entirely closed. She opened them and looked at me, and I could see that her regurgitated memories had been sorrowful ones. That is the problem with Jackson's syndrome. You remember. You can't help remembering. "Oh, Doctor Wilkes. My mama. My sweet, sweet mama. She's dead."

The announcement did not astonish me. Had either of Mae Holloway's parents been alive I would have been astonished. I started to tell her that, but my words came out surprisingly gentle. "It happened a long time ago," I told her. "It's a hurt long over."

She shook her head. "No. It happened this morning. I saw Pa leaning over my bed. Oh, such a strong, young man he was! But he'd been crying. His eyes were red and his beard and hair weren't combed. He told me that my mama was dead at last and she weren't a-hurtin' no more."

Mae Holloway pulled me down to sit beside her on the hard, cold bench, and she curled against me for all the world like a little girl. I hesitated and almost pulled away; but I am not without pity, even for an old woman who half-thought she was a child.

"He told me it was my fault."

"What?" Her voice had been muffled against my jacket.

"He told me it was my fault."

"Who? Your father told you that? That was…cruel."

She spoke in a high-pitched, childish voice. "He tol' me that mama never gotten well since I was borned. There was something about my birthin' that hurt her inside. I was six and I never seen my mama when she weren't a-bed…"

She couldn't finish. Awkwardly, I put an arm around her shoulder. A husband who lost his wife to childbirth would blame the child, whether consciously or not. Especially a husband in the full flush of youth. Worse still, if it was a lingering death. If for years the juices of life had drained away, leaving a gasping, joyless husk behind.

"I have to get back to my office," I said, standing abruptly. "There may be a patient waiting. Is there anything I can get you? A sedative?"

She shook her head slowly back and forth several times. When she spoke, she sounded more like the adult Mae. "No. No, thank you. I ain't—haven't had these memories for so long that I got to feel them now, even when it pains me. There'll be worse coming back to me, by and by. And better, too. The Good Man'll help me bear it."

It wasn't until I was back behind my desk and had made some notes about her recollection for my projected book that I was struck with an annoying inconsistency. If Mae's mother had died from complications of childbirth, where did her "little brother Zach" come from?

Step-brother, probably. A young man like her father would have sought a new bride before too long. Eventually, we put tragedy behind us and get on with life. But if I was going to analyze the progress of Mae's condition, I would need to confirm her recollections. After all, memories are tricky things. The memories of the old, trickier than most.

Peaches in the summertime,
Apples in the fall;
If I can't have the girl I love,
I won't have none at all.

There was music in the air when I returned home, and I followed the thread of it through the garage and into the backyard, where I found Consuela sitting on a blanket of red, orange, and brown, swathed in a flowing, pale green muumuu, and Deirdre beside her playing on the cane flute. Dee-dee's thin, knobby fingers moved haltingly and the notes were flat, but I actually recognized the tune. Something about a spider and a waterspout.

"Hello, Dee-dee. Hello, Consuela."

Deirdre turned. "Daddy!" she said. She pulled herself erect on Consuela's gown and hobbled across the grass to me. I crouched down and hugged her. "Dee-dee, you're outside playing."

"Connie said it was all right."

"Of course, it's all right. I wish you would come out more often."

A cloud passed across the sunshine. "Connie said no one can see me in the yard." A hesitation.

"And Mommy's not home."

No one to tell her how awful she looked. No cruel, taunting children. No thoughtlessly sympathetic adults offering useless condolences. Nothing but Connie, and me, and the afternoon sun. I looked over Dee-dee's shoulder. "Thank you, nur— Thank you, Connie."

She blinked at my use of her familiar name, but made no comment. "The sunshine is good for her."

"She *is* my sunshine. Aren't you, Dee-dee?" *You are my sunshine, my only sunshine.* A fragment of tune. Only, how did the rest of it go?

"Oh, Daddy…"

"So, has Connie been teaching you to play the flute?"

"Yes. And she showed me lots of things. Did you know there are zillions of different bugs in our grass?"

"Are there?" *You make me happy when skies are gray.*

"Yeah. There's ants and centipedes and…and mites? And honey bees. Honey bees like these little white flowers." And she showed me a ball of clover she had tucked behind her ear.

"You better watch that," I said, "or the bees will come after you, too."

"Oh, Daddy…"

"Because you're so sweet." *You'll never know, dear, how much I love you.*

"Daaaddyyy. I saw some spiders, too."

"Going up the waterspout?"

She giggled. "There are different kinds of spiders, too. They're like eensy-weensy tigers, Connie says. They eat flies and other bugs. Yuck! I wouldn't want to be a spider, would you?"

"No."

"But you are!" Secret triumph in her voice. She had just tricked me, somehow. "There was this spider that was nothing but a little brown ball with legs *this* long!" She held her arms far enough apart to cause horror movie buffs to blanch. "They named it after you," she added with another giggle. "They call it a Daddy-long-legs. You're a daddy and you have long legs, so you must be a spider, too."

"Then…I've got you in my web!" I grabbed her and she squealed. "And now I'm going to gobble you up!" I started kissing her on the cheeks. She giggled and made a pretense of escape. I held her all the tighter. *Please don't take my sunshine away.*

We sat for a while on the blanket, just the three of us. Consuela told us stories from Guatemala. How a rabbit had gotten deeply into debt and then tricked his creditors into eating one another. How a disobedient child was turned into a monkey. Dee-dee giggled at that and said she would *like* to be a monkey. I told them about Mae Holloway.

"She didn't give me any new songs today," I said, "but she finally remembered something from her childhood." I explained how her mother had died and her father had blamed her for it.

"Poor girl!" Consuela said, looking past me. "It's not right for a little girl to grow up without a mother."

"Deirdre Wilkes! What on *earth* are you doing out*side* in the *dirt*?"

Dee-dee stiffened in my arms. I turned and saw Brenda in the open garage door, straight as a rod. A navy blue business suit with white ruffled blouse. Matching overcoat, hanging open. A suitbag slung from one shoulder; a briefcase clenched in the other hand. "Brenda," I said, standing up with Dee-dee in my arm. "We didn't expect you until Monday."

She looked at each of us. "Evidently not."

"Dee-dee was just getting a little sunshine."

Brenda stepped close and whispered. "The neighbors might see."

I wanted to say, So what? But I held my peace. You learn there are times when it is best to say nothing at all. You learn.

"Nurse." She spoke to Consuela. "Aren't you dressed a bit casually?"

"Yes, señora. It is after five." When she had to, Consuela could remember what was in her contract.

"A professional does not watch the clock. And a professional dresses appropriately for her practice. How do you think it would look if I went to the office in blouse and skirt instead of a suit? Take Deirdre inside. Don't you know there are all sorts of bugs and dirt out here? What if she were stung by a bee? Or bitten by a deer tick?"

"Brenda," I said, "I don't think—"

She turned to me. "Yes, exactly. You didn't think. How could you have allowed this, Paul? Look, in her hand. That's Nurse's whistle, or whatever it is. Has Deirdre been playing it? Putting it in her mouth. How unsanitary! And there are weeds in her hair. For God's sake, Paul, you're a doctor. You should have said something."

Sometimes I thought Brenda had been raised in a sterile bubble. The least little thing out of place, the least little thing done wrong, was enough to set her off. Dust was a hanging offense. She hadn't always been that way. At school, she'd been reasonably tidy, but not obsessed. It had only been in the last few years that cleanliness and order had begun to consume her life. Each year, I could see the watchspring wound tighter and tighter.

Consuela bundled up flute, blanket, and Dee-dee and took them inside, leaving me alone with Brenda. I tried to give her a hug, and she endured it briefly. "Welcome home."

"Christ, Paul. I go away for two weeks and everything is falling apart."

"No, Nurse was right to bring her outside. Deirdre should have as much normal activity as possible. There is nothing wrong with her mind. It's just her body aging too fast." That wasn't strictly true. Hutchinson-Gilford was sometimes called *progeria*, but it differed in some of its particulars from normal senile aging.

Brenda swatted at a swarm of midges. "There are too many bugs out here," she said. "Let's go inside. Carry my suitbag for me."

I took it from her and followed her inside the house. She dropped her briefcase on the sofa in the living room and continued to the hall closet, where she shed her overcoat. "You're home early," I said again.

"That's right. Surprised?" She draped her overcoat carefully across a hanger.

"Well…" *Yes, I was.* "Did Crowe drop you off?"

She shoved the other coats aside with a hard swipe. "Yes." Then she turned and started up the stairs. I closed the closet door for her.

"How was Washington?" I asked. "Did you impress the Supremes?"

She didn't answer and I followed her up the stairs. I found her in our bedroom, shedding her travel clothes. I hung the suitbag on the closet door. "Did you hear me? I asked how—"

"I heard you." She dropped her skirt to the floor and sent it in the direction of the hamper with a flick of her foot. "Walther offered me a partnership."

"Did he?" I retrieved her skirt and put it in the hamper. "That's great news!" It was. Partners made a bundle. They took a cut of the fees the associates charged. "It opens up all sorts of opportunities."

Brenda gave me a funny look. "Yes," she said. "It does." If I hadn't known better, I would have said she looked distressed. It was hard to imagine Brenda being unsure.

"What's wrong?" I said.

"Nothing. It's just that there are conditions attached."

"What conditions? A probationary period? You've been an associate there for seven years. They should know your work by now."

"It isn't that."

"Then, what…"

Deirdre interrupted us. She stood in the doorway of our bedroom, one foot crossed pigeon-toed over the other, a gnarled finger tucked in one shrunken cheek. "Mommy?"

Brenda looked at a point on the door jamb a quarter inch above Dee-dee's head. "What is it, honey."

"I should tell you 'welcome home' and 'I missed you.'"

I could almost hear *Connie said…* in front of that statement and I wondered if Brenda could hear it, too.

"I missed you, too, honey," Brenda told the door knob.

"I've got to take my bath, now."

"Good. Be sure to get all that dirt washed off."

"Okay, Mommy." A brief catch, and then, "I love you, Mommy."

Brenda nodded. "Yes."

Dee-dee waited a moment longer, then turned and bolted for the bathroom. I could hear Connie already running the water. I waited until the bathroom door closed before I turned to Brenda.

"You could have told her that you loved her, too."

"I do," she said, pulling on a pair of slacks. "She knows I do."

"Not unless you tell her once in a while."

She flashed me an irritated look, but made no reply. She took a blouse from her closet and held it in front of her while she stood before the mirror. "Let's go out to eat tonight."

"Go out? Well, you know that Dee-dee doesn't like to leave the house, but…"

"Take Deirdre with us? Whatever are you thinking of, Paul? She would be horribly embarrassed. Think of the stares she'd get! No, Consuela can feed her that Mexican goulash she's cooking."

"Guatemalan."

"What?"

"It's Guatemalan, whatever it is."

"Do you have to argue with everything I say?"

"I thought, with you being just back and all, that the three of us—" *The four of us.* "—could eat dinner together, for a change."

"I won't expose Deirdre to the rudeness of strangers."

"No, not when she can get it at home." I don't know why I said that. It just came out.

Brenda stiffened. "What does that crack mean?"

I turned away. "Nothing."

"No, tell me!"

I turned back and faced her. "All right. You treat Dee-dee like a non-person. She's sick, Brenda, and it's not contagious and it's not her fault."

"Then whose fault is it?"

"That's lawyer talk. It's no one's fault. It just happens. We've been over that and over that. There is no treatment for progeria."

"And, oh, how it gnaws at you! *You can't cure her!*"

"No one can!"

"But especially you."

No one could cure Dee-dee. I knew that. It was helplessness, not failure. I had accepted that long ago. "And *you're* angry and bitter," I replied, "because there's nobody you can sue!"

She flung her blouse aside and it landed in a wad in the corner. "Maybe," she said through clenched teeth, "Maybe I'll take that partnership offer, after all."

It was not until much later that evening, as I lay awake in bed, Brenda a thousand miles away on the other side, that I remembered Consuela's remark. *It's not right for a little girl to grow up without a mother.* I wondered. Had she been making a comment, or making an offer?

> *I don't want to play in your yard.*
> *I don't like you anymore.*
> *You'll be sorry when you see me*
> *Sliding down our cellar door.*

The next time I saw Mae Holloway, we quarreled.

Perhaps it was her own constant sourness coming to the fore; or perhaps it was her fear of insanity returning. But it may have been a bad humor that I carried with me from Brenda's homecoming. We had smoothed things out, Brenda and I, but it was a fragile repair, the cracks plastered over with I-was-tired and I-didn't-mean-it, and we both feared to press too hard, lest it buckle on us. At dinner, she had told me about the case she had helped argue, and I told her about Mae Holloway and we both pretended to care. But it was all monologue. Listening holds fewer risks than response; and an attentive smile, less peril than engagement.

Mae wouldn't look at me when I greeted her. She stared resolutely at the floor, at the medicine cabinet, out the window. Sometimes, she stared into another world. I noticed how she gnawed on her lips.

"We have a couple of days to catch up on, Mrs. Holloway," I said. "I hope you've been making notes, like I asked."

She shook her head slowly, but in a distracted way. She was not responding to my statement, but to some inner reality. "I just keep remembering and remembering, doc. There's music all the time, and that double vision—"

"Consciousness doubling."

"It's like I'm in two places at once. Sometimes, I forget which is which, and I try to step around things only I cain't, because they're only ghosts, only ghosts. And sometimes, I recollect things that couldn't have…"

The "dreamy states" of Jackson patients often grow deeper and more frequent. In one woman, they had occupied nearly her entire day; and, in the end, they had crowded out her normal consciousness entirely. "I could prescribe something, if you like," I said. "These spells of yours are similar to epileptic seizures. So, there are drugs that…"

She shook her head again. "No. I won't take drugs." She looked directly at me at last. "Don't you understand? I've got to know. It's always been bits and pieces. Just flashes. A jimble-jamble that never made sense. Now…" She paused and took a deep breath. "Now, at least, I'll know."

"Know what, Mrs. Holloway."

"About…Everything." She looked away again. Talking with her today was like pulling teeth.

"What about the songs, Mae? We didn't get anything useful on Wednesday and I wasn't here Tuesday or yesterday, so that's three days we have to catch up on."

Mae turned and studied me with lips as thin as broth. "You don't care about any of this, do you? It's all professional; not like you and I are friends. You don't care if'n I live or die; and I don't care if'n you do."

"Mrs. Holloway, I…"

"Good." She gave a sharp nod of her head. "That's jake with me. Because I don't like having friends," she said. "I decided a long time ago if'n I don't have 'em, I won't miss 'em when they cut out. So let's just keep this doc and old lady." Her stare was half admonition, half challenge, as if she dared me to leap the barriers she had set down around her.

I shrugged. Keep things professional. That was fine with me, too. A crabby old lady like her, it was no wonder they all ran out on her.

She handed over a crumpled, yellow sheet of lined paper, which I flattened out on my desk. She had written in a soft pencil, so I smeared some of the writing and smudged my palm. I set a stack of fresh index cards by and began to copy the song titles for later research. *Where Did You Get That Hat? Com-rades. The Fountain in the Park. Love's Old Sweet Song.* While I worked, I could hear Mae humming to herself. I knew without looking that she had her eyes closed, that she was living more and more in another world, gradually leaving this one behind. *White Wings. Walking for That Cake. My Grandfather's Clock. In the Gloaming. Silver Threads Among the Gold. The Mulligan Guard.* Mae was her own Hit Parade. Though if the music did play continually, as she said, this list could only be a sample of what she had heard over the last three days. *The Man on the Flying Trapeze. Sweet Genevieve. Champagne Charlie. You Naughty, Naughty Men. When You and I Were Young, Maggie. Beautiful Dreamer.* Three days' worth of unclaimed memories.

I noticed that she had recorded no doubling episodes, this time. Because she had not had any? It seemed doubtful, considering. But one entry had been crossed out; rubbed over with the pencil until there was nothing but a black smear and a small hole in the paper where the pencil point had worn through. I held it up to the light, but could make out nothing.

I heard Mae draw in her breath and looked up in time to see a mien on her face almost of ecstasy. "What is it?"

"I'm standing out in a meadow. There's a sparkling stream meandering through it, and great, gray, rocky mountains rearing all around. Yellow flowers shivering in the breeze and I think how awful purty and peaceful it is." She sighed. "Oh, doc, sometimes, just for a second, we can be so happy."

Jackson had often described his patients' "dreamy states" as being accompanied by intense feelings of euphoria; sudden bursts of child-like joy. No doubt some endorphin released in the brain.

"There's a fellow coming up toward me from the ranch," she continued, trepidation edging into her voice. "My age, maybe a little older. Might be Mister's younger brother, because he favors him some. He's a-weeping something awful. I reach out to him and he puts his head on my shoulder and says…" Mae stopped and winced in pain. She sucked in her breath and held it. Then she let it out slowly. "And he says how Sweet Annie is dead and the baby, too; and there was nothing the sawbones could do. Nothing at all. And I think, *Thank you, Goodman Lord. Thank you, that she won't suffer the way that Ma did.* And then a mockingbird takes wing from the aspen tree right in front of me and I think how awful peaceful the meadow is now that the screaming has stopped."

She wiped at her nose with her sleeve. "Listen to it. Can you hear it, doc? There ain't a sound but for the breeze and that old mockingbird." The look on her face changed somehow, changed subtly. "Listen to the mockingbird," she croaked. "Listen to the mockingbird. Oh, the mockingbird still singing o'er her grave…"

Then she looked about in sudden surprise. "Land's sake! Now, how did I get here? Why, everybody's so happy; singing the mockingbird song and dancing all over the lawn and a-hugging each other." A smile slowly came over her face. She had apparently tripped from one doubling episode directly into another, due to some association with the song, and the imprinted emotions were playing back with it, overwriting the melancholy of the first episode. Or else she had seized on the remembered joy herself, and had wrapped herself in it against the cold.

"I'm a-wearing my Sanitary Commission uniform," she went on, preening her shabby, faded gown. She shot her cuffs, straightened something at her throat that wasn't there. "I was a nurse, you know; and when the news come that the war was finally over we all hied over to the White House and had ourselves a party on the lawn, the whole kit 'n boodle of us. Then the President his-self come out and joined us." She turned in her seat and pointed toward the medicine cabinet. "Here he comes now!"

And in that instant, her joy became absolute terror. "Him?" Her smile stretched to a ghastly rictus and she cowered into her chair, covering her eyes with her hand. But you can't close your eyes to memory. You can't. "No! I kin still see him!" she said.

What was so terrifying about seeing president Wilson close up? "What's wrong, Mrs. Holloway?"

"They shot him."

"What, on the White House lawn? No president has been shot there…" And certainly not Wilson.

She took her hands away from her eyes, glanced warily left, then right. Slowly, she relaxed, though her hands continued to tremble. Then, she looked at me. "No, the shooting happened later," she snapped, anger blossoming from her fear. Then she closed up and her eyes took on a haunted look. "I'm taking up too much of your time, doc," she said, creaking to her feet.

"No, you're not. Really," I told her.

"Then you're taking up too much of mine." I thought her blackthorn stick would punch holes in the floor tiles as she left.

After a moment's hesitation, I followed. She had recalled her father's death. She had remembered that her birth had killed her mother and that her father had blamed her for it. She had remembered her husband going off to war, never to return. Sad memories, sorrowful memories; but there was something about this new recollection that terrified her.

She thought she was going crazy.

It was easy to track her through the garden. Deep holes punched into the sod marked her trail among the flower beds. When I caught up with her, she was leaning over a plot of gold and crimson marigolds. "You know, I remember exactly where I was when President Kennedy was shot," I said by way of easing her into conversation.

Mae Holloway scowled and bent over the flower bed. "Don't make no difference no-how," she said. "He's dead either way, ain't he?" She turned her back on me.

"No particular reason." I had figured it out. She had seen McKinley, not Wilson; and her husband had fought in the Spanish-American War, not World War I.

She turned her dried-out old face to me. "Think I'm getting senile, doc? Why aren't you back in your office reading on your books? You might have a patient to ignore."

"They'll find me if they need me."

"I tol' you the songs I been remembering. Why did you follow me out here, anyway?"

I had better things to do than have a bitter old woman berate me. "If you feel in a friendlier mood later," I said, "you know where to find me."

Back in my office, I began checking the latest tunes against the song encyclopedia. The mindless transcription kept me busy, so that I did not dwell on Mae's intransigence. Let her stew in her own sour juices.

But I soon noticed a disturbing trend in the data. *Champagne Charlie* was written in 1868. *You Naughty,*

Naughty Men ("When married how you treat us and of each fond hope defeat us, and there's some will even beat us…") had created a scandal at Niblo's Gardens in 1866. And *Beautiful Dreamer* dated from *1864*. Mae could not have heard those songs when they were new. Born in the early seventies at best, tucked away back in the hills of Tennessee—"So far back in the hollers," she had said one time, "that they had to pipe in the daylight."—She must have heard them later.

And if a little bit later, why not a whole lot later?

And there went the whole rationale for my book.

The problem with assigning dates to Mae's neurological hootenanny was that she could have heard the songs at any time. A melody written in the Twenties, like *The Red, Red Robin*, is heard and sung by millions of children today. Scott Joplin created his piano rags at the turn of the century; yet most people knew them from *The Sting*, a movie made in the Seventies and set in the Thirties, an era when ragtime had been long out of fashion.

(The telescoping effect of distance. From this far down the river of years, who can distinguish the Mauve Decade from the Thirties? Henry James and Upton Sinclair and Ernest Hemingway came of age in very different worlds; but they seem alike to us because they are just dead people in funny clothing, singing quaint, antique songs. "Old-fashioned" is enough to blur them together.)

Face it. Many of those old songs were still being sung and recorded when *I* was young. Lawrence Welk. Mitch Miller. Preservation Hall. Leon Redbone had warbled *Champagne Charlie* on the Tonight Show in front of God and everybody. Wasn't it far more likely that Mae had heard it then, than that she had heard it in 1868?

A Hundred and Twentysomething. I had deduced a remarkable age for Mae from the dates of the songs she remembered. If that was a will-o'-the-wisp, what was the point? There was no teleology to interest the professionals; no hook to grab the public. How many people would care about an old woman's recollections? Not enough to make a best seller.

And what right had that old bat, what right had anyone, to live so long when *children* were dying? What use were a few extra years remembering the past when there were others who would never have a future?

Damn! I saw that I had torn the index card. I rummaged in the drawer for tape, found none, and wondered if it made any sense to bother recopying the information. The whole effort was a waste of time. I picked up the deck of index cards and threw them. I missed the wastebasket and they fluttered like dead leaves across the room.

Oh, how old is she, Billy Boy, Billy Boy?
Oh, how old is she, charming Billy?
She's twice six and she's twice seven,
Forty-eight and eleven.

She's a young thing that cannot leave her mother.

I could have gone home, instead, and gotten an early start on the weekend.

I had planned to visit the National Archives today, but to continue the book project now seemed pointless. The whole rationale had collapsed; and Mae had withdrawn into that fearful isolation in which I had found her. There was no reason not to go home. Brenda had taken the day off to recuperate from her trip. She was probably waiting for me. So, I closed the clinic at noon and took the Transit to Newark's Penn Station, where I transferred to the PATH train into the World Trade Center. From there a cab dropped me at Varick and Houston in lower Manhattan.

If we did not meet, we could not quarrel.

The young woman behind the information desk was a pixie: short, with serious bangs and serious, round glasses. Her name tag read Sara. "Green?" she said when I had explained my mission. "What an odd name. It might be a nickname. You know, like 'Red.' One of my grandfathers was called 'Blackie' because his family name was White. She took out a sheet of scratch paper and made some notes on it. "I'd suggest you start with the 1910 Census and look for Green Holloway in the Soundex."

"Soundex?" I said. "What is that?"

"It's like an Index, but it's based on sounds, not spelling. Which is good, since the enumerators didn't always spell the names right. Holloway might have been recorded as, oh, H-a-l-i-w-a-y, for example, or even H-a-l-l-w-a-y; but the Soundex code would be the same."

"I see. Clever."

She took out a brochure and jotted another note on the scratch pad. "Holloway would be…H. Then L is a 4, and the W and Y don't count. That's H400. There will be a lot of other names listed under H400, like Holly and Hall, but that should narrow your search." She filled out a request voucher for me. "Even with the Soundex," she said as she wrote, "there are no guarantees. There are all sorts of omissions, duplicates, wrong names, wrong ages. Dad missed his great-grandmother in the 1900 Census, because she was living with her son-in-law and the enumerator had listed her with the son-in-law's family name. One of my great-great-grandfathers 'aged' fourteen years between the 1870 and 1880 censuses; and his wife-to-be was listed twice in 1860. People weren't always home; so, the enumerator would try to get the information from a neighbor, who didn't always know. So you should always cross-check your information."

She directed me to an empty carrel, and shortly after, an older man delivered the 1910 Soundex for Blount County, Tennessee. I threaded the microfilm spool into the viewer and spun forward, looking for H400. Each frame was an index card with the head of household on top and everyone else listed below with their ages and relationships.

I slowed when I started to see first names starting with G:

Gary…George…Gerhard…Glenn…Granville… Gretchen…Gus…No Green. I backed up and checked each of the G's, one by one, thinking Green might be out of sequence.

Still, no luck. And I couldn't think of any other way "Green" might be spelled. Unless it was a nickname, in which case, forget it. I scrolled ahead to the M's. If the census taker had interviewed Mae, Green might be listed as "Mister."

But…No "Mister." Then I checked the M's again, this time searching for "Mae" or "May," because if Mister had died in the Spanish-American War rather than World War I, Mae herself would have been listed as head-of-household in 1910.

Still nothing. It was a fool's errand, anyway. For all I knew, Mae was really Anna-Mae or Lulu-Mae

or some other such Appalachianism, which would make finding her close to impossible.

I tried the 1900 Soundex next. But I came up dry on that, too. No Green, no Mister, no Mae. Eventually, I gave up.

I leaned back in the chair and stretched my arms over my head. Now what? *We lived so far back in the hollers they had to pipe in the daylight.* It could be that the census takers had flat out missed her. Or she had already left the hills by 1900. In which case, I did not know where to search. She had gone to Cincinnati, I remembered. And to California. At one time or another, she had mentioned San Francisco, and Chicago, and Wyoming, and even New York City. The old bag had a lot of travel stickers on her.

I took a walk to stretch my legs. If I left now, and the trains were on time, and the traffic was light, I could still be home in time to tuck Dee-dee in. But a check of the sidewalk outside the building showed the crowds running thick. The Financial District was getting an early start on the weekend. Not a good time to be leaving the City. Not a good time at all. Traffic heading for the tunnels sat at a standstill. Tightly-packed herds of humans trampled the sidewalks. I would have likened them to sheep, but for the in-your-face single-mindedness with which they marched toward their parking lots and subway entrances.

The trains would be SRO, packed in with tired, sweaty office workers chattering about Fashion Statements or Sunday's Big Game; or (the occasional Type A personality) hunched over their laptops, working feverishly on their next deal or their next angina, whichever came first. Was there ever a time when the New York crowds thinned out? Perhaps there was a continual stream of drones flowing through the streets of Manhattan twenty-four hours a day. Or maybe they were simply walking around and around this one block just to fool me. A Potemkin Crowd.

I returned to the information desk. "I guess as long as I'm stuck here I'll check 1890." That would be before the Spanish-American War, so Green might be alive and listed.

"I'm sorry," Sara told me. "The 1890 Census was destroyed in a fire in 1921, and only a few fragments survived."

I sighed. "Dead end, I guess. I'm sorry I took up so much of your time."

"That's what I'm here for. You could try 1880, though, and look for the parents. There's a partial Soundex for households with children aged ten and under. If the woman was born in the 1870s like you think…"

I shook my head. "No. I know she was born a Murray, but I don't know her father's name." Checking each and every M600 for a young child named Mae was not an appealing task. I might only be killing time; but I had no intention of bludgeoning it to death. I'd have a better chance hunting Holloways, because Green's name was so out of the ordinary. But I'd have to go frame-by-frame there, too, since I didn't know his parents' names, either. That sort of painstaking research was the reason why God invented professionals.

Sara pointed to a row of shelves near the carrels. "There is one other option. There are printed indices of Heads of Households for 1870 and earlier."

I shook my head. "The grandparents? I don't know their names, either."

"Did she have a brother?"

"Zach," I said. "Just the two of them, as far as I know. At least, she's never mentioned any other siblings."

"Children sometimes were given their grandparents' names. Maybe her father's parents were Zach and Mae Murray. It's a shot in the dark, but what do you have to lose? If you don't look, you'll never find anything."

"Okay, thanks." I wandered over to the row of index volumes and studied them. I was blowing off the time now and I knew it. Still, I could always strike it lucky.

The indices for Tennessee ran from 1820 through 1860. Thick, bound volumes on heavy paper. No Soundex here. I'd have to remember to check alternate spellings. I pulled out the volume for 1860 and flipped through the pages until I found Murray. Murrays were "thick as ticks on a hound dog's hide," but none of them were named Zach. However, when I checked *H*, I did find a "Green Holloway" in District 2, Greenback, Tennessee. Mister's grandfather? How many Green Holloways could there be? I copied the information and put in a request for the spool; then, just for luck, I checked 1850, as well.

The 1850 Census listed a "Greenberry Holloway," also in District 2, Greenback P.O. I chuckled. Greenberry? Imagine sending a kid to school with a name like Greenberry!

Green appeared in the 1840 and 1830 indices, too. And 1830 listed a "Josh Murry" in the same census district as Green. Mae's great-grandfather? Worth a look, anyway.

The trail ended there. The Blount County returns for 1820 were lost, and all the earlier censuses had all been destroyed when the British burned Washington in 1814.

I put the volumes back on the shelf. There was a thick atlas on a reading stand next to the indices and, out of curiosity, I turned it open to Tennessee. It took me a while to find Greenback. When I finally did, I saw that it lay in Loudon County, not Blount.

"That doesn't make any sense," I muttered.

"What doesn't?" A shriveled, dried-up old man with wire-frame glasses was standing by my elbow waiting to use the atlas.

"The indices all say Blount County, but the town is in Loudon." I didn't bother to explain. It wasn't any of his business. There could be any number of reasons for the discrepancy. The Greenback post office could have serviced parts of Blount County.

The man adjusted his glasses and peered at the map. I stepped aside. "It's all yours," I said.

"Now, hold on, sonny." He opened his satchel, something halfway between a purse and a briefcase, and pulled out a dog-eared, soft-bound red book. He licked his forefinger and rubbed pages aside. He hummed and nodded as he read. "Here's your answer," he said, jabbing a finger at a table. "Loudon County was erected in 1870 from parts of Blount and neighboring counties. Greenback was in the part that became Loudon County. See?" He closed the book one-handed with a snap. "It's simple."

I guess if hanging around musty old records is your whole life, it's easy to sound like an expert. He looked like something the Archives would have in storage anyway. "Thanks," I said.

The whole afternoon had been a waste of time. I had been searching in the wrong county. Blast the forgetfulness of age! Mae had said she had been born in Blount County, so I had looked in Blount County. And all the while, the records were tucked safely away under Loudon.

I checked the clock on the wall. Four-thirty? Too late to start over. Time to pack it in and catch the train.

When I returned to my carrel, however, I found the spool for 1860 Blount County had already been delivered. I considered sending it back, but decided to give it a fast read before leaving. I mounted the spool and spun the fast forward, slowing when I reached District 2. About a third of the way through, I stopped.

NAMES	AGE	SEX	COLOR	OCCUPATION ETC	VALUE OF REAL ESTATE	VALUE OF PERSONAL PROPERTY	BIRTH PLACE
Holloway Green	56	M	W	Farmer	$800	$100	Tenn
"	37	F					"
Mabel	22	M					"
Zachary							

Hah! There it was. Success—of sorts—at last! This Green Holloway must have been the same one whose Civil War records I had gotten. Green and Mabel Holloway begat Zach Holloway, who must have begat Green "Mister" Holloway. Jesus. If those ages were correct, Mabel was only fifteen when she did her begatting. Who said babies having babies was a modern thing? But, kids grew up faster back then. They took on a lot of adult responsibilities at fifteen or sixteen. Today, they behave like juveniles into their late twenties.

Now that I knew what I was looking for and where it was, it didn't take me very long to check the 1850 Census, as well.

NAMES	AGE	SEX	COLOR	OCCUPATION ETC	VALUE OF REAL ESTATE	BIRTH PLACE
Holloway Greenberry	45	M	W	Farmer	$250	Tenn
"	32	F	"			"
" Mae	12	M	"			"
" Zach						

Those names…The eerie coincidence gave me a queer feeling. And Mabel should have been twenty-seven, not thirty-two. (Or else she should have been forty-two in 1860.) But then I remembered Sara's cautions. How easy it was for enumerators to get names and ages wrong; and how the same names were used generation after generation.

Just one more spool, I promised myself. Then I head home.

Uncle Sugar had been less nosy in 1840. The census listed only heads of households.

Everyone else was tallied by age bracket.

The "white female" was surely Mabel, and she was in her twenties. So her age in 1860 had been wrong. She must have been forty-two, not thirty-seven. Twenty-two, thirty-two, forty-two. That made sense. I folded the sheet with the information and stuffed it in my briefcase. Sara had been right about cross checking the documentation. The census takers had not always gotten the straight skinny. Mabel had probably looked younger than her years in 1860 and a neighbor, asked for the data, had guessed low.

"She looks younger than her years." The phrase wriggled through my mind and I thought fleetingly of Dee-dee looking older than her years. For every yin there is a yang, and if the universe did balance… If for some reason Mabel herself never spoke to the enumerator and a neighbor in the next holler guessed her age instead, the guess would be low. So, twenty-seven, thirty-two, thirty-seven made a weird kind of sense, too. And it actually agreed better with the written documents!

And what if she kept it up? I laughed to myself. Now there was a crazy thought! Aging five years to the decade, by 1870 she would have seemed…mmm, forty-two. And today? Add another sixty-odd years, and Mabel would appear to be…A hundred and five or thereabouts. About as old as Mae seemed to be.

I paused with one arm in my jacket.

About as old as Mae seemed to be? I stared at the spool boxes stacked in the carrel, ready for pick-up.

Greenberry and Mabel. Green and Mae? No, it was absurd. A wild coincidence of names. The census records are not that reliable. And it's only that Dee-dee is aging too fast that you even thought about someone aging too slow. I took a few steps toward the door.

And the 1830 Census? I hadn't bothered checking it. What if it listed a Green Holloway aged 20–29 and a "white female" *still* aged 20–29?

I turned and looked back at the reading room and my heart began to pound in my ears, and all of a sudden I knew why Dr. Bench had figured Mae for eighty-five three decades ago, and why Mae had feared for her sanity all her life.

> So early in the month of May,
> As the green buds were a-swelling,
> A young man on his death-bed lay,
> For the love of Barbry Ellen.

It was pitch black out when I finally arrived home. There was a light on in the kitchen, none above-stairs. I parked in the driveway and got out and walked around the end of the garage through the gate into the backyard. The crickets were chirruping like a swing with a squeaky hinge. Lightning bugs drifted lazily through the air. I walked all the way to the back of the yard, to the edge of the woods and leaned against a bent gum tree. The ground around me was littered with last year's prickly balls. I listened to the night sounds.

I had checked 1830 and found…I didn't know what I had found. Nothing. Everything. A few tantalizing hints. Greenberry, Mabel, and Zachary. Mister, Mae, and…Zach? Not a younger brother, but a son? And another entry: *Wm. Biddle, Jr., a free man of color.* Mae had spoken of "Will Biddle who farmed two hollers over from us when I was a child…" But in 1830? In *1830*?

There was a logical part of my mind that rejected those hints. Each had an alternative explanation. Coincidence of names. Clerical errors. Senile memory.

Sometimes we remember things only because we have been told them so often. I remember that I stepped in a birthday cake when I was two years old. It had been placed on the floor in the back of the family car and I had climbed over the seat and… But do I *remember* it? Or do I remember my parents telling me the story—and showing me the snapshot—so many times over the years that it has become real to me. Mae could be remembering family tales she had heard, scrambled and made *hers* by a slowly short-circuiting brain.

But there was another part of me that embraced those hints; that wanted to believe that Mae had known Margaret Sanger, had voted for Teddy Roosevelt, had danced on the White House lawn in a Sanitary Commission uniform, because if they were true…

I stepped away from the tree and a rabbit shot suddenly left to right in front of me. I watched it bound away…And spied figures moving about in the Carters' backyard. Henry and Barbara. I watched them for a while, wondering idly what they were up to. Then I recalled Henry's nickname for his wife— and a song that Mae had known.

I took the same route the rabbit had taken. Last year's dead leaves crackled and dry twigs snapped beneath my feet. I saw one of the Carters—Henry, I thought—come suddenly erect and look my way. I hoped he wouldn't call the police. Then I thought, Christ, they're newlyweds. What sort of backyard shenanigans was I about to walk in on?

I stopped and waved a hand. "That you, Henry? Barbara? It's Paul Wilkes."

A second shadow stood erect by the first. "What's wrong?" It was Barbara's voice.

"I—I saw you moving around back there and thought it might be prowlers. Is everything all right?"

"Sure," said Henry. "Come on out. You'll get tick-bitten if you stay in there."

"Why don't you have your yard light on?" I asked as I stepped from the woods. Stupid question. I could think of a couple of reasons. Brenda and I had once gone skinny dipping in our pool at three in the morning. *Stifled laughter and urgent play, and the water glistening like pearls on her skin.* That had been years ago, of course; but sometimes it was good to remember that there had once been times like that.

"It would spoil the viewing," Henry said.

Now that I was close enough, I saw that they had a telescope set up on a tripod. It was a big one. "Oh. Are you an astronomer?"

Henry shook his head. "I'm a genetic engineer, or I will be when I finish my dissertation. Barbry's going to be a biochemist. Astronomy is our hobby."

"I see." I felt uncomfortable, an intruder; but I had come there with a purpose. I made as if to turn away and then turned back. "Say, as long as I'm here, there is a question you might be able to answer for me."

"Sure." They were an obliging couple. The moon was half-full, the air was spring evening cool, they did not really want me there interrupting whatever it was that the sky-gazing would have led to.

"I've heard Henry call you Barbry," I said to Barbara. "And…Do you know a song called *Barbry Ellen?*"

She laughed. "You mean *Barbara Allen.* Sure. That's where Henry came up with the nickname. He's into folk singing. *Barbry Ellen* is an older version."

"Well, someone told me it was the 'old president's favorite song,' and I wondered if you knew—"

"Which old president? That's easy. George Washington. You see, he had this secret crush on his best friend's wife, and…"

"George Washington? Are you sure?"

"Well, there might have been other presidents who liked it. But Washington's partiality is on the record, and the song has been out of vogue a long, long time."

"Was that all you wanted to know?" asked Henry. There was something in his voice that sounded a lot like "good bye." He wasn't happy, I could tell. I had spoiled the mood for him.

"Yes, certainly," I said. "I thought you might have been prowlers." I backed away into the woods, then turned and walked quickly home.

I learned me that 'un when I was knee-high to a grasshopper. Pa told me it was the President's favorite song. The old President, from when his Pappy fought in the War.

The old President, from when his Pappy fought in the War.

Lost my partner, what'll I do?
Lost my partner, what'll I do?
Lost my partner, what'll I do?
Skip to my love, my darling.

Brenda drank tea. She always allowed the bag to steep for a precise five minutes (read the package) and always squeezed it dry with her teaspoon. She always disposed of the bag in the trash before drinking from the cup. When she drank, she held the saucer in her left hand and the cup in her right

and hugged her elbows close to her body. She stood near the French doors in the family room, gazing out toward the backyard and the woods beyond. I had no idea if she had heard me.

"I said, I think I'll go over to Sunny Dale today and look in on Mrs. Holloway."

Brenda held herself so still she was nearly rigid. Not because she was reacting to what I had said. She always stood that way. She spent her life at attention.

"You didn't have any plans, did you?"

A small, precise shake of the head. "No. No plans. We never have any plans." A sip of tea that might have been measured in minims. "Maybe I'll go into the office, too. There are always cases to work on."

I hesitated a moment longer before leaving. When I reached the front door, I heard her call.

"Paul?"

"Yes?" Down the length of the hall I could see her framed by the glass doors at the far end. She had turned around and was facing me. "What?"

"Why do you have to go in today? It's Saturday."

"It's…nothing I can talk about yet. A wild notion. It might be nothing more than a senile woman's ravings, but it might be the most important discovery of the century. Brenda, if I'm right, it could change our lives."

Even from where I stood I could see the faint smile that trembled on her lips. "Yes, it could, at that." She turned around and faced the glass again. "You do what you have to do, Paul. So will I."

It was odd, but I suddenly remembered how much we had once done together. Silly things, simple things. Football games, Scrabble, Broadway shows. Moments public and private. The party had asked Brenda to run for the state legislature one time, and I had urged her to accept, but the baby had been due and…Somehow, now we stood at opposite ends of the house. I thought for a moment of asking her to come with me to the Home, but thought better of it. Brenda would find those old, gray creatures more distressing than I did. "Look," I said, "this should only take a couple hours. I'll call you and we'll do something together this afternoon. Take in a movie, maybe."

She nodded in her distracted way. I saw that she had spilled tea into her saucer.

(to be continued in issue #14)